Praise for Elizabeth St. Michel

The Winds of Fate Reviews:
myBook.to/TheWindsofFate
The Winds of Fate "…captivating romance that takes us to the world of seventeenth-century London…Sexual tension and legal and familial intrigue ensue with the reader cheering on the lovely pair."
—Publishers Weekly
The Winds of Fate "has everything…full of passion, betrayal, mystery and all the good stuff readers love."
—ABNA Reviewer
"Original…strong-willed heroine…I love all of it…the unlikely premise of a female member of the aristocracy visiting a man who is condemned to die and asking him to marry her."
—ABNA Reviewer

Surrender the Wind Reviews:
http://hyperurl.co/qnu96k
Surrender the Wind "The lush descriptions of the southern countryside, the witty repartee between the characters, the factual descriptions of battles woven into the storylines, and the rich characters kept me glued to the pages."
—Alwyztrouble's Romance Reviews
Surrender the Wind received the "Crowned Heart" and National "RONE AWARD" finalist for excellence. "With twists and turns… and several related subplots woven in, no emotional stone is left unturned in this romance."
—InD'tale Magazine

Only You
Duke of Rutland Series III

Only You
by Elizabeth St. Michel
Award winning author Elizabeth St. Michel masterfully creates a remarkable heroine, and an unforgettable passion, in this powerfully moving love story, *Only You.*

The series centers on the Duke of Rutland, a widower, and his four strong-willed offspring. The Duke has formidable enemies determined to destroy his family.

The third installment involves Nicholas, heir to the Duke of Rutland, kidnapped and imprisoned aboard a Portuguese slaver. Nicholas learns that his family members have been either captured or slain—but a mysterious woman allays his despair.

Fellow prisoner, Alexandra has overheard that his family is safe. But can he believe her? She claims to be a woman of status, but as she cannot prove her story, Nicholas assumes she is a thief. They are in the same predicament, however, and he and Alexandra form a friendship.

When a hurricane destroys the ship and Alexandra rescues Nicholas from certain death, he must discover the truth about her. They wash up on a deserted island, where her survival skills come to the fore. As an aristocrat, Nicholas feels unequipped to handle the situation, but he watches Alexandra with growing admiration—and hears her account of how she, the daughter of a baron, came to be so resourceful.

Nicholas yearns to leave the island and seek revenge on his captors, yet he can no longer deny his growing passion for Alexandra. Of noble birth herself, she is an appropriate match for Nicholas. Yet Alexandra has more secrets—and one of them could doom their love.

Only You

Elizabeth St. Michel

ISBN: 099748246X
ISBN: 9780997482461
Library of Congress Control Number: 2017917475
CreateSpace Independent Publishing Platform
North Charleston, South Carolina

For J.
You make me smile.

Part One

Chapter 1

Atlantic Ocean 1777

*N*icholas Rutland, heir apparent of the fourth Duke of Rutland shook his head to erase a thick fog that crowded his brain. Where was he? He eased his aching body into a seated position where rough wood, greased with muck, slicked his fingers.

He groaned, the same sludge saturated his backside. If only the damn swaying would stop. Doused with water, he sputtered and choked. He squinted at the bright sun coming through the grate above. A man pressed his pock-marked face against rusty iron, his ferret-like eyes, dancing with gleeful malevolence, the obvious sponsor of the bucket of water thrown on him.

"His Lordship's awake, Capitan," Pockmark said, sneering at Nicholas. "How's that knock on your head?"

Nicholas raised an unsteady hand, sweated with the effort. His fingers touched a lump at the back of his head. White starbursts of light popped. His arm went limp and dropped against the wall of his prison. A five-by-six cube, he guessed. Barely enough room for a man to lie down. "Why don't you come down here and we'll find out?"

"Got some fight in you, eh? You're shaking. Wet your breeches?" Pockmark laughed.

Nicholas clenched his hands, his blood rushing with the urge to slam his fist into the man's pitted face.

"Move aside, Damiano." Overhead, sails snapped and shadowed a groomed man of forty. "Move aside, Damiano," the man repeated, his high thin voice squealed in heavily accented English. Not Dutch like the droll Van Dyke beard he bore. Spanish?

"Welcome aboard the *Santanas*, Lord Rutland. I am Capitan Diogo."

Nicolas's gaze clouded as he fumbled with memories. Who was Capitan Diogo? And why was he imprisoned? "I am at a loss for I do not know you. Perhaps you can enlighten me."

"Who I am does not matter other than I have been well-compensated for your voyage." The captain looked down his nose and sniffed.

Kidnapped. Shadows clawed his mind, churning and rising. His sister, Abby's betrothal party at his ancestral home at Belvoir Castle. He had been summoned by his father to attend an important meeting. A shockwave hit him and he'd been thrown to the ground in front of his brother's laboratory. Fire. Heat had singed his face. Crushing pain in the back of his skull.

"My father will pay for my return," he rasped.

"Your father is dead," Captain Diogo said matter of fact.

"Dead?" Nicolas swallowed the nausea that rolled through his stomach. *Not true.*

"Everyone dies…a bitter unchangeable law of life." Diogo shrugged, his eyes dull. "The *Senor* who paid me gave instructions to inform you that your father, Duke Richard Rutland, and your brother, Anthony, were lured to the laboratory and killed in an explosion. Your sister, Abigail has been put on a ship to suffer your same fate."

4

Bile clawed in his throat. *Dead? Killed? No. It can't be.* Except his shackles said otherwise. His soul splintered like shards of glass. "Why?"

"You do not think the Rutland's would have enemies?"

Nicholas glared. "Return me at once. I'll pay you twice as much."

Capitan Diogo stroked his beard. "I think not. The risk of entering the Thames again is troublesome. I'll make additional profit from Brazilian slavers for a buck like you."

Not a chance in hell was he going to be anyone's slave. "I demand to know who paid you."

Captain Diogo laughed. "You are not in a situation to demand anything, Lord Rutland. Enjoy our hospitality, I will see you again."

"I'll see you in hell," Nicholas called after the lowlife scum, then rolled over and heaved his insides. He wiped his mouth on his jacket, then sat huddled, arms wrapped around his drawn-up knees for warmth.

His father? Anthony? Dead? No. Poor Abby. How vulnerable she was. He scrubbed his face with his hands remembering the terrible fight he'd had with his father in the library during the ball about changes he wanted to make to the estate...and his father's stubborn refusal.

Hot blood rushed through his veins. He stabbed stiff fingers through his matted hair. The years he'd spent adhering to his father's obsolete, fruitless policies. All the arguments, the harsh words. For naught. His chest seized. *Oh, God.* Tears welled. If only he could take it all back.

But he couldn't. Words once said can never be taken back. He straightened, sucking in a deep breath. He swore Captain Diogo and the crew of the *Santanas* to perdition.

The sail high atop cracked and flapped violently. If his Maker delivered him from this hell, he would find whomever had done this to his family. He would make them pay. He would make them all pay. Nicholas slammed his fist into the wall.

"Hold my hand."

Nicholas jerked his head back, stared at a filthy hand stuck through an apple-sized hole in the wall in front of his chest. A woman?

"Please hold my hand."

Her small voice broke. Well-shaped fingers, filthy yet unlike the ill-bred inhabitants of St. Giles with their twisted, claw-like talons. A lady's hand? He accepted what was offered.

"I heard the captain's orders to stop dosing you with laudanum yesterday. The nausea, sweating, headaches and fatigue will wear off."

Laudanum. Of course. He'd deduced as much. How else would they have managed to imprison him without his knowledge.

Warmed by her touch and soft voice, he gently closed his fingers around her trembling hand.

"You fought like a bull every time you woke. They were afraid you would hurt yourself and deprive them of their profit. They kept you drugged."

"More likely, I would hurt them." He snorted. "You are a prisoner?"

"We are the only two prisoners aboard. The scoundrels on the dock in London who paid Captain Diogo made sure there were no witnesses to our abduction and that we'd never reach the coasts of England again."

"Who are you and why have you earned this voyage?"

"I was caught in Baron Sutherland's home."

He had heard of Baron Sutherland. A good friend of his now dead father. "You are a thief." He withdrew his hand, but she held fast.

"I am not a thief."

"If you say so."

"If I told you the truth would you believe me?"

"A thief? Plying your trade, not only stealing everything that is nailed down but the nails as well."

He heard her intake of breath like the indrawn wind that filled the long sweeps, tilting the ship to a sharp angle.

He had difficulties with thieves, had come to blows with a horde who had invaded the Rutland townhouse. He would not forget that night when they were bent on killing him, and neither would the thieves he had dispatched one by one.

Yet the woman didn't have to tell him she was caught in the Baron's home. She could've made up a story. He was kidnapped and he didn't do anything. What if she wasn't a thief? But what other reasonable explanation was there?

He kicked a chamber pot and it clanged in the corner.

"Think what you wish. You may be a murderer for all I know, but since we're in this together, I'll allow your illusions," she said.

"My illusions? Am I to take that from someone whose tools may be deception and misdirection?"

The iron framework of the hatch that sealed them was divided, half in his four-walled cell and half in hers. Her arm filled the tiny hole, barring a glimpse of her. How old was his traveling companion? Young? No. A safe bet, she existed as a hoary bent crone predisposed to a life of crime. Yet her voice possessed a musical quality and intimated something sacred and pure in her humanity—like his sister's.

Abby. How was she faring? Gently reared, she would not survive the rigors at sea under ruthless men. He didn't want to think of the horrors she'd encounter. Gloom darkened his cell. He had quarreled with his sister, had caught her in a grievous lie.

She had faked an engagement to her best friend, Sir Humphrey until she decided what she wanted to do with her life. Nicholas had ordered her to marry Humphrey and live with the consequences. To marry a man she did not love.

A vein throbbed in his jaw. Like Nicholas, forced by his iron-handed father to marry a woman he had no feelings for to fulfill his duty. To accept the responsibility that came with being a Rutland.

"How long have we been sailing?" Nicholas shook his head, the effect of the drug, tunneling his vision and pounding his head.

"I tugged out a loose nail in the floor and scratched twenty-seven marks on the wall, four weeks into the Atlantic, and too far to swim back to London."

His chin sunk into his chest. He would not last long enslaved in Brazil. Whomever was his enemy wanted a slow death. A fitting end for killing a man in self-defense? He stared at her hand. Her fate was worse than his. He could imagine what evil men did to a female slave.

Sailors yelled orders to each other high in the shrouds. He heard a bucket of water sloshed onto the deck and the swish of a mop.

"They are lying," she whispered.

"Go on."

She gripped his hand, apparently afraid he'd let go. To assure her, he rubbed his thumb over her knuckles, smeared the dirt.

"I didn't know until Captain Diogo conveyed his message to you now from the man who had you kidnapped. On the docks in England, you were lying down and bound behind me. The laudanum given me had worn off. I feigned sleep. Your sister must have been kept in the room next to ours for they referred to her as Lady Abigail. They took her and another man, embarking on a ship before us."

"Outside our building, a very angry gentleman shouted at Captain Diogo, demanding he disappear to Brazil at once. The gentleman complained about a delay and said *they* left the laboratory too soon. Could he have been talking about your father and your brother? Do you think they left before the explosion and that's why the gentleman hastened your departure?"

The ship tilted again and latticed sunlight from above chased away the shadows of his cell. His blood rushed. He tightened his grip on her hand. "The gentleman, was he in charge? Did you get a look at him? Are you sure of what you heard?"

"You'll have to take the word of a thief." She withdrew her hand.

He deserved her scorn. Strange as it was, he missed the human contact of her hand, missed her warmth.

"I did not see the gentleman and he was definitely giving the commands."

Nicholas swallowed, his throat dry as sand. "Lady Abigail is my sister. At her betrothal ball, I called her out on her sham engagement. I argued her case with my father as well as my own complaints. He wouldn't listen, intolerant of any breach to his authority.

I went to the stables to cool my temper and was intercepted by a servant with a message to meet my father in my brother's laboratory. How strange when I had left him seconds before."

"Do you think your disagreement delayed your father and saved his life?"

The woman had given him possibilities—had given him hope. He owed her a debt of gratitude. *By God, if I ever get free of this hellhole, I'll go back home and do whatever my father demands.*

He heard voices above. The hatch above was thrown open. "Dinner time." Damiano lowered a bucket to the woman on the other side of the wall. "I should come down and help you eat? Eh, *senhorita?*"

Like his sister, Abby, his fellow prisoner was a woman without protection. "Leave her alone, swine."

"Insolent dog. You will be sent deep inside the jungles of Brasilia where you will die toiling in the hot tropical sun. Impossible to escape." Damiano hurled the contents of a bucket on Nicholas and slammed the grate. "Eat like a swine, your lordship. There won't be any more until tomorrow."

Nick wiped cold suet and watery rice off his shoulder. He doubted if any of it was edible. A rat scurried over his boot intent on the garbage. Nicholas kicked the offending rodent.

"I fear Damiano," the woman said. "He is worse than the captain," said his fellow prisoner.

Nicholas grunted and peered through the hole, but the fading gray light, filtering from above kept his traveling companion obscure.

She shoved her fist through the opening, unfolded a hand of food. "Eat. Keep up your strength. To escape."

"In the middle of the Atlantic?" He scoffed. Ridiculous. But she was right about needing strength...for whenever the time came. He took the proffered food, and then eating, he sank into a sea of silence.

The words, degrading and dehumanizing, were something he preferred not to think about, reminding him of the filthy wretch he'd become. His clothes were torn by his captors.

He wrinkled his nose at a stink that rivaled the worst of London's sewers. The lack of water to wash and several weeks' growth of beard was far from the cleanliness to which he was accustomed. His valet would have an opinion.

To escape, she'd said. Pretty transparent, it was...trying to jerk him from sinking into despondency. She did not know despair had no chance with him.

Vengeance had emerged as his new master.

Alexandra Sutherland shivered in the darkness. Hours passed since they had spoken. "Lord Rutland, have you wondered about the name of this ship and its crewmate? *Santanas* means Satan. Damiano means to kill."

"You know Portuguese?"

The mockery in his voice set her teeth on edge. *Thief* had branded his thoughts. Let him think what he wanted. "I learned a little Portuguese at my employer's."

"And he is a thief, too?"

Stubborn, spoiled man. Certainly, not a Sir Galahad. Vicar Thompson was the gentle soul who had educated her and far from a thief. "He was very giving toward me."

"So, you stole for him and he offered you a warm bed."

Heat rose to her face. "You insufferable clod. How dare you insinuate——" She bit back the rest of the scathing words on her tongue. She needed an ally, not an enemy. Taking a deep breath, she shoved more food through the hole again. If only she could thrust it down his throat. "Be forewarned, you should not bite the hand that feeds you, and——I refuse to answer any more of your provocations."

"Provocation? A sophisticated word. Well-learned——"

"For a thief? I read."

He grunted his disbelief. "What did you read last?"

Despite his antagonism, the deep timbre of his voice was like an eternal god, commanding denizens of the earth. As if she needed the sound of his voice to feel his very presence taking up the space all around her.

No doubt he was intelligent and had been educated in the best of England's schools. She gritted her teeth. With certainty, he considered her illiterate. "Something you should read. *Common Sense.*"

"You approve of the American, Thomas Paine's clear and per-suasive prose, inciting the common people of the Colonies to revolt against the King?"

Clever to test her. Well, if he wanted a challenge... "I believe the author marshals moral and political arguments for an egalitar-ian government."

He scoffed. "You agree with Paine's claim that a mind is a vessel not to be filled, but a fire to be kindled?"

She smiled for the first time in a long while. "Not Paine, but Plutarch. Anymore questions, Lord Rutland?"

"Proves you are a weed among stones. So, I'm in the company of an educated thief. Your name?"

His voice boomed like a thunderclap, a demand not a request. She stiffened, her emotions too raw for his scorn. No reason to go into her real history, unable to prove her true ancestry in any event. She chose to give her adopted name. "Alexandra Elwins."

"Miss Elwins," he repeated.

She looked heavenward. His reckless defiance of Damiano and Captain Diogo, left no doubt of his authoritative nature. With all the ferocity of a winter tempest, he dared to quarrel with his captors. She reversed her earlier opinion of his intelligence. He was insane or feeble-minded. "Why did you champion me?"

He sighed. "You needed my protection."

"I am grateful." Regardless of his belligerence, she needed someone to communicate with as much as the air she breathed. "What do you think motivated the man who abducted you and your sister, and lured your father and brother to the laboratory?"

"If I knew—"

His voice deepened, too complicated to point to one single emotion.

"I am unable to explain anything," he said, the sharpness in his voice betraying his unwillingness to do so. If he wanted to keep his own counsel, then fine.

Alexandra closed her eyes, fighting an onslaught of images that flashed through her head. The leering Damiano dropping into her cell, his rough hands and drooling mouth moving over her body. So far, he'd been put off by the captain's watchful eye.

The smirking Damiano indulged in countless taunts of the new hell awaiting her. The terrors she would face in Brazil. Stripped naked, men groping her breasts, to be prodded and probed in the most intimate places, and then sold to the highest bidder. To be used by men to satisfy their lusts. Her mind spun with the odious insults Damiano had described over the past weeks, in lurid detail, what ghastly fate was in store for her.

She squeezed her eyes shut. *Think of other things.* Positive things. How to escape…or the low, deep and commanding voice of her fellow prisoner.

Was the man on the other side of the wall the heir to the Duke of Rutland? She had seen him once, two years before, while visiting London. He was talking to friends in front of the Palace of Westminster. Molly's friend had affirmed the Rutland ducal coach and Alexandra had glimpsed him from behind. Dark-haired. Broad-shouldered. Would a handsome face match that rich masculine voice of his? Perhaps not. More a haughty, pinched-faced aristocrat, pale, and possessing a penchant to wipe his beak-nose.

She recalled a scandal following Lord Rutland, a noted pugilist after someone had died at his hands. No wonder Captain Damiano kept him drugged. The newspapers had trumpeted that Lord Rutland had committed murder with one fatal punch to another Lord. Competing testimony by witnesses, fanned by sensational articles in the London Chronicle had moved public opinion against Lord Rutland. She shrugged, unable to determine his guilt or not.

In her cell for days, Alexandra had counted each grain and knot in the planks. She peered through the hatch, every inch of canvas fully drawn, the bellies so rounded and hard they looked ready to burst, and speeding her away from her beloved England. She sat in the gloom, her companion choosing to sink into his sullen reflections. His silence taunted her, reminding her how she had arrived at this wretched point in her life.

Isolated in Deconshire, Alexandra had felt different from the people who resided there, different in her way of growing up. Old memories taunted her of a far easier life, and goaded misplaced childhood years to the surface. Driven by curiosity and frustrated by her adoptive parents' lack of information, Alexandra had resorted to snooping. She tore the cottage apart and found a gold covered Bible, far more elegant than anything Molly and Samuel could afford.

Written in the family Bible were her real parent's names. She had confronted Molly and Samuel Elwins who had posed as her parents. To have been lied to all those years.

Molly and Samuel sat her down and talked. Her real mother, Lady Lucy Sutherland had died during childbirth. Molly Elwins had been hired as Alexandra's wet nurse and nanny, nurturing Alexandra. Two years later, her real father, Baron Stephen Sutherland had remarried and soon afterward, died.

Molly had doubts about the new baroness. When Baron Sutherland had died suddenly while in good health, Molly became even more suspicious and started eavesdropping. From an overheard conversation Molly had learned Alexandra's stepmother, Lady Ursula Sutherland, had poisoned the baron, thus enabling her own son, Willean, to become the heir of the barony.

What terrified Molly was an unfortunate accident planned for the three-year old Alexandra to ensure Willean's inheritance. Powerless to prove the foul deed, and to protect the little girl, Molly and Samuel had swept the child, Alexandra away in the middle of the night, leaving no trace of their footsteps. For seventeen

years, they hid in the small fishing village of Deconshire in southern England where they provided a simple and good life.

Despite Molly and Samuel's good intentions, Alexandra, at
twenty years, simmered with a fury for being deceived for so long
and had refused to speak to them. She had waited for Molly to leave
for London to visit a friend. Part in rebellion of their deception and
mainly because she needed answers, Alexandra put on Samuel's
sturdy woolen coat and had set out on foot, leaving Deconshire
behind her. Catching a ride on a miller's wagon to the next town,
she bought passage by coach and traveled to her ancestral home.

Despite the danger, and under cover of darkness, she broke
into the library.

The key to her heritage was there. All her life, visions of her
real father had haunted her. The wainscoting, his desk, the smell
of leather volumes filling the shelves triggered a flood of memories—riding her Shetland pony, parties with cakes, her first puppy,
sliding down a bannister, her father's laughter. She had wiped away
a sudden rush of tears and rifled through the desk. A lamp fell.
Footsteps beat a staccato rhythm in the hall. Willean appeared and
overpowered her, and then Ursula, summoned from her chambers, materialized. Willean refused his mother's demands to kill
Alexandra, and then solved their problem by shipping her off with
Captain Diogo, a smuggler and business associate.

The *Santanas* careened to the right. Alexandra flailed her arms,
slapping her hands against the greasy planks to catch her balance.
Rats scratched against the wall. She had no one to blame but herself
for her miserable destiny.

Beyond the wall, Lord Rutland remained cast in stygian darkness. He did not offer his thoughts. Had the residual laudanum

made him fall to sleep? Tucking her tattered woolen skirts about her drawn-up knees, she adjusted her filthy linen blouse, and then snuggled beneath Samuel's woolen coat, grateful she had taken it for the warmth it provided. She leaned back, tilted her head up. Through the shrouds, the heavens chased the day into night, the glimmering of stars her only companions. A shadow passed over the grate. The figure of a man. A key rasped in a lock. The hatch scraped open. *Damiano.*

He swung his feet over the edge.

"No," she cried and scrambled to her feet, arms waving and pummeling his legs.

He dropped onto her. "Senhorita, you will experience a man." He covered her mouth, the rancid odor of rum and fish penetrated her cell.

"Leave her alone! Fight me, Portuguese scum," bellowed Lord Rutland. He kicked the walls, making a racket to alert the captain. "Captain Diogo! Captain Diogo!"

"Shut-up, Rutland, before I run you through," Damiano warned, his voice harsh and gravely.

"And I'll kill you if you touch her."

Damiano laughed. "Brave words from the other side of the wall. You are useless."

Alexandra clamped her teeth on Damiano's hand. The ugly man cursed and swung out with a powerful blow across her face. Her head snapped back, stars exploded in front of her eyes. Damiano reached out, grabbed her by the shoulders and slammed her to the floor. He thrust his hand down her bodice. Pinched her nipples, sucked her lips, bit her neck. She raised clenched fists, swinging wildly, pummeling at the side of his head.

He grabbed both of her hands and held them together over her head. "I like a woman with fight in her." As he yanked up her skirts, her screams were drowned by Lord Rutland's shouts. Damiano punched her on the side of the head. She stared out the opened hatch, helpless to fight anymore.

Through a haze, a figure in the darkness appeared at the aperture above, then in one swift move, he dropped onto her assailant. Damiano's weight abruptly lifted off her. She rolled away, cringing and pulling into herself.

"You swine," snarled Lord Rutland.

How had Lord Rutland come to be in her cell?

In the darkness, the thud of a fist buried into flesh. Air wheezed from someone's lungs. The outline of broad shoulders charged against another dark outline. She scrambled into the corner, the tiny confines of her cell, making it impossible to avoid the two men. Fists flew as hard and fast as the curses between blows. Knuckles crunched against jawbone again and again. Her food bucket rattled against the wall.

"I promise you, Damiano," Lord Rutland growled as they banged around in the small space. "You will be weeping with the devil when I'm done with you." Fists pounded into flesh.

Boots hammered above her across the deck. She glanced to the hatch. Damiano had left the hatch open and unlocked. That's how Lord Rutland had gotten in. Their jailer had inadvertently freed him.

"Damiano," Captain Diogo roared and pointed his pistols. "Stop or I'll shoot you both." Within minutes, two deckhands lowered a ladder and hauled both men from her cell. A lantern held by one of the sailors blinded her view.

"Damiano tried to attack her," Nicholas said on the way out. "Your profit will diminish if she is defiled, Captain Diogo."

Alexandra's heart sank with the truth of his words. A virgin was a highly-prized commodity on the slave market. Lord Rutland was protecting her by striking the captain with his greed.

"You would lose a substantial amount." Nicholas pressed when Captain Diogo hesitated. "Damiano should be punished to set an example."

"There is truth in what you say, Lord Rutland. But this is my ship and under my command. Get back into your cell." And at the captain's nod, a deckhand shoved Nicholas and sent him tumbling into his cell. Diogo turned to Damiano. "I have warned you to stay away from the woman. I will not have you lashed because I need every available seaman. But I'm taking away your profit share from this voyage. Consider my orders a mercy for disobeying me."

Damiano leaned away from his guards and spat into the grate. "Lord Rutland, you will pay. And to you, my lady. Think how it will be if there is a storm and you are locked below to suffer the fates of the sea as the ship sinks and the water rises over your head."

"I will have you tied to the mast if you disobey my orders," Captain Diogo warned. "I lose my patience when my sleep is disturbed."

The hatch dropped with a thud, a lock clicked, sealing them in their separate cells once again. Alexandra sank to the floor, covered her face with her hands and wept.

Nicholas thrust his hand through the hole. "Hold my hand," he commanded.

Fingers shaking, she lifted her hand and clasped his. Like the force of a thousand burning suns, the heat of his strength and energy surged through her.

"Are you hurt?" She hated the idea of Lord Rutland being injured on her behalf.

"Half of the blows he initiated never landed."

With her other hand, she ran her fingers over his knuckles, and like a blind child would, caressed their breadth and width and power. So much could be told about a person's hands, and his were calloused like a blacksmith's. She frowned with the incongruity. Aristocrats never labored. "Damiano will remember his humiliation."

"Oh, he will get even, if given the opportunity. I await the occasion with pleasure."

Her hand felt at home in his, like it should be meant for all time. "I hope Captain Diogo will keep a stern eye on him."

"I wish I could lash him until he could not breathe," said Nicholas.

A smile touched her lips. She sensed he bore his imprisonment with solid indifference, his fearlessness allowing him to escape any tragedy. He was heroic for sure, for he had come to her rescue.

What if they were free from these wretched conditions, and had met under normal circumstances? Where the element of her birthright was proven and her rank in society solidified. Would they be friends? Would he court her?

No. Too many impossibilities and too much dreaming. They weren't free. They may never be free. Their fate lay in the hands of their captors.

"Thank you…again," she whispered. How she wanted to tear down the wall, to be comforted in his strong arms. But for now, she received some solace that his shoulder was leaned against hers with the wall between them.

"I did nothing. You were very brave."

His voice came swift and sharp and sure like the thundering of the surf against the hull, making her feel safe. As safe as one could feel in such a situation. "You did," she said. She held his hand and a warm feeling gushed through her. Never had she been so forward in her life to allow the intimacy of holding a man's hand.

In the darkness, the light of consolation had come from a stranger who wouldn't desert her. She turned his hand over, drawing a trail from his wrist, across the palm to the tip of the longest finger. His hand flexed and straightened, then she folded his hand into hers and kissed his raw knuckles.

"Tell me about your family," he asked softly through the darkness.

Where should she begin? Her heart caught in her chest. "My mother stayed at home, tending a garden. My father was a sea captain, traveling the oceans for many years until he retired. He shared his love of the sea. I helped him untangle his nets. He taught me how to whittle and use a machete."

"Where did you live?"

"I…uh—" she coughed, stalling. If she gave out too much, Ursula might… "—lived in a quiet little fishing village in the south of England. Nothing remarkable. People eke out a living however they can. Very modest." She knew what he was thinking about her. How had a nice family yielded a thief? She did not want to travel that path. Not now. "We must think of the possibility of escape."

"I'm listening."

"You fought with Damiano like a demon," she whispered. "Your skill could come in handy when we arrive in Brazil. For now, we should pretend we are sick, malnourished and getting weaker. They will think we have no strength. Once we make port, we could fight them off and run. With my limited Portuguese, we could get help from someone, don't you think?"

From up above, Damiano leaned against the grate, looking furtively about. "There will be no help when you reach Brasilia, Senorita."

Alexandra touched her throat. Had Damiano heard what she'd said? No, the wind was too high.

Damiano drooled, his saliva dropped next to her foot. "Have I told you of the Senor in Brasilia you are promised to? He's gonna take you home once we get there. He wanted a light-haired woman and a virgin and was willing to pay a pretty price. His practices are extreme. Your arms and legs will be tied to the four corners of a bed. He loves a woman's screams. Takes pleasure in it. No one will come to your aid for he is enormously rich. You will feel a hot surge in your loins repeatedly. And did I mention the toys he uses on his women? When he tires of you, he lets his friends have a turn."

"Go to hell, Damiano." Nicholas leaped, grabbed the grate and pushed his fist through.

Damiano reared back, missing the blow and clucked. "All his women have a bad end...they are torn apart from stem to stern."

Damiano continued his rant. "Lord Rutland, there will be no escape for you in the heart of the jungle, surrounded by venomous snakes...and insects as long as your hand that suck your blood.

And in the jungle, there are very large cats that will sneak up on you, not to mention the piranha in the river, their sharp teeth can devour a man in seconds. You will die, too."

Alexandra smoothed her trembling fingers over her filthy skirts. She swallowed hard, her situation dire, and what she wanted of Lord Rutland was so profound that it lay balled in the bottom of her throat. In the universe, she was insignificant and forgotten. To know of the merciless violence that was her future, to be a slave to a man who used her body for his malicious cravings. She needed a way to get out of being sold to this sadistic man. If she could figure out a way to darken and cut her hair…and if she was no longer a virgin, he wouldn't want her.

To simplify what was complicated.

She had never lain with a man before and if it was going to happen she wanted her first to be with someone she might have chosen anyway. She might even have chosen Lord Rutland to be her first.

With a shattering breath, she whispered, "Lord Rutland, if you could get through this wall…I want you to…"

Oh, her entreaty to Lord Rutland. She felt herself blush from her toes to the roots of her hair. Salt air stung her nose, and the wind whipped around the ship and beat against the sails while she waited for his response.

He cleared his throat. "Impossible."

Her spine curved into the damp boards. If only she could disappear into the wood grain. What he must think of her, giving so cavalier a request. "If you take my virginity then that man would no longer want me."

"We are not discussing the sale of oats."

23

Her breath burned in and out of her lungs. "I know you are a man of honor—"

"You will still be sold and our prison holds me bound. Our captors will make sure we are kept separate."

He did not say no. "If you could breach the wall that divides us, would you?"

His voice went softer, but she heard it as if he had whispered in her ear. "Hear this, I will kill anyone who lays a hand on you."

She pressed her palms together and breathed a prayer for Lord Rutland.

Chapter 2

*A*lexandra awoke to see another bucket of slop sluiced onto Nicholas. Was it to be a daily ritual?

Damiano cupped his hands around his ears, his pockmarked face possessing the appearance of a pebbled goblin. "Enjoy your garbage with the rats."

Alexandra shared her better rations with Nicholas, experiencing the heat of his fingers touching hers.

She put her shoulders back, refusing to succumb to the feeling of helplessness in the face of her hideous fate. "Don't let your thoughts fall prey to the must not's, the don'ts, or the impossible. We will escape," Alexandra confirmed to Lord Rutland to keep her optimism alive.

She burrowed into her father's coat, inhaling his scent, and then moved her hands into the pockets and pulled out his spectacles, fingering the thick lenses. How he needed them to see. She gulped. Even that small luxury she had taken from him. She pinned the cool lenses into her bodice, a silly gesture to keep him close to her heart.

Lord Rutland broke through her reverie. "It will be an absolute triumph if I can hold down the garbage they give us for food. Despite your happy confidence, we are heading to a country controlled by

Portugal, far from England, a different language and a sea captain bent on his profits."

"There is no room for petty doubt," she sighed, clinging to the hope of seeing her father again. To ask for his forgiveness. "We must exercise to keep our muscles from weakening, and to use our energies to devise our escape, to imagine what scenarios we might encounter. We will survive. I feel it in my bones." Her breath caught in her chest, less sure of the outcome than she touted.

"Keep wiggling that worm of hope. We'll give the escape a try."

A storm was coming. She could smell the thickness in the air. Her hearing adjusted itself beyond the crack of sails and the plunging sweep of spray around the hull.

The wave-racked confluence of the westerlies moving across the Atlantic now battled with the easterlies off the coast of Africa. Such forces she had learned about from her sea captain father.

Hurricane.

Destructive storms that raged across the sea, leaving no soul alive. The rusty lock on the hatch stayed secure. Cold ropy tentacles of fear wrapped around her chest and suddenly she couldn't breathe. Would she die a prisoner in a watery grave at the bottom of the sea as Damiano had predicted?

The masthead lookout's cry was muffled by the wind and the lively pop of sails. The seas grew choppier, and then gigantic waves swept over the decks, rushing like a fierce terrier.

For four days, the wind raged with terrible ferocity, the *Santanas* and its crew at the mercy of the storm, scudding away to be swallowed up by the sea.

"Let us out," demanded Nicolas, but his voice was lost to the wind and fury. Alexandra jumped, grabbed the grate, swinging back and forth. She stuck her free hand out and waved. "Have mercy. Let us out." Seawater rushed over the hatch, Alexandra fell, sputtering, gagging. She stood again, gasping for air. The ship lifted and a wave ripped along the *Santanas* port beams, then wallowed over, throwing the ship backward. Alexandra slipped and slid. She could imagine any man not tied to the decks aloft survived.

Damiano clutched the grate. "*Senhorita*, I will give you pleasure now."

"You dare to go against Captain Diogo?" Nicholas snarled, his demand drowned out by the wind.

"I killed him. We are all going to die from this storm, but I will have the woman before I do." Damiano threw open the hatch. Alexandra bared her teeth, but her knees shook. "I will not make it easy for you."

Damiano laughed.

At the same time, Nicholas leaped upward, head butted him. Damiano fell back. Nicholas hurdled from the hold, thrust his hand down for Alexandra. She grabbed on. Nicholas yanked her upward with such strength she rammed into him and flattened him to the deck. The *Santanas* tacked violently, her sails in confusion as she plunged into the storm.

"Tie yourself to something," Nicholas ordered like he was Poseidon.

She rolled off him, crawled across the slippery planks, curling her fingers over the edge of the iron hatch.

Damiano came to his feet and lunged. "I will make you pay, Lord Rutland for making me look a fool."

She watched Nicholas sidestep and bring his right forearm viciously down across the back of the seaman's neck. A wave swept over the ship, carrying the two across the deck and slamming them into the rails. Damiano rose first, his lip bleeding where his teeth went through. He wiped his mouth on his shirt and leaped on Nicholas.

With a deceptive lunge to the right, followed by a snake-like twist to the left, Nicholas swung his powerful right fist into Damiano's face. As the Portuguese sailor's head snapped back, Nicholas doubled-up his own head and shoulder and drove into the man's stomach like a battering ram.

Alexandra rose to her feet. The canvas slapped around her ears and still the men fought on. Madness. That was what it was. Pure insanity. The planks beneath her vibrated with the storm's fury. The hull staggered violently, blocks screamed, the *Santanas* heeled steeply to take the wind under her stern sails, lifting then filled to its thrust. The mast topgallant seemed to bend forward, the masthead pendant flicking straight out towards the bows, as if to point the way.

Through the slanting rain, a few men stood like men facing an execution, so stricken they were unable to think or respond. Others fought the wind, and pushed a lifeboat over the gunnels, and then scrambled into the vessel. Someone shouted a warning. The ship heaved. Alexandra fell, hurled on her back. She reached out, clawed at the capstan.

Damiano staggered backward, fell onto the deck, rose and came at Nicholas with a barrage of fists, punching Nicholas's head hard with the force of a bull. Nicholas slipped on the wet deck and Damiano dropped onto him. Nicholas flicked the wet hair from his forehead. Looking weakened and thin from lack of nutrition, he feinted to the right and then the left and dodged the fists coming at him. He needed help.

Just as she thought it, a belaying pin rolled by Alexandra. She stretched her fingers and snatched it up. She let go of the capstan, and inched toward the rail, her eyes passing over swivel gunners, the unprotected wheel, two grim-faced sailors stringing futilely at the sails above. The most forward shrouds and rigging hung like black weeds above the *Santanas* deck, the brig staggering drunkenly under the onslaught.

A seaman shrieked as he fell from the yardarm above, his body making a sickening thud on impact, landing on the deck next to her. His eyes and mouth still open, blood pooled around his head. The *Santanas* gave a violent shudder, tacking listlessly to the side.

Alexandra slammed into the rail. The dead seaman rolled over her and into the sea. Water churned below, the waves like tumbling white-horses. Gone was the lifeboat, into the sea upside down, men's cries to their savior lost in the screaming wind.

Hand over hand she pulled on one pilaster and then another. Nicholas and Damiano tumbled on the deck, fists flying and cursing at each other. The *Santanas'* fore and mainmasts staggered and then began to topple sideways, the sails jerking to the bombardment of wind.

A crippled wreck, the frigate's sails ripped and punctured like rags. Lightning exploded, and the ships' foremast vanished in a mass of rigging and ripped canvas. Still clutching the belaying pin, she edged toward the men. Damiano pulled a knife from his belt.

Death coming up the hawse, Nicholas dodged Damiano's knife thrusts. She stared at Lord Rutland, her eyes critical. For just those few moments, she had seen the real man beneath and it frightened her. Nicholas punched, feinted, and taunted Damiano again and again, never giving the sailor a chance to recover.

Alexandra reached the quarterdeck, yanked her wet hair from her eyes. The mast was shattering and ready to fall. "Watch out, Nicholas."

Damiano bellowed, dropped his knife. Nicholas broke off as the splintering crash of the main topgallant canted over, the sail whipping madly in a web of parted rigging, while the yard itself snapped into equal halves before pitching toward the sea. Alexandra covered her head as an avalanche of wood and cording suddenly rained down upon her. Where was Nicholas? On her hands and knees, the slippery deck raised as she crawled over fallen rigging.

Damiano. Her gaze went to his corpse, his body severed by the weight of the cordage draped over the larboard and trailing along the sea. She swallowed the sour bile in her mouth, squeezed her eyes shut and forced her limbs to creep around Damiano's body to find Nicholas.

Below, flotsam clawed at the *Santanas*, the storm a battering ram splitting her seams wide open. Alexandra combed the deck and the sea. Rain slashed at different angles from the wind changing direction and blinding her. Through the haze, she saw Nicholas bobbing on the mast dragged from the ship, the foremast shrouds catching him in a giant web. The *Santanas* shrieked, tilted more to port. Alexandra screamed, stretched her arms out, freed the halyard and grasped Damiano's knife. In a matter of seconds the ship would sink, the rigging trapping Nicolas and dragging him into the jaws of the sea.

Clasping the knife between her teeth, she dove into the water, her skirts and coat, a lodestone, that dragged her downward to a watery grave. She tore them off and kicked. The sea tumbled her round and round in a rolling motion. In the dark waters, she had no idea what was up or what was down. She could drown and no one would know.

No. She was not going to die in the sea. *Swim.* She had to *swim.* Her lungs about to burst, she gave another valiant kick. *Swim, Alexandra.* The muscles in her body ached. Her shoulders burned. Lights danced in front of her eyes.

At last, she broke the surface, grabbed the knife from her mouth, and spitting water, sucked in a lungful of air before another wave rolled over her. With saltwater stinging her eyes as she peered through the grey mist, she called out, "Nicholas!"

She pulled in another long draught of oxygen, dove and came up through the rigging. Found Nicholas limp, and with blood pouring from an ugly gash across his forehead. *No. No.* She heard a moan. Nicholas? Or was that the wind? She placed trembling fingers on his chest, felt a slight movement, then a thump under her fingers. Tears welled in her eyes. Her chest squeezed. *Oh, God. Thank God.*

But, like the tentacles of an octopus, the rigging held him fast. Suddenly numb to the storm, she sawed at his bonds, looking behind, the ship yawed over them. Any minute it would succumb to its weight and carry them below. She tugged the last rope free. His wrists slipped from her grasp and she lunged, grabbing one of his hands. *Hold on. Don't let go.*

Spray dashed across their heads, and then a wave curled over them, sucking them down in its wrath. One. Two. Three...ten seconds elapsed before they surfaced in the air. So little time. Grabbing flotsam large enough for one person, and with long portions of the remaining rope, she tied him to the top of it, wrapped a rope around his wrist to hers, and then secured herself on top of him, tucking her precious knife in her bodice with her father's spectacles. She kicked her little craft away from the straying rigging.

She looked up as a giant wall of water crashed over them, possessing an otherworldly, wicked force. Its curved hollow felt like the inside of a clenching fist as it hurled them across the unknown waters of the Atlantic. They fell into another trough, and again the wave threw them into its belly. No air. Her head exploded. Lights went out in her brain. Air. Death. *We are the interlopers.* The sea will have its retaliation. It will devour us.

For hours, feathers of spray lifted from wave after wave, spinning, and then plunging their little craft hard into the grey crescents, surrendering them to the mercy of the long-drawn out shrieking of the wind as if a thousand devils had been freed from the sea itself.

Currents whirled them toward a shadowy land form. Sharp rocks loomed, the land more dangerous than the sea. A raging, mountain-like wave rolled astern with such fury and was their final *coup de grâce*. In a chest-squeezing panic, a sense arose within that the ocean held all the power.

Shadows blanketed and fogged at the edges of her mind, in time with the sea that undulated and yawed. So weak. Losing all sense of where and who she was...she wanted to let go. Fatigue settled in, and with it, she allowed the monster to swallow her up.

Chapter 3

*G*entle surf rolled in at his feet causing Nicholas to snap his eyes open. He stared through a mesh of leaves. He glanced around. What the... He pushed off the palm fronds scattered over him, rose, and clutched his pounding head, the throbbing about to split his head open.

He staggered a few feet, and then collapsed near a coconut log and rested his back against it. He squinted at the blue sky with cloud racks piled upon the horizon, and parallel to him lay the sea, the restless, turbulent sea, now at peace.

His energy depleted, he sat there allowing the sun to beat down upon him. His stomach had long since contracted into a hard, little fist, shrunk to nothing. With neither food nor adequate water, he sweated little. His stomach gurgled with hunger and every muscle in his body ached from the hammering blows delivered by Damiano.

He brushed a sandy hand through his hair, remembered the mast falling on him. How had his life been delivered? He looked about. Nothing to eat or drink and...no weapons.

Worse than the prospect of perishing from hunger or being devoured by beasts in this godforsaken end of the world, was finding himself alone. To watch the sun, rise in the east, cross the sky and sink into the west while listening to the echoes of his own thoughts, and finding no other inspiration, would break him.

Entertaining the melancholy of his isolation, he narrowed his eyes on a trail of footsteps along the beach. He saw her then, with barely a stitch of clothing on, walking down the shoreline like a goddess, a knife tucked in her bodice.

Bright as the morning's light, she was the symbol of the earth, the movement of waves, and the song at night. Blood pounded in his temples as he absorbed the movement of her hips beneath the sheer fabric of her chemise, and the way she wore her hair, long, wavy, gleaming gold tumbling down her back. The sight of well-shaped breasts unconfined by the normal female frivolities, stirred-up the heat in his loins and muddled his wits.

He scrubbed a hand across his face. He must be delirious with dehydration.

"Oh, you're awake," said his hallucination. She clutched a coconut to her chest, used it as a ridiculous shield of modesty.

He closed his eyes tight shut and opened them again to make sure he was not dreaming.

"Is it my state of undress, Lord Rutland?"

The vision knew his name? He stared at her as if she might escape if he didn't hold her with his gaze. "Am I hallucinating?"

"If you were, how would asking me, help?" She laughed at her own wit.

Stunned by the truth of that logic, he fumbled with his recollection. Had they been introduced? Her voice had a sweet, innocent quality... "Alexandra?"

She nodded. Good God. How could he have thought the breathtakingly beautiful woman standing over him was a hoary old crone? When he pulled her out of the hold, he'd been too busy with fighting Damiano and hadn't looked at her.

No wonder Damiano chose to suffer a lashing and loss of profit to have her. If he were not a gentleman, he'd have torn down the wall himself.

A blush stole across her sun-kissed cheeks. "I had to divest my skirts and overcoat when I dove in the ocean to save you."

Nicholas jerked his head back. "You dove off the ship? In that storm?"

She rubbed her hand over a long thigh, an unconscious act of smoothing out skirts that no doubt lingered at the bottom of the ocean. "When the mast fell, you were pitched into the sea... trapped in the rigging. I freed you...tied you to floating wreckage...the storm pushed us to this place." She concentrated on her toe, liberating a shell from the sand.

He frowned, taking in the extraordinary events since his imprisonment aboard the *Santanas*. "I am indebted to you."

The lacy fringe of her lashes lifted and he felt as if a thread went taut between them, connecting them, alone together on this wretched beach.

"You've had another knock on the head. I worried if you would regain consciousness or become demented."

"I assure you, I have all of my wits."

She laughed at his grimness, picked up the shell she had unearthed, waded into the sea and filled it with water. "You were too heavy to drag up the beach, so I covered you with palm fronds to shield you from the sun."

She ripped off the hem of her chemise, knelt beside him, and washed his face. Her fingers trembled. He flinched not only from her touch but the sight of long shapely calves.

"You have a gash across your forehead but it will heal."

"I feel like dying."

"I'll decide when you die, Lord Rutland, not you. Although, I should have let the sea have you when you kept up that witless fight with Damiano."

He glanced around. "Damiano?"

She shuddered. "The mast cut him in two."

"It was no more than the swine deserved. Are there any other survivors?" Nicholas started to rise, but fell back against the log.

She brushed her long golden mane behind her shoulders and peered toward the west. "I walked the beach for miles and didn't see evidence of any others. Not even a drift of flotsam from the *Santanas* to mark its existence. Not that I would welcome Damiano, Capitan Diogo or his crew's hellish company. I desire no remembrance of them."

He attempted to rise again. She waylaid him by taking hold of his face with both her hands, and rubbing her thumbs along his jaw. He felt as though he were being stroked by the wings of an angel. She looked like an angel too, damn it all, with those enchanting turquoise eyes that matched the sea. He liked her cool hands upon his face, but it made it damned hard to concentrate on what to do about this predicament. She had no idea how her touch seemed to make him a bumbling idiot. Perhaps he was demented.

Maybe, if he didn't look at her mouth again he'd be able to think. But damn if he didn't look anyway. It was impossible to not look at those full luscious lips that were meant to be kissed.

She withdrew her hands. "I'll scout around and find something to make a poultice."

"You know of such things?"

She sat back on her heels. "You find it remarkable that a thief would have healing knowledge?"

"We are on equal footing, Miss Elwins. We have survived thus far and will need each other to continue to do so."

She smiled with his concession and her face took on a mesmerizing radiance. She leaned over to pick up the coconut she dropped, giving him a tantalizing view of her full breasts and rosy nipples. He cleared his throat, listening to the thudding of her smashing through the grassy husk, pounding the inner shell on a rock until it cracked open. She offered the crude vessel to him. He lifted the sweet water into his parched mouth, amazed by her resourcefulness, from diving off the ship, cutting through rigging, covering him with palm fronds and gathering coconuts.

"Eat the coconut meat inside," she ordered.

Not accustomed to taking orders, he slanted a look at her.

"We are on equal footing, Lord Rutland," she repeated his words. "You need your nourishment if you are to be of help to me."

With avid interest, he saw a spark in her eyes and an amused twitch of her mouth. She was a dazzling vision and like a schoolboy with his first infatuation, she could cut him out into little stars if she had the whim.

What other secrets lay behind her playful smile? The innocent appeal of a thief this beautiful could easily operate undetected by charming her victims. Why, she could steal the Crown jewels out of London Tower and be long gone before anyone noticed. He grunted. Despite her past crimes, he needed her.

He chewed on a piece of fibrous coconut and his strength seemed fairly restored. "Are we on an island or a continent?"

She shielded her eyes, scanning the treetops and the mountain behind. "On board the ship, I observed the stars through the shrouds. I think we are in the northern region of the Caribbean. Whether we are on an island or continent, I cannot tell."

"Your knowledge of the sea?" he said, more of a question than a statement.

"My father kindled my imagination and set fire my thirst for learning, taking great delight in sharing his knowledge of the ocean. He spent many hours taking me out in his dingy, catching fish, teaching me how to use a knife and how to live off the sea. During those idyllic days, he instructed me about the stars."

"Did he ever take you on his voyages?"

"I never accompanied him but he told me tales about the places he visited especially the Caribbean. He returned with books, shells, and rare fruits. With some accuracy, I'll be able to identify what we can eat."

She gestured with a coconut chunk. "To think one of my favorite books was *Robinson Crusoe* and here we are living Defoe's imaginings. Who would have thought?"

"Reading fiction and surviving it are two different experiences."

He followed her searching gaze out over the horizon, a thin seam where the crown of the sky and the flat of the sea hemmed each other into a line of sapphire. The harsh cry of a seagull fractured the serenity. "We will explore later to find out if we are on an island. For the time being, we need to deal with necessities like food, water and shelter."

He glanced at the palm trees with their giant fronds and vines clinging to their massive trunks. Shelter would be easy enough to do. "We will build a signal fire first to herald a passing ship." Now that he had a thread of hope that his father and brother might yet live, he had to get off this godforsaken patch of earth.

"We will not."

He turned so fast a muscle in his neck snapped. "Excuse me. Did I hear you right? We have to get off this barbaric coast. I have to rescue my sister and find out who committed this horrendous act to my family." He clawed at the sand at his side, his soul burning at his inability to protect them. Of one thing, he was sure. He would not fail to find who was responsible and make them pay. "We will build a signal fire first to herald a passing ship."

"No, we will not."

"Did I hear you right?"

She stood there, her posture, ramrod straight, a mutinous expression on her face. "Oh, you are favored by the gods, Lord Nicholas? Shall we hail a Spanish ship and become slaves of the Spaniards? They make the Portuguese look like saints. Or the Caribes? A lovely indigenous Indian group that resides on this tail end of the earth and who are predisposed to cannibalism. Perchance you are inclined to be someone's dinner."

Heat burned in his chest. There was nothing demure about the woman. Didn't she realize as a gentleman, he knew best? "I'll take that risk. We can live on coconuts for the time being," he said with enough glaring force that would make his tenants cower.

"And you are expert at starting fires?" She made an outrageously exaggerated curtsy. "Where is your tinderbox?"

"You do not believe I can perform the task?" Shaking off his dizziness, he stood, towered over her. Most women would take a step back. Miss Elwins stood her ground. He gritted his teeth, regretting the part about being on equal footing. Miss Elwins was demonstrating she had the upper hand.

"I suppose being a gentleman, you know a great deal about setting fires," she sniffed, her tone inferring that since he was really a softly reared aristocrat, he knew nothing.

He needed to set clear boundaries, and the sooner she realized he was the one who possessed the sounder logic the better off their relationship would be. "Your suggestion of obtaining food is admirable, but for today, I want you to pick-up driftwood."

"Suit yourself, Lord Rutland. I wish you luck building your fire. I'm off to scavenge for food which is a greater priority." She headed down the beach, kicking up puffs of sand from her heels.

He tore off his coat and threw it on the ground. Miss Elwins thought he couldn't build a fire. She could curtsy herself all the way to Windsor Castle and back. He'd show her.

Chapter 4

$\mathcal{A}$lexandra stomped down the beach, kicked a coconut out of the way. A sharp pain jagged from toe to ankle. Cursing, she hopped on her good foot while holding her injured toe. Apart from the King, Lord Rutland was the most dignified and memorable man she had ever met....and he knew it. Oh, to take him down a peg.

She sat down on a log and massaged her foot. To think she had saved his life and he commanded her like she was one of his servants.

Yet, she could not quell the rioting in her stomach. She had studied him while he was unconscious, reposed like a warrior taking his rest. Regardless of his pathetic state, he was the most beautiful man she'd ever seen. His face was shockingly handsome with high cheekbones and full lips. His bearded jaw spoke of determination and...stubbornness. Or did it hide a weak chin?

His thick wildly unkempt hair, dark in the sunlight, waved over his temple. And he had a patrician nose. A giggle bubbled up from deep in her throat from her imaginings on the ship. Beak nosed? What would his imperial majesty think about that notion?

While he'd been unconscious, she checked for bone breaks. His arms and legs were sound, but would have been thinner if she had not fed him aboard the *Santanas*. His coat had parted. She had walked her fingers over his ribs, skipped them over his abdomen, stopped at the waistband of his breeches. How shameless she had been. Her cheeks reddened from the memory.

Oh, when he was awake and stood up, he was a ferocious man, and how those blue eyes of his had raked her. Heat flooded her with his awareness of her attire. She shook her head. Not much to do about the thin chemise that stuck to her skin. If he couldn't stomach the impropriety, then she should have let him go down with the ship.

Would he hurt her? How he had fought Damiano with his powerful fists. Instinct told her he would not hurt her.

Why did she let him continue to let him believe she was a thief? The overwhelming culpability of what happened to Molly she had not been able to come to terms with yet. Like a bird grounded with a broken wing, guilt kept her a prisoner.

"I'm so sorry, Molly."

There was no echo, nor reverberation. If anything, the firmament consumed her words and her infinite, hopeless apology. But not her memories. She would never be rid of those.

And then to, days of secrets, hiding still another truth weighed on her shoulders with backbreaking force. Her throat constricted. Best to keep her identity as a ship captain's daughter. Too many questions would follow and she had no means of answering them.

Apart from her musings of Lord Nicholas, her spirits soared as food was in abundance. Their newly acquired diet would restore their health from the deprivations they had suffered aboard the *Santanas*. Fresh fruit hung heavily from the trees and her arms ached with the weight of mangoes, bananas and coconuts she had collected. She passed a herd of wild pigs, grazing on the edge of the beach, and then waded into the sea to cool her skin. Colorful fish darted around her knees, so plentiful and tame, and if her arms weren't full for fruit, she could pick them up.

Despite being God knew where, she took a deep breath of satisfaction. The wind was freshening and waved through the palms lining the deserted pink sand beach on which she followed her solitary footsteps. A sea hawk with its wings spread wide, floated motionless upon the updrafts issued from the land, and in the distance, the frothy creaming of waves broke upon an outer reef.

Her father had described this quarter of the earth, but his descriptions were nothing in compare to the soft, compelling beauty of these seas, and the endlessly changing shades of turquoise, greens and blues. The scenery induced her soul to complacency for it seemed incredible that here nature could prove to be an adversary...much like Lord Rutland.

She smiled. No matter his prevailing pride, she was blessed with such an agreeable climate and situation, and she would not be alone. This land with its bountiful fruits was far superior to being a prisoner on a ship and to be sold as a sex slave to a sadistic man.

Lord Rutland was not where she had left him. She followed a muttered curse and pushed through a canopy of palms. He stooped over a pile of driftwood, spinning a crude arrangement of twine procured from a vine, and a stick, reminiscent of Cro-Magnon man. At least he took her advice and moved the unlikely inferno away from the sea and potential hostile intruders. "How is the fire-starting?"

He threw down his contraption and stared at the bounty in her arms. "Food. I'm starved."

Cro-Magnon. She clutched the fruit to her breast. "I thought you said food was not a requirement." She held up a mango, dangling it back and forth. He cut the distance between them with long purposeful strides, snatching the ripened fruit from her hands. Lord Rutland's predictability was a supreme art. "You may want to peel it first," she suggested.

He ripped open the peel and sank his teeth into the fruit. "I know what a mango is, they are grown in our conservatory at Belvoir Castle." Juices flowed down his bearded chin. He was barefoot, his stockings and boots propped upside down on a log to dry. His shirt sleeves were rolled up over his elbows and his breeches were torn and filthy, his appearance contradictory to the well-spoken aristocrat.

"We should demonstrate some refinement and chew our food before we swallow. After surviving infinite probabilities, I'd hate to see you choke to death." She sat cross-legged in the velvety sand, and peeled a banana, popped a piece in her mouth, savoring the sweetness. She had eaten small amounts during the day, careful not to overdo.

"Not when you haven't had anything to crow about in your stomach for a month." He sucked the pit, threw it aside, grabbed a bunch of bananas and devoured the lot of them.

She wagged a finger at him. "It is dangerous to stuff yourself. Be mindful that people who have suffered starvation, follow their instincts to consume a lot of food, and then die."

He grabbed a coconut and started smashing it on the limestone rock. "I waited all day for you to return with food."

"Surely you jest."

"It is not in my nature to joke about food when I'm starving."

She gave a weary sigh. "This morning you brushed away my ideas of procuring food and water, claiming a fire was more important."

He pounded the coconut with renewed vigor. "When I went hunting at home, I crafted fires easily enough. Without a tinderbox, I'm having the toughest time getting one started."

He hated being useless. Alexandra was less forgiving. "I'll start a fire if it makes you happy."

"Be my guest. He bowed with the scornful elegance of a haughty aristocrat and waved his hand toward the pile of wood.

So, it would be a contest of wills. Alexandra stood, dusting sand off her bottom and gathered a dry coconut husk he'd chipped off. She stared at him, her fingers deftly separating the hairs, but the intensity of his gaze sucked the air out of her lungs. She turned her back to him and knelt by his stack of wood. With shaking hands, she sculpted a dome of fibers.

From inside her bodice, she unpinned her father's spectacles. Her heart squeezed as she smoothed her fingers over the polished glass, thanking providence for this useful part that belonged to Samuel. She squinted to find the sun behind her, and then turned, focusing the rays through a lens, and onto the coconut strands. Smoke curled. Sparks flared. She blew into the husk fibers, adding twigs, then breaking up branches until a fire commenced, and then glanced over her shoulder for his Lordship's approval. The look of incredulity on his face was priceless.

"That is unfair, Miss Elwins."

His tone was irascible.

"You let me waste an entire day——"

"You needed a little humbling, Lord Rutland." She turned back to the fire. "That knock on your head has left you overbearing."

He did not answer her rebuke. His face paled from grey to that of a tallow-hued cadaver. He rushed to a palm tree, bent over and relieved himself of his dinner.

Alexandra looked to the heavens. "I could say, I told you so—not to stuff the food down your throat because your stomach has shrunk, but you wouldn't want to hear that would you, Lord Rutland?"

He collapsed by the fire, holding his head in his hands. "How I value your recommendations, shot from the quiver of infallible wisdom. What other sufferings do you live to taunt me with, Miss Elwins?"

Her lips twitched with his disgruntlement. She picked up a leaf she had collected from her scavenging. "You bring misfortunes on yourself. I found some medicine, Lord Rutland that will help your head wound heal."

He slid down, propping his head against a log. "Call me Nicholas. I think we can exclude with formality. There is no society here to condemn us."

She nodded her head. "And call me Alexandra." She knelt beside him, split open an aloe leaf, dug her finger into the sticky gel, and applied it to his wound. When he flinched, she lifted an eyebrow.

How easy to imitate Molly's treatment of patients in Deconshire, smearing the balm over his gash. Molly, who had cared for her all her life and taught her herbal skills.

Her stepmother, Lady Ursula's last words reverberated in her head. *Met Molly in London. She refused to tell me your whereabouts. I hired a thug from St. Giles, took pleasure in watching Molly turn purple... how she struggled to pull his hands from her throat, gasping for her last breath.*

Aware he was staring at her, she picked up a coconut vessel, and lifted his head to drink. She laid him back down, turned and broke up small pieces of banana, placing them in the coconut shell. "Eat one at a time and—slowly."

"Alexandra?"

She didn't want to get into a discussion. No. Not about Molly. Not about her own past. She crossed to the opposite side of the fire, breaking up small twigs. Sparks crackled and hissed, rising once, and then sinking back to earth.

The silence of the night murmured with a rustle from under the palms, small nocturnal creatures seeking a meal. If not for the horrific events of the past few days, they wouldn't be there either. She scrubbed a hand over her face. A profound weariness seeped through her bones as her mind replayed each nerve-shattering hour of their time on the *Santanas*. Lord Rutland's fight with Damiano, the storm and her current fate.

With her back to him, she laid down, crossed her arms and curled into herself. Tears welled. She drew a shattered breath and then another, desperate to hold back the flood that would surely erupt if she let go. She deserved everything that had happened to her.

A shadow loomed and she looked up. Nicholas reached down and tucked his coat around her. "You need this more than I, Alexandra."

"But I couldn't possibly——" His coat slipped off her shoulder and he pushed it back up.

"Yes you can. I insist. You've been stronger than any woman I've known, facing unbelievable terrors.

You have cheered and consoled me. You have fed and cared for me. You have put up with my brutish moods." His voice deepened. "You have saved my life."

His mouth quirked as he slanted his handsome head to the palm tree where he had tossed the contents of his stomach. "You even possess the indelicate art of telling me, *I told you so.*"

Her bottom lip quivered. She didn't deserve his praise. Whatever she'd done was purely for self-preservation. Survival. Two people had a much better chance fighting off their captors and, in fact, it was Lord Rutland who'd fought off Damiano. She would never have had a chance against the beast.

Maybe Lord Rutland wasn't the rude man she'd thought him to be. Perhaps his condescending, boorish behavior was his shield to keep from getting hurt. That he thought to praise her, to give her credit for saving his life… She had to be wrong about him. A warm feeling flowed through her. Her stomach fluttered.

Nodding, he pulled a long breath. "You are like a sister to me, Alexandra."

"Sister?" The apology she was about to give died on her tongue.

His chin rose ever so slightly, as if satisfied with himself.

So, they were sister and brother. Apparently he thought it wise to be straight forward with their relationship. Being stranded on a deserted patch of earth and all.

Alexandra offered a weak smile.

She rolled over, hiding beneath his coat, grateful for the warmth. Did he think she had insinuated a romantic inclination? Unable to think of anything she had said to make him think of that possibility, she burrowed further beneath his coat, her humiliation complete. She was powerless to escape her reality...and... his scent.

An affiliation with a duke would be impossible. With her vague history, she was far beneath that connection.

If only she could cork her melancholy in a bottle and cast it into the sea.

He moved to his log and soon his gentle rhythmic snoring could be heard in tandem with the waves that washed upon the beach. He lay huddled in a ball to keep warm. In his weakened state, what if he caught a chill and died? Alexandra sighed. She rose, clutching his coat to her. For the first time in her life, she laid next to a man, covering them both with his coat and sharing their body warmth. Just like on the ship...this was about survival. They needed one another.

Chapter 5

Nicholas sat up, his coat sliding off. Where was Alexandra? He shielded his eyes from the sun's brilliant rays and scanned the horizon. Perched like an ancient warrior princess, her knife cleaved to a long stick with twine, she stood poised atop a rock with teeth-gritting determination. She pulled back and threw. Her spear whooshed through the water.

Alexandra squealed, pinning her spear to the sandy bottom. "Nicholas, I have caught a fish."

He splashed into the water, grabbing hold of her silvery prize before it slipped away. "You are worth your weight in guineas, Alexandra."

He hauled the flapping treasure ashore in his arms, whistling a jaunty tune while gutting the fish. Real food. Alexandra laid the fish's body over hot coals and it steamed its fragrance. Nicholas washed his hands in the surf. He scanned the beach and did a double-take. An indentation in the sand was grooved next to where he had slept. His whistling dropped in a rapid decrescendo. Had she lay beside him?

"You were cold and I-I—"

The air grew thick. Errant strands of gold hair clung to the perspiration that glistened on her pinkened cheeks. Did her bottom lip tremble? Nice and full.

Tight and controlled, his breath eased out in a low delay. "Kept me warm. We've stared into the face of death, Alexandra. Conforming to conventional standards departed with the outgoing tide. Your kindness speaks volumes. Please know, I am a gentleman and honorable."

After a short breakfast, they set out to explore the earth on which they inhabited. The air, redolent of wildflowers and the sweet scent of sea breezes caressed the high valleys, rolling up over the green covered peaks, and then rising to touch the bluest sky.

As they walked, the jungle came to life. Birds twittered, a coconut plopped on the ground, triggering small animals to scamper under Casuarinas. He spotted an occasional, curly-tailed lizard sunning itself upon a slab of limestone and a herd of goats strike a path up the mountain. Beasts of prey seemed nonexistent. No tracks in the soft earth to mark their presence other than the hooves of swine and goats.

The going was not easy, having to stop every few minutes to regain his breath. Despite the fish, his stomach gnawed with hunger. To mark a trail, he broke limbs and slashed trees with Alexandra's knife. The sun heated the skin on his back and arms. Alexandra pulled up beside him, her breathing coming in short spurts, fracturing the quiet.

How did she evoke such innocence? As a thief, she had seen more of the world than he had. Had more skills apparently.

He exhaled on a note of regret. "Kidnapped, stripped of everything, dealing with Portuguese slavers and now cast upon this infernal earth, I realize how ill-equipped I am to survive. I have no knowledge, tools or weapons other than the knife you possess. I am useless."

"You are hungry and it's hot," she said, resting her hand on one hip and wiping her brow with the other. "Are you so woeful because you are used to an army of servants waiting on you?"

Is that what she thought of him? A macaroni who could not fend for himself? His nerves tensed. "I will die here and no one will know where I've been cast-a-way."

She laughed at him, and then fingered a tall orange and blue flower. "I'm selfish, Nicholas. You need to build me a shelter before you die. I need protection from wind and rain." She smiled, the kind of smile that could melt his old Jesuit tutor and make him forget his vows.

"Bird of Paradise."

"I have never seen such majestic colors. I can breathe the colors."

Breathing? He stopped breathing for a moment, mesmerized by the color of her eyes, dark-ringed with golden lights in pools of turquoise. He shook his head and stooped to pick up a coconut from the many that spread across the ground. Anything to remove himself from her enchantment. He cracked open the coconut, drank and pressed the vessel into her hands to drink.

"We must find a water source." He chewed a piece of coconut and pushed on. "To capture one of those fat swine I saw herding through the forests, consumes me. If only I had a bow and arrow, or better, I could try your spear. If we are to survive, I will have to hunt for food to supplement our diet. The coconut and fish have revitalized me, but I will get sick of the redundancy."

"Do you hear it?" She turned west, cutting through thick vegetation. He followed. She leapt over strangler vines and roots, fast and independent as the caprices of the wind. A stitch grew in his side. Drawing closer, the thunder grew louder.

She drove through head-high elephant leaves, halted, her mouth dropping open. He came up beside her, and he, too, stood in awe, his world full of magic things.

The most desirable spot in the world with beauty beyond his wildest imagination lay before him. Cascading plumes of sweet water tumbled down a fern softened cliff, dancing with multi-colored hues, and then blending into a cobalt melting of silver mist before plunging into a deep jungle pool. Lime bursts of parrots chattered in the tree tops. Beneath a cerulean sky, a carpet of scarlet, yellow and orange flowers sparkled with droplets. He filled his lungs with the fragrance and warm tropical air.

She laughed and dove in, splashing the water up over her with the gleeful state of a child. He dove in after her, taking great gulps of fresh water. He back-floated for a while, watching her out of the corner of his eye. Likely owed to her sea captain father, she swam with elegant ease, wild and natural as the gulls that soared above the sea. She dove under the fall, surfacing and lifting her head to the flowing water. Nicholas followed, her innocent enthusiasm contagious, the water rushing over him, cleaning away sweat and salt and grime.

She crawled up on a flat moss-covered rock, her chest heaving with exertion and lay in the sun. He hitched himself up on the same rock, sitting next to her. The trees murmured to one another, swaying in a gentle breeze, smelling of allspice and flowers. A half rainbow descended from the mists over the glade.

But it was her dazzling beauty that arrested his attention. Her hand lay over her heart, concealing one breast. A dark nipple puckered and protruded through the fabric of her other breast. Golden hair fanned out from beneath her and there was color to her face, a flush that lent her skin a radiant glow.

Sister? Had he really called her a sister? It was all he could do not to crawl on top of her and… he raked his fingers through his damp hair.

"Nicholas, you will not die here. You must agree we have been blessed with this boon." She waved a hand to the trees that bordered the lagoon. "I have never seen a place so lovely. Bright colored orchids and fruit hang everywhere."

He wasn't thinking about orchids and fruit. The garment she wore was completely diaphanous. He tried not to look at how her chemise stuck to her like a second skin, tried not to look at the curls of the deep vee between her legs. His hands fisted with the criminality of a woman to appear like that. But who was present to enforce the law?

A hummingbird flew suspended over the pool. Beneath, the current swelled and elongated. Nicholas shifted. The ease in which she displayed herself cemented his theory on her profession. He remembered her request aboard the *Santanas*, and that request lingered, evoking all kinds of depraved imaginings. She had wanted him to—

"In time, I know you will catch us a pig to roast."

"Pigs?" Wicked and carnal came to mind, leaving his personal pride and integrity in tatters. Had she no idea how his principles were tested?

He stood, turned to hide his physical reaction to her. "Let's go," he groused. "The sun is high and I want to explore more." He glanced over his shoulder, saw how disappointed she was to leave. "We can come back again. The lagoon is an excellent water source."

He shouldered through colossal ferns, keeping ahead of her. He enjoyed women, some unique and adventurous creatures welcomed his attentions in and out of bed. There was one actress he still recalled with a degree of fondness.

This nymph could care less about him.

Her prophecy that he would not die in this place irked him. "You won't allow me to be gloomy, will you, Alexandra?"

"There is no time to be gloomy. We must catch fish to smoke and preserve, and gather fruit to dry in the sun."

"None of which I have any experience in doing."

"I will teach you and we will do everything together."

"We will be here for a long time, won't we," he said, not really a question.

She shrugged. "Perhaps. A month? A year? A decade? Who knows?"

He did not have a month or a year, much less a decade. The uncertainty would surely drive him mad. He had to get back to England. Stumbling over a lumpy ground root, he clung to a curling vine that snaked around the tree's trunk in suffocating loops. "How will we build a shelter with your knife as our only tool?"

"There is that," she conceded. "We will make do."

"I wish I had your optimism."

She sighed. "Have you always been this miserable, Lord Rutland? I don't like gloomy. I like people who make me laugh. I honestly think it is the thing I like most, to laugh. I think it cures a multitude of ills and sure beats crying and whining."

"I prefer to be moody and grim."

"I can tell. You're very good at it. Must have practiced your whole life. Your spirit of pessimism is to be admired."

Nicholas grumbled.

"You think you are cast upon a horrible desolate habitation, void of all hope. But you are alive. You are no longer a prisoner bound for a life of slavery in some godforsaken place. You are not starved, and perishing in a barren location that affords no sustenance. There appears to be no wild beasts to hurt you. The climate is agreeable. And you are not alone. You have me to speak to. You must count your blessings."

She was right. He was a master at despondency. He must shake off the past of anger, blame and guilt over his father.

The spongy ground sank beneath his step with decayed vegetation. He scraped his chest, easing through a stand of bamboo, and then ran his hands along the tall sturdy trunks. He could build houses, had helped several of his tenants at one time. "This would make an excellent building material."

"That's the way I like you to think, Nicholas."

"The problem is cutting it without proper tools." Never had he felt so impotent.

He continued for an hour, trekking through the dense green undergrowth, dodging around a swarm of leaf-cutter ants. The air grew thick and heavy, his stamina tested with the heat and climbing. He held back branches for Alexandra to pass through and she smiled up to him.

What circumstances had led her to the lifestyle of a thief? Had she been orphaned by the sea captain with no one to turn to other than the streets, and then choked by the thorns and brambles of early adversity? She had offered no explanation of her history and he would respect her privacy.

"Why not treat our sojourn here as a quest?"

"A quest? To what end?"

She pushed a tendril of hair back from her eyes. "I haven't decided yet. But when I discover one, I'll let you know."

"What you have offered so far, Miss Elwins, is denial of our grim reality."

"You are just like Jay Thompson, defiant as a bear in defeat."

His nostrils flared with the smell of rotting fruit. Pieces and parts of her didn't add up. She could swim, cut rigging and could read, yet she was a thief. Did she have a lover in England? On the ship, hadn't she intimated a relationship with a man who was kind and giving? "Who is Jay Thompson?"

The ferocity of his question startled her, and they stood so close his breath stirred the wisps of golden silk that framed her face.

"I cared for him. Whenever things didn't go his way, he'd stamp his foot and pout."

Nicholas glowered. "Sounds immature for a man."

Her laughter tinkled over the mountain and he couldn't help but be ensnared by it.

"Goodness, no. Jay is nine years old, a little mulish and at times, peevish and impatient. Did my best to tease him out of his doldrums. He was a mischievous boy, prone to throw apples off the cliff at the Cornett sisters when their carriage passed the road below."

Nicolas scowled. He did not like being compared to an intractable nine-year old. "You did not correct him?"

She kept a straight face but her lips quaked. "I might have tossed a few down myself."

He gave a look of mock horror. "Very improper, Miss Elwins."

"To think I am in the esteemed company of the Lord of Virtue who never performed one mischievous thing in his life."

He couldn't deny the way she challenged him nor her infectious laughter. "I might have tossed a tomato or two." He stopped and leaned against a tree, swiping at the sweat across his face.

She patted his shoulder. "It will take a while before your strength returns." She produced a mango and they feasted on the sweet orange flesh.

"What I wouldn't do for a round of beef," he said.

She skipped ahead of him, following a well-worn animal path. Nicholas threw down the suck-cleaned seed. He didn't like being led, in fact, the view annoyed him. She had long legs, well-rounded hips. He snapped a branch in two.

What matter to worry about the distant shores beyond them when he saw the dancing light in her eyes, which were continually filled with excitement? He studied this woman-child who could look so far ahead. Mayhap they would be rescued within a month. They would return home, he to his family and Alexandra to what? Save for this interlude, he'd probably never see her again.

He watched the sway of her hips and the ripe bounce of her full breasts. *Mistress?* He could set her up in a home near his London townhouse, visit her whenever he had the inclination...all the time. He'd buy her gowns and jewels...take her to the opera...interludes in the country. Alexandra stretched out over satin sheets, her golden hair fanned out over a pillow, her body quivering with the pleasure he'd give her. She was a narcotic, an opiate. He could not get enough of her.

She had saved his life.

She deserved better. He frowned. He didn't like the idea of her living a life of crime. He'd return her to her sea captain father and settle an amount on her so she could live without the risk of having a noose around her neck.

Nicolas swallowed. *How was he going to keep his hands off her?*

They came out on a cliff overlooking the sea. "I don't like the look of those clouds forming. We need shelter. So far, we have experienced gentle weather and warm trade winds. Exposed to the elements for long, we will perish," he said.

As if he divined the heavens, the skies opened-up and doused them. Huddling beneath an outcrop of rock, and shivering, Nicholas said, "Exactly my point. I regret spending so much time at the lagoon. The sun is past its zenith, descending to the west. We will have to return. We can't make it to the summit in time." He was ornery and knew it.

"Oh, Nicholas, how you cleave to an abiding sense of tragedy." She waved an airy hand over the glistening palms, as if ordering the deluge to stop. "See, the rain has abated as quickly as it arrived and a brilliant pearl of a sun has lifted in its wake."

His mouth went slack. Had she divined the heavens? When he turned to follow their path back to the beach, a great gust of wind blew from across the sea, laying its hand upon the land and billowing out his shirt.

Alexandra squealed. "Look, down there. Do you see it?" Without waiting for him to answer, she plunged into the forest, descending the mountain. Nothing. There was nothing to be seen. The woman was crazy.

She disappeared in the dense growth, her chattering and exclamations marking her progress. "Hurry, Nicholas. You must see."

Nicholas skulked down the steep incline. He loathed wasting energy and time on a useless gambit. The earth buckled out from beneath him. His arms flailed in the air. Everything sailed past him. Plummeting down a steep embankment, he grabbed at vines, branches, clawing roots, and dirt to brake his fall. A thorn jabbed in his backside. He slammed into wet leaf mold, his breath whooshing out of him. His shirtsleeve was torn. Not bloody likely he could summon his valet and order a new shirt.

"Hurry, Nicholas," prompted the source of his demise.

He pushed through ropy vines, forded a small river, tripped on a rock and fell into a depression. His head sank beneath the surface of the water. He burst to the top, shaking his head. He'd break his neck if she had her way.

He moved into a small clearing, radiating with light. He found her then, standing next to a dome of vines. Nick massaged the back of his neck. "What?"

She whirled in delight, "Oh Nicholas, we are saved. I worried about a shelter and here we are."

He drew closer, blinked. Vines grew wildly over an edifice and cloaked its existence. "I can't believe this. It is a miracle you saw this place, Alexandra."

She tipped-up on her toes. Never would he forget the rapture lighting her face, the triumph in her eyes, and the satisfaction in her smile. He crossed the distance between them, picked her up and twirled her around, a prisoner to the joy emanating from her soul.

They had shelter.

He put her down and she blushed. How he longed to sample her full, moist lips. No. That would be crossing a line he didn't want to cross.

She cleared her throat. "No one has lived here for a long time."

"Must be fifteen years of growth, but hard to tell, things grow faster in the tropics." He pulled the knife from his belt, slashed through the tangle blocking the entry while Alexandra yanked the loosened creepers, tossing them in a growing pile. Nicholas grabbed a black pod and sniffed. "Must be vanilla bean." He held it to her nose.

"Heavenly. I can cook with this," she said delighted. "If I had milk, I could make a pudding."

An entry emerged flanked by hand-hued coral limestone blocks. Nick lifted the handle. The door stuck. He put a shoulder to it, and shoved. Dust colored the air and settled on his head. He entered the dark interior. "Civilization."

Alexandra followed, then crossed the room to open a window shutter. "We need to remove more vines to let in the light."

Nicholas went outside and removed the growth around the windows. She pushed and he pulled. The shutter fell off. "That will have to be fixed."

He worked his way around the house, cutting the vines, releasing the windows from their prison. Fresh air and sunshine spread into the domicile, chasing away years of musty gloom. He passed a lean-to he'd explore later.

With the added light, he surveyed the interior. Tools hung on the walls. Machetes. Drills, hammers. Two flint lock dueling pistols ornately engraved. Two muskets. Numerous barrels were stacked in the corner. He cranked open lids. He sifted his hands through five barrels of wheat berries, one moldy and four good, worthy to be ground into flour for bread. A barrel filled with cones of sugar and one of salt. They were like children experiencing a million Christmases and drunk with joy.

"Whoever occupied this dwelling, did so for the long haul." He took one of the muskets off the wall. "A Brown Bess, range eighty yards. I'll take down one of those wild pigs that roam. The gun is a little rusty but filing it down with sand, I can return it to its original condition. Not much use unless we have gunpowder." He checked the powder horn on the wall and grimaced. "The contents are trifling."

A bed filled one corner covered with quilts. He saw where her gaze was riveted, the way her hands twisted together. She caught him staring at her, cleared her throat.

He took a breath, satisfied with her embarrassment, and appraised her sudden attention to the cottage's contents. Was she more innocent than he had presumed?

She ran her finger through the dust across a table, and then pointed to objects. How he relished her delight over benches, chairs, iron pots, copper pans, knives, forks, a tea kettle, a tea set decorated with roses and violets, pewter plates and tankards, forks and knives, box of beeswax candles, a compass, books, seeds, even a Bible.

She held up a silver chess set. "Will you teach me how to play?"

He laughed. "Adversaries claim I'm brutal. I play to win."

"Then I shall find you a wonderful tutor," she laughed.

She dusted a clock on the shelf. "Will you wind it?"

Nick turned the key. The clock started ticking.

"Oh, you are wonderful." Alexandra clapped her hands together as if he had parted the Red Sea.

She held up the quilt to the window. Light poured through moth eaten holes. "I will wash and mend this and it will be good as new."

When her back was turned, Nick tugged canvas from beneath the bed, inspecting its condition. Good enough to use as a hammock. He kicked the canvas back under, preferring not to say anything about the sleeping arrangements, the devil in him choosing to draw out her discomfiture.

"We will clean this out. Here is a broom. Start sweeping," Alexandra ordered, her face lit with pure resolve.

Nicholas stared at the broom she'd placed in his hands, as foreign as any object he'd ever observed.

He handed it back to her and she stamped her dainty foot. "We have to start somewhere."

"I'll look under the lean-to."

When he crossed the threshold, he heard her mumble, "typical man," as he headed to the rear of the house. He shoved open the door of the lean-to, assessed the contents, shovels, hoes, pick-axes, three iron crows, a wheelbarrow, a dozen hatchets, a grindstone for sharpening knives and tools, three barrels of musket bullets, another fowling piece, kegs of gunpowder, boards, sword, barrels of nails, two buckets, a screw-jack, adze, ropes, crocks, a couple of empty barrels, good for storing rainwater. In the rafters, he had discovered a sealed wooden box full of reams of muslin, linen, and cotton. He returned to Alexandra.

"Good news, we have a hogshead of rum."

"Of course, the rum, a vital necessity for you," she teased, opening a basket. "Needles and threads. I can improve my wardrobe if there is any fabric." She flipped through the last trunk and sighed. "Naught. Did you find a chest of fabric in the lean-to?" she said hopefully.

"Nothing." He lied smoothly. Did he have any remorse? No. As far as he was concerned, the sheer Irish linen shift she wore, as revealing as a cobweb was just fine.

Her shoulders dropped. To take away her disappointment, he said, "There is another structure we need to investigate." He didn't need to look back, perceived her footsteps in his wake. They worked together pulling vines off a small domed structure. He frowned. "What is it?"

Her mouth tilted into a smile. "My father told me of such a device. A beehive oven used for cooking outside to spare the heat in the house." She pointed to the lower cavity scorched with soot. "Wood is fired in the lower chamber, heating the closed area up above to bake breads. There is an iron shaft for turning meats to roast." She swung a bar back and forth to demonstrate, and then studied the mysterious door in the back, her face lighting with approval.

"This oven is more sophisticated than I have seen. You can divert the smoke from the fire to a back chamber for smoking meats."

"We can preserve meats?" he said and watched her scan the unchecked vegetation that rioted across the terrain.

"Oh," she said breathlessly. "All of this was once a well-tended garden."

She bent to pluck a green plant and sniffed. "Rosemary. I can use this in stews." She traversed the grounds, growing more excited, pointing and naming everything. "Mangos, papayas, lemons, oranges, limes, tomatoes, sugar cane, licorice pods, bananas and plantains. Some of the fruits are varieties I've never seen.

Everything will have to be trimmed and cut down to allow sunlight for our gardens."

His leg brushed against spikey plants and he cursed.

"Nicholas, you have found us pineapple, and it is ripe." She twisted and twisted until the fruit cracked and raised her trophy in her hands. Dinner."

He strode to the front. A great many feet below, palms fringed like a green necklace along a stark, white beach, and a frothy creaming of waves broke upon an outer reef. Nicholas was again struck by the soft, compelling beauty of these seas. "Whoever built this dwelling did well to conceal its location. There is a fair view of the sea beneath, the angle and height of the cliff, obscures the house from the sea and hostile intruders, yet offers the inhabitants a clear vantage point of anyone who comes close."

Curling a lock of hair around her finger she considered what he said, and then took a breath. "I wonder who lived here and what happened to him."

"He probably died."

Fists plunked on her hips, she said, "Must you always be so cheerful?"

He grinned. "Why? When you will guarantee a list of sunny optimisms."

"You are smiling, Nicholas, and I'll remind you that to tug that smile out of you has been a colossal effort."

He smiled and it felt good. She ran into the house, retrieved two buckets. "The stream I passed through may be far away but at least it is a source. Please, get water so I may start cleaning, and don't tell me you have to look in the lean-to."

Alexandra commenced dusting and sweeping, and putting things to order. Starting from the top down, she took the broom and standing on a chair, brushed the cobwebs from the rafters. Remembering Lord Rutland's reaction when she had given him the broom to sweep, she laughed. How his lips had twisted with the kind of grimace that made her feel she was an unwelcome guest at a party and couldn't find the door.

With certainty, he was accustomed to servants attending him. Cast ashore with nothing, he'd have to learn to endure and work with his hands. A little humility was good for him.

A breeze blew in from the sea, lifting her filthy chemise. She heard the slosh of water from behind, felt him staring at her. He must think her a ragamuffin. Or worse. He had assumed on the ship she was a thief and a loose woman, and now with her lower legs exposed, she must have confirmed the foulest of his suspicions.

She dropped the broom and stepped down from her chair. Nicholas placed the buckets filled with water on the table. He peeled a banana, taking overlong to eat the fruit. Her palms sweated and the fluttering behind her ribs increased until it felt like a hundred hummingbirds were trapped there, desperate to escape.

She straightened, swept back the damp hair from her face. *Be calm, Alexandra. Be dignified.* "If the wind hadn't blown I would never have seen the house."

She stopped midstream, rag held in her hand. Even she had possessed uncertainties about their future, but had hidden her fears from Nicholas. Now all those doubts were erased.

"Very lucky," Nicholas said with a smile, a smile with enough quiet charm to send every single young lady in London to dreaming.

She plunged the rag in water. "Not luck. Providential. Fate brought on by more than coincidence. Think about it. We have survived the evil of the *Santanas*. We have survived a hurricane when seemingly not one member of the crew endured. We were spared from being smashed against sharp rocks, delivered to a sandy beach, and have found shelter when we needed it the most."

She took the quilts outside and shook them free of dust, laying the bedding on top of brightly colored crotons to air out in the sunshine. She returned to the house, perusing what else had to be done. "Never in my wildest imagination did I expect to have nearly all the pleasures of home and I vow to be judicious of what has come into our possession."

From an opened chest, Nicholas lifted a telescope, hooked his leg over the window frame and perused the sea, looking for nonexistent ships. "Tomorrow I will travel to the beach to retrieve my coat." He restored the scope in the trunk, and per her instructions, lifted the heavy feather mattress off the rope bed, placing it on a huge boulder outside.

She followed him outside. "Why do you have to perform an insignificant task when there is so much to do? I need your help weeding out the extra vegetation." With the broom, she beat the mattress free of dust, pretending it was his lordship.

"There is no pressing need to be anywhere. While I'm at the beach, I will build a pile of driftwood to set a signal fire in case I see a friendly ship."

That was the real reason. Stubborn man. "Ships sailing by are not as frequent as they are on the Thames and I doubt if we shall see a ship for a month." She angled her head to the overgrown garden. "We need to start there."

A muscle tensed in his jaw. "I'm going to the beach."

"Teaching a bear to genuflect is easier than getting you to work." A gust of wind wafted the choking bite of dust motes around them to underscore her words.

"Pardon me," he thundered.

How dare he try to stare her down. "You are free to do whatever you like while I am left to do everything."

"Michel de Montaigne."

Her broom froze mid-air. "Pardon me?"

"You quoted a French statesman," he bellowed.

"You are like a blast of trumpets wasting moments in loudness, and I'm ready to add my own quote but I don't think you'd like it," she snapped.

He grumbled a lot but made many trips with fresh pails of water, helping her to move the heavy trunks aside, while she dusted and washed down the shelves, walls, drawers, table, and chairs.

"You surprise me with your industry."

"You think I'm immune to labor?"

Didn't he look like St. Sebastian, pierced with a million arrows? Of course, he'd seethed martyrdom. In four long strides, he loomed over her. Mocking him and his damned integrity had been a miscalculation on her part.

"A fire swept through one of the villages of the Rutland Estate. With my own hands, I helped rebuild several cottages, and then helped the tenants get their crops in the field." His voice dropped lower, husky. "I have many other skills that you are unaware of, Miss Elwins."

Her mouth opened and closed, skewered with his double entendre. He was gone in a trice, buckets banging against the doorframe and his long legs churning up the distance to the stream.

She had hit a nerve. Her energy flagged, and she didn't want to start an altercation. Dusk settled over the house. So much more to do. Tomorrow she'd sweep and mop the floorboards until they shined.

The feather mattress had been returned to the rope bed and quilts thrown on top. She swallowed. The bed yielded an intimacy she could not allow. Last night, Lord Rutland had been asleep when she had moved next to him. *Safe.*

Nicholas set buckets of water on the table and dropped into a chair. His long legs stretched out in front of him, and he turned the pineapple in his hands, scrutinizing it. How he arrested her attention. Without considering the propriety of it, she studied him with thoughtful curiosity, tall, lean, full dark beard, and a countenance revealing every arrogant line of his aristocratic features. She even found beautiful the hand that rose to wipe the moisture from his brow, and the most amazing blue eyes—and realized they were staring back at her.

Startled, her heart shuddered, stopping for a moment, and then began beating anew at a frantic pace. He'd been angry most of the day, had pushed long and hard through the jungle, and made her leave the lagoon with barely an explanation. She had discounted his annoyance from not knowing what had happened to his family and being stranded in a foreign environment.

Yet, she didn't know what emotion it was he caused to rise within her. It could not be fear. She grew flustered. It wasn't fear. She resisted the same curious sensations as she observed him. Something leaped along her spine. He was devastatingly handsome, forbiddingly severe. Overall, she thought his countenance one of the most compelling and fiercest she had ever seen.

He was all a Duke would be.

Her face grew warm as the seconds eclipsed and nothing was said. Her embarrassment became complete when she beheld his half naked dress. He had no shirt and his breeches were wet and clung to powerful thighs, the corded muscles rippling beneath, in what could only be considered indecent. She raised her eyes, the expanse of muscles in his arms and chest weren't dissimilar, but with the lean grace of gentlemen she'd seen in London.

How disgraceful she was to gawk at him.

She looked across the room, at anything to thwart the heat of his gaze.

"I bathed in the river. I'm exhausted and need sleep."

She looked at the bed and cleared her throat. No way could they share the same bed.

"You haven't had much to eat," she said, the words tumbling off her tongue as if she were no more than a simpleton. His state of undress bunched her thoughts together like overcooked porridge, and because she couldn't think of anything less mundane to say, she looked twice as obtuse.

She took the pineapple, sliced it in half and shoved it toward him. Moaning, he ate greedily, plunging his mouth into the fruit and sucking the sweet juices from the skin. Alexandra nibbled at her portion.

When he finished his repast, which wasn't anywhere quick enough, he stood. All she could focus on was his impressively wide shoulders, the light furring on his chest, following a line down to his waist. He chuckled and her eyes snapped to his face. Did he think she was inspecting him?

Her heart raced as he leaned toward her and wiped a drop of juice from her chin. "You missed that."

Her breath caught.

She stepped back to allow him room to pull canvas from beneath the bed and watched him saunter outside. "Where are you going?"

He strung a contraption between two palms, devising a hammock.

She marched to the doorway. "What if it rains?"

He hefted himself up and into his bed. "The skies are clear and the air is warm."

There was nothing for her to do but retire for the night. The coal-black darkness of the night hushed upon her. Satisfied that Nicholas could probably not see his hand stretched in front of him, she removed her shift, washed it in the water bucket, and laid it over a chair to dry. She sank into the bed beneath the quilts. How gallant Nicholas was.

Last night she had slept next to him because she was afraid. Afraid he'd disappear and she'd be alone. What if pirates or cannibals came to the island? She'd have no one to protect her. She missed him by her side.

"Nicholas, are you asleep?"

"Would we be having a discussion if I was?"

"Nicholas?"

He groaned. "Yes?"

"About last night—"

"What about last night?"

She took a deep breath. "The reason I slept next to you was not only for warmth but because I was afraid. Will you protect me?"

Silence lay infringed by his snores. Asleep. Wouldn't the night air grow damp and chill? Wrapping one quilt around her, she gathered up the other, tip-toed outside and tucked it around him.

Chapter 6

*A*lexandra stretched, dreaming of her room in Deconshire. Overhead, bound reed thatching lay on dark wooden beams, securing the house against the winds and cold. Giving the delicacy of Wedgewood pottery, the white stucco walls were decorated with Molly's pictures of pressed violets. Even Samuel's touches were present with an oak chair and carved headboard hewn from his hands.

The rasp of metal filled her ears as Molly moved kettles below in the kitchen. Soon bacon would crackle and Alexandra would rise and have honeyed tea, scones with jam and clotted cream while Samuel filled his pipe and spun a yarn.

She sighed, cuddling into her pillow. Familiar waves beat upon the shore and the ever-present wind rushed through the trees. She frowned in her dream. Trees clacked together, a wholly different sound.

Her eyes flew open. Palm trees. Not the sound that swept through the willows, yellow dunes and marram grasses or green hills of her beloved Deconshire. She sat up, bit down on her knuckles, smothering a sob.

She was not home. God only knew when she would be…if ever.

Poor Samuel. He must be sick with worry and grief, believing she was dead. She clenched her fingers into fists, rendering half-moon marks in her palms. If there was God, she'd bring Ursula and Willean to justice.

The grinding sound quit. Nicholas sat on the threshold, sanding the musket, rust dustings and sand peppered the floor. She clutched the quilt to her neck, concealing her naked state beneath. Had she kicked the covers off during the night? Heat rose to her cheeks.

"Good morning," Nicholas greeted, and commenced polishing the barrel to a blue-black patina as if nothing was untoward.

Her shift lay across the chair. Not that the dratted garment concealed much.

"Something the matter?"

The soft tone in his voice startled her. Had she said something in her sleep? Oh, to tell him the truth of her past. She couldn't. Her grief and childish rebellion against Molly and Samuel released a heavy anchor of shame. She shook off the thought. She couldn't think about that now. Not when they had to survive long enough to be rescued.

So much work lay ahead of them. Gardens to clear and plant. Hauling water, a constant chore. Shutters had to be fixed before another storm hit the island. Her breath hitched. No. She could not talk about home.

"I thought you were going to get your coat," she said.

"I'll do some hunting." Gun in hand, Nicholas rose, towering over her. With the tip of the barrel he lifted her shift off the chair, only to dangle the garment over her.

She snatched at it.

"When you want to talk, Alexandra, I'm here for you." His deep baritone voice was quiet. Infinitely patient.

In the pearly morning light, Alexandra swallowed the lump in her throat and whispered through parched lips, "I-I can't."

He angled his head toward a bunch of bananas on the table. "I went out early and acquired breakfast."

He took the powder horn off the wall, stuck the knife in his belt. He had his shirt back on with his sleeves rolled up. "I'd prefer a rare sirloin, coddled eggs, bacon, with warm cinnamon bread and butter, but that is not on the menu. I'm good at hunting." He bowed and strode out the door, his lithe muscled form moving with perfect grace.

He vanished like vapor before the sun, the forest swallowing him up. Alexandra missed him the minute he left. To take up the time, she swept the cottage, and then getting on her hands and knees, scrubbed the floor until it gleamed like beaten moonbeams. She made two trips to the river to get water, the heat of the day rising with the sun. On the last trip, she dipped in the river, enjoying a midmorning bath.

Carrying the buckets back to the house, she picked two mauve orchids, and then placed them in a flagon on the table. Savoring a sweet banana, she prided herself on her hard work in transforming the fresh condition of the house.

Her shoulders slumped as she scrutinized the massive job of clearing the garden. Tugging at bristly vines, her hands grew raw, piling a large heap to burn later. She sat back on her heels, observing the rich surrounding greenness, the bright and solitary loveliness of a new world emerging, quieting all her qualms. Kneeling, she stuck her hands into the deep rich loam, awed by her connection to the earth, the soil so much better than in Deconshire. Everything would grow here.

A shot rang out. Close. She cupped her hands and shouted up the mountainside. "Nicholas, are you all right?" No answer. She bit her lip, how he wanted to prove to her he could hunt—that he was useful. Had he shot himself? She started up the slope.

Between two palmettos, a gigantic boar charged.

"Nicholas!"

Sharp tusks protruded from the beast. She picked up a rock and threw, the missile sailing over its bristled back. *Run. Move! Now!* Spinning around, she leapt through the pineapple plants mindless of the razor-sharp leaves, cutting her legs. She looked over her shoulder, the beast's eyes bulged, grunting, thrashing through the vegetation, head lowered ready to pierce her with its sharp tusks. She tripped on a root and sprawled in the dirt, her hands skidding through briars.

She jumped to her feet. An impossible wall of undergrowth trapped her. A tree loomed three feet away, and she leapt, reaching high to grab the lower branch. Her sweat-slicked palms slipped off and she crumpled to the ground. The boar stopped, clawed the ground with his pointed hooves, bloodlust in its eyes. "Nicholas!"

Where was Nicholas? She scuttled farther, pressing into the bush. The boar charged. She screamed, thrusting her hands up in front of her.

A shot exploded. The boar dropped. Nicholas appeared, smoke curling from his musket. Alexandra pressed her hands to her face and cried. He pulled her up and put his arm around her.

She pushed him away. "That pig nearly killed me. What took you so long?"

"I thought you'd be congratulating me on my excellent marksmanship," he said, his smile jubilant. "We have dinner, breakfast and supper for the next several days."

Breathing hard, she pushed her toe into the beast to make sure it was dead. "Is that all you can think of is your stomach?"

He dropped the carcass under the shade of a lignum vitae, the blue flowers so beautiful and at odds with the macabre process below. His forehead furrowed when she rolled a crock from the lean to, filling it with water and mixing in a measure of salt.

"To make a brine, we shall soak most of the meat before smoking to preserve." She took a chunk of meat and submerged it in the brine, still waiting for her racing pulse to slow.

Alexandra gathered wood and started a fire in the lower berth of the beehive oven. After procuring a rib section, she placed it on a spit to roast. Nicholas finished his task, filling the crock to the brim and burying the remains.

Her mind still reeling from her near death, she said, "Thank you for saving my life."

"I'll keep you safe," he said over his shoulder as if it was no great feat, and then joined her by the oven with two fresh buckets of water.

"Hauling water is an onerous task. I wish there was a well closer to the house."

"Let me worry about the water. I don't want you lifting buckets." He had bathed in the river, his shirt spread out over a croton bush to dry, and she marveled at how she was becoming accustomed to his half-naked splendor. He brushed back his sinfully thick black hair and a damp strand still stuck to his forehead. She itched to smooth it back.

"You have provided us with worthy sustenance. I don't think that there is a thing you cannot do." She sprinkled salt and patted rosemary leaves onto the roasting meat.

Nicholas plunked down in the grass, stretching his long legs in front of him. "There's plenty I can't do." His laughter had an edge.

"I find that hard to believe."

"Ask my father. My greatest critic."

Perhaps the relationship with his father caused his anger. She turned the spit, keeping her eyes on the meat. "He is disapproving?"

"There are many things I want to do to develop the estate. But my father won't listen. He is stuck with the old ways and won't listen to any of my ideas." He plucked the grass and chewed it. "It doesn't matter now. Despite the fact, that I haven't given up hope that my father is yet alive, I remain at the edge of the world and unable to implement any of my concepts anyway."

She smiled at him. He did not fit the prescription of an ordinary aristocrat. His awareness, and confidence belied undertones of a man who cut his teeth by rolling up his sleeves and working with the peasantry. Hadn't he said he worked with his tenants, helping them to rebuild their homes after fire swept through the village? With his arms behind his head, studying the golden coconuts bunched in the tree above, she felt he was a man who had the ability to command everyone's attention, a man born to lead.

More commendable was his intense and admirable desire to succeed. "Tell me what you want to do. I'd love to hear your plans."

"Alternating pastures with planting grains. At the minimum, plant clover in place of fallow."

She paused to wipe her hands. "It would increase arable land but digging up established pastures is hard work."

He sat up, his arm bent over his knee. "My father called my ideas folly. He's not forward thinking enough. The grain yields would be fantastic."

"How?" She wanted him to defend his beliefs his father had disregarded.

"Clover enriches the soil, works as a fertilizer. The clover can support livestock, turning out more milk, cheese, meat. The manure left behind maintains soil fertility."

To her eye, Nicholas seemed fiercely independent and demonstrated excessive pride in his ideas. To grow up with an equally independent and dominating father? She blew out a breath. The relationship between father and son was an explosive formula. "Brilliant. What other ideas do you have?"

He stood, paced a few steps and came back again, his expression thoughtful. "Land conversions, land drains and reclamation, irrigation, four crop rotation."

Heavens, the man was something to look at, so enthused was she by his vision. "What is four crop rotation?"

"Growing a series of crops in the same area in sequenced seasons."

"For instance?"

He threw up his hands, gesturing like an orator. "It is not a new idea, been practiced by Mid-eastern farmers for six thousand years, yet timeless in its applicability. Crops of wheat, turnips, barley and clover are alternated each year. The soil will not be robbed of one kind of nutrient, reducing pathogens and pests that occur in the lands when planted with the same crop."

His deep baritone held excitement and promise. "With the increase in produce, the tenants could sell their surplus for their own profit to distant localities that were experiencing shortages. Thus, improving the lives of the tenants on the estates."

Her little village in southern England raised corn, wheat, cows and other crops. His ideas were revolutionary and could help Deconshire. "How could it work? There is price fixing and tariffs from town to town. And—I doubt the Lords would allow such power in the hands of the tenants."

"Once I am duke and take my place in the House of Lords, I'll use my political influence to develop a national market, free of tariffs, tolls and custom barriers. The point I'll drive home is the farmers will be more effective land managers by becoming low cost producers, and enrich everyone. It is a win, win. What do you think?"

Alexandra stared at him, completely absorbed, trying to grasp the significance of his groundbreaking ingenuity. "The quiet cough of a rich man is louder than the braying of six paupers. If anyone can do it, it would be you, Nicholas." She drew her finger across the meat and sucked the juice off. "I can't understand why your father would reject your ideas."

"I'm the oldest, the heir and he demanded the best from me. When my mother died, our family was irrevocably broken. Without her calming presence, he ramped up his demands on his children through his expectations of education and marrying well. He became silent, distant, a kind of shadow presence, hiding in his office behind closed doors."

"He was in mourning."

"But the mourning has lasted for years." Disgust lined his voice. "Not that I was a perfect son. I embarrassed my father with my brawling.

Fortunately, my Uncle Cornelius stepped in, becoming my surrogate father. Unusual, because he's not really my uncle but a close friend of the family. When I was snagged into trouble at Eton, Uncle Cornelius intervened and made sure I wasn't thrown out. When I was taken advantage of by a card shark, he rescued me from a gambling debt. And after I graduated from college, he took me on a European tour."

"You were lucky to have your Uncle Cornelius." Alexandra now understood how horrible that time must have been for Nicholas, provided with every luxury and advantage, yet absent, were the needs of the heart—the necessary connection between father and son. She pulled the roast off the skewer and placed it on a pewter platter. "Let's eat."

Nicholas ogled the succulent meat, dripping with juices, and placed the platter on the table. Alexandra lit one of the precious beeswax candles. He sliced the meat, while she peeled and sliced orange papaya. The pewter plates she had washed were heaped with yams and carrots and their tankards filled with water. He seated her, and then sat at the head of the table.

"Excellent," said Nicholas, sampling a sweet honeyed yam, and then savoring the fruit.

She smiled and they ate in silence. Outside, palms swayed in the breeze, the soft sound like whispering secrets. Over the brim of her tankard, she studied him, a glimmer of the man whose journey she shared had come to light. Unfair discipline and rigid rules left

Nicholas without the ability to display vulnerability. When life was tough, negative feelings were to be suffered and internalized. His stubbornness, sometimes unsympathetic and definitely—dominating flaws became exaggerated. His darkness was held within. He hid behind his hurt.

Nicholas's mind reeled like a hunting dog backtracking through the country, turning back and turning back, tracing out the way it had come. To block the dog, who wanted to lurk in all those dark places, he could remember his mother and her sweet face and matching disposition. How she would stroke his head when he was ill and tell him everything would be fine. How she had been the softening touch to his father's sternness.

How she died in her husband's arms. How they loved one another. To have a love like that was once in infinity.

The loss of his mother had been monumental for the whole family. His father's grief magnified the severity of her passing. He refused to listen to Nicholas's ideas on improvements on the estate. With all his children, he bully-whipped them to marry spouses that enriched the Rutland legacy. His father had thrust upon him the beautiful and most sought after, Lady Susannah Tomkins. She possessed impeccable breeding and would bring added social, political and financial power to the Rutland family.

Lady Susannah was—too perfect. Like a prize mare, she had been coifed and coddled from birth. Stuffy, of little learning and spirit, she was far from the spectrum of Nicholas's interest.

The dread that was inescapable rose, the explosion. His father. Nicholas swallowed a knotted lump in his throat. He didn't want to think of the possibility his father might be dead. He forced the cruel notion down. So much left unsaid. So much to undo.

A fonder memory drifted into Nicholas's mind...of his father's natural inclination toward his first-born son as a source of pride. The Duke, sitting at the table after a meal with a roomful of guests or at his desk with his solicitors and secretary about. He would pull Nicholas up into his lap to pat and hug him. Sometimes they would ride around the estate to visit the tenants. His father lifting him up on the saddle in front of him, the high-headed bay cantering to the duke's instruction. He could still feel his father's hand and forearm crooked around his waist. While his father conducted business, Nicholas played with the tenant children. At those times, he was always aware his father kept a kind of vigil over him. He would look up from his play to see his father gazing at him. His father would smile and nod, or he would raise his hand in a kind of salute. The wonderful companionship he had with his father during his youth was a tender kindness that he would remember with pleasure and with regret.

Nicholas cut his meat in exact pieces. "I had a terrible fight with my father before my abduction. I have many regrets."

"What happened?"

"What I had built up inside for a long time exploded. I told him how he was destroying the family."

"Go on."

"Due to my father's unbending and stubborn nature, my sister, Abigail rebelled, becoming a bit of a hoyden. Nothing bad, but the threat of scandal existed. My father was adamant on all of us marrying to gain privilege, esteem, and lands to enhance the Rutland name."

Nicholas stabbed meat from the platter and put it on his plate. "To correct the problem, my father insisted Abigail marry right away, giving her two months to select from many of the swains who camped on the doorstep. If she didn't choose a spouse during the allotted time, he'd make the decision for her."

"Abigail begged him to relent. She did not want to marry, at least not yet. Stubborn by nature, and driven to extraordinary measures, she faked an engagement to a man she didn't love. I confronted my father, insisting he was handling Abigail all wrong. Told him he was being premature and unfair."

"How did he take that?"

"Not well. The argument burst into a shouting match. I threw out all my pent-up animosity. Absent father...my brother, Joshua disappearing in the wilderness of the Colonies to get away from him... my brother, Anthony pressed to marry a selfish immature shrew who spent troves of his money and, who I suspected, had cuckolded him. I said everything I could to hurt my father. Felt good, lashing out at him. The real reason was that I loathed the dukedom under his reign. I was born to command, felt my abilities in my blood."

She looked out the window, silent in her circumspection. His good mood from hours before fell away devolving into a morose brooding as another, morbid memory rose that included killing a man in self-defense. Not a part of him he was proud of, nor a part of him he'd reveal to her. A breeze rattled palm fronds together. Hands fisted, he waited. Her opinion meant more than he'd realized...or cared to admit.

"We all do things we wish desperately we could undo. Those regrets become a lodestone around our neck. To waste time, trying to change that, is like chasing the moon."

Her voice was quiet, reflective. Was she was speaking from experience?

She turned her gaze on him, her face playing a million emotions in the wavering candlelight. Hurt? Guilt? Remorse? What?

Nicholas bit out, "But you didn't see my father's tortured face. And now, I'm not to know if he lived or died. That last moment with my father...I threw away in anger."

"It is not a perfect world, Nicholas. It's when you feel regret all the time and can't do anything about it——" She looked down at her hands then looked at him again. "From what you've said, it's obvious your father loves you. He probably grew distant because he didn't want to risk losing you like he lost your mother."

He rose and moved to the window overlooking the ocean. The sun set over the mountain behind them and splashed scorching oranges, pinks and reds, like a burnt poppy, across the sea.

"People react differently when they mourn." He heard the scrape of her chair as she pushed it back, felt her come up next to him. "I'm sure your father is alive, Nicholas. Have faith in that."

There was a long pause as the late moon climbed out of the sea in the perpetual mystery of the tropics. Along the house, a coconut palm dipped and the night grew heavy, bearing down on the world.

With his fingertips, he gently lifted her chin and gazed down into her turquoise eyes. Alexandra, with her hair braided and secured with twine and her thin shift dirty from the day's work. She did not break like a porcelain doll. She was so unlike Lady Susannah.

He considered her seriously. This woman-child had a self-possession which went far beyond anything he had ever encountered before. In many ways, it was disturbing and impossible to think of her in a sisterly manner. "You are a very lovely girl, Miss Elwins. Don't let anything or anyone change you, including me."

The way the light caught her eyes, he imagined he could see into her, see her clarity, an openness that drew men. No. Couldn't get close. Wouldn't be fair to her. When rescued, he'd go back to England and resume his life.

Nicolas lowered his hand, regretted the confusion reflected in her face. Turning, he strode outside before he began something he couldn't stop. He plopped into his hammock, the blackness of night creating a strange uncertainty, the sky seeming to go round, and round like a circle with no beginning and no end.

Chapter 7

*N*icholas saluted her with a tankard of rum. "Would you like a flagon?"

Alexandra grimaced. "No, thank you."

"Suit yourself." He took a long draught, plunking shaving materials, and then a water basin, splashing the contents over the table. With his tankard of rum, he was more cautious. Not one drop did he allow to escape. With ceremony, he angled a mirror up against a pot to examine his face.

"The ration of rum should leave many a scar. Oh, to be witness to a senseless casualty." Alexandra dragged a chair to the far side of the room and stood on top. She rearranged the overhead shelves, finding herself peeking, and then leaning to see what sort of barbarous face had been concealed by his thick black beard. No doubt it would reveal a weak chin.

"You lean any further, you will fall off that chair."

She had been leaning so far to the left, she could not recover her balance quickly enough to pretend she hadn't been doing exactly that. She caught the shelf with her hands before she plummeted to the floor. Reflected in the mirror, she jerked her gaze from his, her face flushing.

"Come down from there and watch me butcher my face. I'm used to having my valet perform the duty."

With him drinking, he'd probably behead himself. She stepped down and rounded the table as he swiped from his throat up to his chin, leaving a red blotch. He attempted another swipe and she winced.

"Damn. I'll bleed to death before the day is out. Here, you do it."

In the bright light of the morning sun, she looked at the heavy beard. Scraping that rug off flesh? She swooned. "I can't."

He pushed the blade across the table. "You can't do any worse."

She had watched Molly shave her father but this was different. With shaking hands, she took the blade, not at all sure about putting a blade to a man's skin. He grabbed her wrist and forced his tankard into her hand. "Drink," he ordered with calm implacable authority that always rankled her. "Will steady your nerves."

She drank a long draught, let it burn down her throat, coughed, then lifted it and drank some more. He removed the flagon from her hands, despite the desire to drink more.

"Not too much, it will blur your vision. I don't desire to have my head on the table. Get on with it."

She winced with the unhappy task. Biting her lip, she carefully scraped along his chin, rinsed the blade in the basin of water and scraped again. Her musings were erroneous. He did not possess a weak chin. On the contrary, it was a square chin denoting strength.

"What do you think?"

Devoid of beard, the beauty of his pure, classical bone structure reminded her of a painting of Admiral Horatio Nelson who she had idolized. Maybe his chin was almost perfect, but just enough off to have character. Below the ridge of his brow, intelligent, probing blue eyes raked her. Her cheeks heated. He was so much handsomer than she expected. "I could be charitable," she teased.

"Be honest."

The man was a force. "You'll fairly do, I suppose."

"Your commentary is hardly charitable. Do you think I'd have a chance with the females of England?"

Alexandra shrugged. "How am I supposed to know? Perhaps a swine herder's, toothless daughter?" She giggled and put the blade to his throat again.

"What made you take up thievery?"

She stopped midstream, her fingers tightening around the handle. She had never denied his assumption. Or was he miffed because she had not called him handsome? She gritted her teeth, refusing, to add to his vanity.

She wiped the blade clean, her heart giving a traitorous leap at the sight of his broad shoulders so close to hers and his sternly handsome face etched with the morning light. "Why do you believe I chose the profession of thief?"

"Why do you always answer a question with a question?"

"Because you are a dim-witted, mulish man bent on believing what he wants." She dropped the blade into the basin. Water splashed on his chest. She turned to leave. He caught her arm.

"Then let's pretend you are not a thief. Why were you caught in Baron Sutherland's library?"

She pried at his fingers, one by one, but he held fast. "I had my reasons."

Nicholas scoffed. "Not good enough. Why would someone go to all the expense to have you privately transported when all they had to do was turn you over to the authorities?"

Alexandra straightened to her full height. "Because they wanted to get rid of me for good. To get rid of the last of my line."

He snorted. "Of a sea captain and his wife?"

Of course, he put no relevant motivation to someone getting rid of another with low-birth lineage. She did not delude herself that she had a choice to tell him her history, however painful it was. Days of secrets, concealing the truth weighed like an iron anchor, sinking her farther into the muck.

She took a deep breath. Would he mock her? "I am not Alexandra Elwins. My real name is Lady Alexandra Sutherland."

Nicholas gave a sharp bark of laughter. "Impossible. Everyone knows, Alexandra Sutherland died when she was a child, accidently dropped out a window by her kidnappers. The disaster was in all the papers, the most famous abduction ever, and the tragedy, on the heels of Baron Sutherland's death."

"The story was spun by my stepmother. To secure the baronetcy for her son...she invented a crime. At the funeral, she dramatically cried over a closed casket of her beloved stepdaughter—except the coffin was empty. Everyone in the country bought her woeful story of bereavement, declaring, 'How could Lady Sutherland handle so much grief?'"

Nicholas stared and released her arm. "The idea is so fantastic. Of course, it is not unheard of, long lost relatives coming forward to claim rights to properties and titles of those who are deceased. It takes years of the court's time to declare who is the official owner."

"My father did not have a natural death. My stepmother poisoned him."

"Poisoned? Those are huge allegations." He inclined his head, mulling the likelihood. "How is it you're alive? Where have you been all these years?"

Alexandra plunged in. "After my mother died, my father hired Molly Elwins as my wet nurse, her own child a stillborn. She stayed on as my nanny and we became very close. My father, Baron Sutherland was lonely, and in his despair easily charmed by Ursula Andrews, and—unaware of his new wife's character.

"Molly grew suspicious when my father died suddenly despite his robust good health. She later eavesdropped on my stepmother, learning Ursula had poisoned my father, and then plotted to kill me. Before my stepmother could perform her evil deed, Molly and Samuel whisked me away in the middle of the night. We hid in southern England under an assumed name."

Nicholas stood. His chair snapped to the floor. "Are you sure?"

Alexandra nodded. "Recently, I found a trapdoor in the kitchen and discovered a Bible gilded with gold and far too costly for a sea captain to possess. My surname, Alexandra Sutherland, not Alexandra Elwins was written in the first few pages with a long line of antecedents. I confronted my adoptive parents."

Nicholas let out a low whistle, righted the chair and paced about the room. "Hard to believe you are the Sutherland baby and have been alive all these years."

"When Molly and Samuel revealed what happened, I became furious with the secret they had kept from me."

He ran his palms down the rough coral brick of the window frame. "You were confused. To feel betrayal and resentment is a normal reaction to news like that. I should know, I shouldered similar feelings toward my father. But why did you go to your ancestral home, knowing the past and the danger?"

"Rebellious and foolish," he answered for her. "There is more to the story. Tell me."

She turned away. The dull ache she carried in her chest grew sharp just thinking about it.

"I'm not here to judge, but to help you, Alexandra." He turned toward her. "We are alone and must help each other."

She swallowed, her voice dropped to a whisper. "Molly had gone to London to visit a friend and on a chance meeting ran into my stepmother. Lady Ursula had Molly followed, hired a thug, and watched while the criminal strangled Molly."

Nicholas swore. "I remember Lady Ursula and Willean, I have seen them at parties. She doesn't seem like a murderer."

"She is the epitome of brutality. Later, when Ursula caught me in the library, she bragged about the murder. Told me she had been enraged when Molly would not disclose my location, but since she had me, her problem was solved...and she was going to kill me. Her son, Baron Willean Sutherland, my stepbrother, held a gun leveled at my chest.

Suddenly cold, Alexandra rubbed her upper arms. "My life literally flashed before my eyes. I remembered Willean tripping me, pushing me down the stairs, holding my puppy over the second-floor balcony and threatening to drop her, putting cockleburs beneath my pony's saddle to make her throw me." "Oh, God." Her voice cracked. She shuddered, blinked back the tears building behind her eyes.

Nicholas crossed the room.

She swiped her cheeks with the back of her hand. She didn't want him to see her cry. To see how weak she really was. "B-but for some reason, Willean refused to kill me and suggested another, crueler solution. He paid to have me put aboard the *Santanas*."

As she said those last words, the true horror hit her and the door to the years of tears she'd held back suddenly opened. Tears slid unbidden down her cheeks.

Nicolas cursed and yanked her into his arms while she wet his shirt with her tears. To think after all these years, the daughter of Lord Sutherland was alive.

"Molly is dead because of me. She protected me. And Samuel, I love him so much. I lied to him about where I was going."

He smoothed his hand over the back of her head. "Cry all you want. You are not responsible for Molly's death. Your stepmother killed Molly."

They stood there for an eternity, every breath, every thought intertwined.

"I admire you, Lady Sutherland."

She halted at the use of her title and her gaze snapped to his face. "You believe me?"

He wiped the tears from her eyes. "Your story is too extraordinary not to believe. My own stupidity was to believe you were a thief. Why did you never tell me?"

She toyed with the mother-of-pearl button on his shirt, driving him mad. "You are a stubborn man bent on believing what he wants to believe."

"There is that," he said. He was an idiot. He'd had questions, but had let his all-important titled existence be his guide, not his gut.

She moved away from him as if realizing the impropriety of their closeness. He desired to snatch her back in his arms, yet hesitated, respecting the distance she sought. He leaned his shoulder against the uneven wall of the cottage, and, frowning, he reconsidered.

She was not a thief. She was an innocent and he took great delight in that notion.

What this lovely woman had faced. Rising above her misfortunes, she had the ability to hope and emerge triumphant. She had the capacity to find light in the darkest corner.

She was an angel.

"All this time, Alexandra you have been positive and I've been moody and recalcitrant. You have survived far more than I ever have. I've been an idiot, an ogre and anything else you wish to call me. I want to apologize to you."

"There is nothing to forgive, Nicholas."

"Alexandra, I vow if we ever get back to England I will help you gain what is rightfully yours, and find justice for Molly and your father, Baron Sutherland. I will protect you."

Chapter 8

From what seemed a wild and horrible nightmare, a semblance of life on the island emerged. They chattered excitedly, digging hands into the soil, feeling its texture. They cleared away the brush from the wild orange and other fruit trees, allowing the caressing warmth of the sun to encourage production.

Nicholas had set spade to earth, and what had been a wasteland of tangled weeds, was now planted with neat little rows of growing lettuces, cabbage, tomatoes and other vegetables. Automatically, Nicholas and Alexandra responded to the novelty and primitive call of the land.

Nicholas was more content than he had ever been in his life.

Days passed and he discovered an order to work on the island that satisfied something deeper in him. An order came from the union of skill and passion. But he had to admit, the driving energy came from working with Alexandra and always toward a goal. Each knowing their role, yet tripping over boundaries to help the other. There was no pause in Alexandra. She worked doggedly to get the job done, and then she would give him that challenging lift to her brow that told him she expected the same or more from him.

Meat had been smoked and hung in the lean-to. The daily routine of obtaining water, although onerous, was maintained. They collected fruit, rendered tallow from the animal fat for lamps, which cut down on the need of their limited beeswax candles. They collected sea grapes on the beach and had great fun crushing the lot so they could ferment in a crock to make wine. He'd gathered a large pile of driftwood and set it on the beach to light a signal fire. He hunted.

As the weeks wore on, he admired her knowledge more and more. She was far better prepared to survive, teaching and inspiring him about planting, food preservation, and collecting healing herbs. He was surprised how much he liked being with her.

A day didn't go by that he didn't try to win her warm smile, taking pleasure, delighting her by something he could accomplish. And those accomplishments were increasing daily. He surprised himself by how much he could do without commanding a servant to do it for him.

With a loop trap, he snagged a female goat, dragging the obstinate bleating creature through the jungle to the garden's edge. Alexandra was on her knees, weeding.

The goat's cries caused her to raise her golden head. She clapped her hands. "Nicholas, you astonish me with your cleverness. How perfect to have a nanny goat to milk and to make cheese and puddings."

He never tired of her exclamations. She made him feel like an emperor—and over a silly goat.

He was free of the awkwardness that comes of the mismatching of two people who are not suited to be together. As with Lady Susannah Tomkins.

He gritted his teeth until his jaw ached. He had promised his father he would marry Lady Susannah Tomkins. If his father were alive, he'd have to honor his wishes.

Alexandra took the tether from him, her hands warm upon his. He jerked back.

She blinked. "Is something the matter?"

"No," he said, harsher than necessary.

She tied the goat in the shade of a Poinciana tree. Flower petals had fallen, creating a thick bright orange carpet on the earth, and like a painting, framed a magnificent backdrop for Alexandra. So happy with her simple gift, she cooed to the beast, calming the animal with her words. Like she did with him.

Nicholas exhaled, so many contrasts between Alexandra and his fiancée. Lady Susannah would be horrified with such an offering. Nicholas' nerves grew taut. He clenched his jaws. To be yoked to a shallow woman satisfied with nothing less than jewels, furs, and the finest of clothes, left a sour taste in his mouth.

"I like your idea of trying different plantings. I think your experimentation will give us a greater yield, Nicholas. I can't wait to see the results."

Alexandra's enthusiasm was infectious. She took joy in what he found important, embracing the simplest things and making every occurrence of every day worth remembering.

Next to Alexandra, Lady Susannah's negative traits magnified. Would Lady Susannah talk about crop rotation? No. She'd yawn, look him up and down with disdain, and then nag him to accompany her to the next ball, tea or entertainment.

He had seen Lady Susannah's sharp tongue toward her servants, giving criticism and instruction rather than praise, even taking a riding crop to a groom who had not helped her dismount quickly enough.

On one occasion, he had business to attend for his father, and was therefore unable to escort her to an opera. How she loved to play the martyr, insisting he reward her tenfold. From his sister and friends, he had learned of Lady Susannah's, constant checking of his whereabouts, and then venting to others, making him look like a fool. He had chosen to be oblivious to all of this...until now.

Nicholas's mind spun, torn between wanting to stay here and continue the pleasant life he and Alexandra enjoyed together, or return to England and take up the mantle his father commanded— if the opportunity ever came to get off the island.

Alexandra's lineage was nebulous, unproven and would be impossible to verify, a result of Lady Ursula, covering her crime well. His father, if alive, would demand an authentic pedigree.

"If we are going to the top of that mountain, we better make the rest of our daylight."

"Is that so?" She laughed and patted the goat as it dunked its head into the bucket for a drink. "I suppose we have worked hard enough that we can spare some time off."

Nicholas slung the Brown Bess and powder horn over his shoulder, and then picked up a machete. The animal path lay dubious and uncertain through thick jungle, leading them through another bamboo forest. Beneath the lush canopy of gleaming leaves, reached snatches of sunlight and sky. They ducked beneath a myriad of roots of an ancient banyan tree and arrived at an open clearing where large spherical fruits hung.

"A calabash tree, Nicholas. My father brought these gourds to England. We can scrape and dry out the fruits, making vessels that will make excellent transports for water when we explore."

He marked trees with his machete for the return trip. After an hour, he climbed to the top of an escarpment buffeted by winds and free of vegetation. To the south, lay the blue sea, like a huge left-handed glove worn by a Medieval knight, the thumb split from the hand. The eastern portion from which they inhabited, undulated with palms and rich verdant green, descending to a white sand beach. Contrasting to the west, or leeward side, were rolling meadows. The northern division was steeped with wretched sharp cliffs that fell straight to the sea.

"Everywhere we are surrounded by water and confirms we are on an island." Nowhere was the landscape so breathtaking. To be on top of the world. He turned around to see her reaction. She was just as taken as he was. He stretched his hand to hers.

When she clasped her palm to his, a current of awareness shot through him with a sweet wash of sensation, like a thousand springs in bloom. A sweetness he had no business feeling, though it brought him a gentle peace. He didn't remember pulling her up beside him. Suddenly, she was standing right next to him and the softness of her arm pressed against his.

"I'm king of this island," he roared over the echoing valley, jolting a pair of flapping egrets from their nests.

"I'm queen of this island," she shouted after him. "And since you are the only male resident, I'll allow you the title of king."

He made an exaggerated bow. "I thank you for your generosity. Still, a compromise is in order. We will rule together, Lady Sutherland, guardians of all we survey."

"On one condition," she said seriously. "That we call this land, Alexandra Island. I've never had anything named after me."

"Then we shall call it Alexandra Island." He'd agree to anything she wanted.

"Isn't it lovely, Nicholas?"

His gaze focused on her. How could he even concentrate? "Very."

He tried to think of a woman of his acquaintance who would hike to the top of a mountain and never complain, finding every day a new adventure. None.

Her chest heaving from the exertion, she scanned the horizon. "There is so much to discover."

Wishing swept through him as he studied her profile. Under no circumstances would he be less than mystified by her eyes, dark ringed with golden lights, mesmerizing, ever-changing from emerald to deep pools of turquoise and fringed with long lashes. Her nose was straight and perfect, and her lips always seemed to hold a hint of a smile.

The way her chin curved, so delicate, made him want to run the pad of his thumb along the angle to see if her bronzed skin, felt as soft as it looked. Her golden braid, reached to her hips. How many times had he resisted the urge to unplait the golden mass? Every time he gazed upon her, tenderness wrapped around him in ever-strengthening layers. He had a fondness for Alexandra, but he suspected she did not for him.

The sting pierced him, but he tried not to let it show. Never, not once had he caught her glancing his way in other than a sisterly fashion. She would be busy doing her everyday chores, chatting up a storm, yet did not notice him the way he desired.

Not that it wasn't his fault. He had been clear about their relationship. Yet, to be alone with her day after day was taxing his reserve. To him, she was far above the price of rubies and he was totally captivated.

Chapter 9

*N*icholas set aside the drilled calabash and washed his hands in the water bucket. His stomach rumbled as he inhaled the savory scent of roasted meat.

"What would I do without you?" she said, waiting in the doorway.

She had that way about her, like she expected lightning to play upon the waves when he did something. Hell, he'd hurl back the Thames to its source if she wanted it.

He scratched a wooden chair across the plank floor as he first seated her, and then himself, maintaining an unstated degree of civilization. Thick wild pork roast slices smothered in gravy with wild sugar yams were heaped on his plate. He helped himself to pink guava slices reminiscent of strawberries and pears combined.

Nicholas ate his fill and massaged his stomach. "I don't think I've ever had such a great meal."

"Would you like some salt beef from the cask aboard the *Santanas*?" she teased him.

Nick eyed her ruefully. "You have a cruel streak. One sight of that muck they gave us would render me stiff as a lifeless rat."

Her eyes twinkled. "I am sure your family had the finest of meals, prepared by the best of chefs, Nicholas."

The way she said his name tugged at his heart. He liked everything about her—the way she drew her bottom lip between her teeth when she concentrated, the care she took with everything, including the way she had sewn his torn shirt with confident stitches.

She rose from the table and moved toward a shelf. He drank in the sight of her. He didn't know why she opened a place inside of him, a deep and vulnerable room he had not known was there.

She picked up a bowl and placed it on the table before him. Her long golden braid entwined with jasmine flowers lay over her breast, and she emanated a breathtakingly beautiful image of breeding and serenity.

"This is a surprise I made just for you since you have had to do without all the luxuries of home in England. Let's see if this competes with one of your cooks. I used vanilla bean and goat milk to make a pudding."

Nicholas dipped his spoon into the creamy mixture layered with honeyed bananas. He groaned, savoring the sweet concoction. "This side of heaven." He scraped his bowl clean and when she bent to take his plates, he stayed her hand. "Let's pretend we are not in a hurry and enjoy some leisure. Get the chess set out and I'll teach you how to play."

He helped her clear the dishes away, and then set-up the board. "I'll go easy on you for the first couple of times until you get the gist of the rules. I was champion at Oxford. I am ruthless."

She bit her lip. "Sounds complicated and formidable. I don't know if I'll make much of a sparring partner. I'll have to pay close attention. And never defeated?"

"Except for my brother, Anthony. No one in England has bested him." For the next several minutes, he described the moves and the importance of each piece. Noting Alexandra's furrowed brow, he wondered if he was explaining the rules too quickly, but let it go because he had plenty of time to teach her. "Tell me about yourself, Alexandra."

She gave a dainty little shrug. "There's nothing remarkable to tell."

Dappled light from the setting sun clung to her, crowning her in an aura of gold. "Enlighten me." He wanted to know everything about her.

"Nothing extraordinary. A normal life where everyone scratched out a living by working hard and making ends meet."

He moved his chess piece forward. He had decided a long time ago wealth did not equate to the goodness inside a person. Having money and privilege did not make someone better than those without. Alexandra's strange history added to her charm and humility.

"You haven't told me what we are playing for. If I win, I want to go to the shore tomorrow...and cement our agreement that we call this place, Alexandra Island."

He contained a snort. "Fair enough. If I win, you'll serve me breakfast in my hammock."

She countered by moving her rook. "When I get rescued, I'll return to my village on the south shores of England."

His throat constricted making it hard to breathe. To think she'd be far from London and even further from Belvoir...from him. He tucked that raw notion in the back of his mind. No ships had been seen and rescue was questionable. "Tell me about your village."

She warmed to the topic. "To the south, fierce winds sweep across a moorland that stretches across barren granite. Wild ponies forage upon the heather that turns from a deep golden in winter to an endless variety of crimson, pinks and purple in the summer. To the north, a river flows into a deep blue harbor where my father kept his ship, and behind are hills of infinite green where sheep and cattle graze. I often walk the crags overlooking the sea. There the earth rises to heaven, life lingers like a last caress, and holds a breath of melody. The cliffs are my favorite place to go when I'm upset and want to think things through."

Her hand fluttered over her heart.

> *"Go travel 'mid the hills! The summer's hand*
> *Hath shaken pleasant freshness o'er them all.*
> *Go, travel 'mid the hills! There, tuneful streams——"*

Nicolas finished for her.

> *"'Are touching myriad stops, invisible;*
> *And winds, and leaves, and birds, and your own thoughts,*
> *Not the least glad in wordless chorus crowd.'"*

"You are a fan of Milton." She smiled.

"*A Sea-Side Meditation.* I had to memorize the poem in my youth."

She gave a heavy sigh. "Molly was a healer. She gardened and grew medicinal herbs. People relied more on her healing skills than the local physician. Samuel retired from the sea, happy to live on his profits from the merchantman and pension due him from his earlier years, serving in His Majesty's Navy."

When Nicholas drew back surprised with that fact, she added, "Aboard the *HMS Victory.*

"Samuel and Molly loved each other very much. Often, I'd see knowing looks between them when they thought I wasn't paying attention. Samuel told wonderful yarns. In our house, there was always love and laughter."

He saw how Alexandra suffered tremendous guilt from Molly's death, struggled underneath her smiling veneer. A tendril of her hair lifted as she looked off in the distance, remembering. How he wished he could wipe that sadness from her.

Best to keep the moment light-hearted. "What else can you share with me?"

"The people in my village were shopkeepers, farmers or fishermen, there was a miller, and blacksmith, much like many other villages in coastal areas of England. "Of course. Growing up in a small community there wasn't much for entertainment."

"There must have been some going's on. My tenant's homes were always a din of activity," Nicholas said.

She fiddled with a vase, focusing on a bouquet of bright yellow hibiscus. He was swimming in a sea of awe. Men drowned in seas like that.

"Well...there was the butcher who cheated people by selling inferior meat and keeping his thumb on the scales."

"Why do I have the impression there was retribution?"

She moved her castle. "I painted red dots on the butcher's chickens and told him they had the pox."

Nicholas laughed and moved his bishop, taking her pawn, thoroughly enjoying himself. In retaliation, she took his knight.

"Excellent," he said.

"Are you complimenting my move or my retribution?"

"So, you believe in mischiefs?"

"You mean as a...concept?"

"No. Entirely in practice."

"You want the short answer or the long one?"

She made another move and he frowned. "You may not want to make that move. It will free me to take your king."

She shrugged. "You said this was a learning venture, did you not? Let's see where it goes."

"Suit yourself. The game will end early and I'll require a plate of bananas, papaya and bread on my hammock as soon as the sun rises."

"The subject is mischief, is it not?" She continued her story, keeping a little pantomime with her hands. "To dazzle the village children, I drilled a hole in an apple and put a beetle in it. I would wave my hands over the apple, divining my great power. The beetle moved the apple, lending credence to my potent magic." She kept a straight face and then broke out in sheer merriment.

"Then there were the cantankerous sisters."

There was nothing more contagious than her laughter. It didn't even have to matter what they were laughing about. "Cantankerous?"

"Well, that wasn't their name. There real name was Cornett like a horn blower and both none too bright. I mentioned them before."

"When you compared my behavior to a nine-year old," he said drily.

She giggled at his offense. "Miss Hortense, had hairs in her ears, curling wondrously out like a bush. She never had a nice word to say about anyone. And then there was her sister, Miss Gertrude, her face, like a drought-ridden earth, laced with a million yawning cracks and equally unpleasant. Both sisters were blessed with an active career as gossipmongers."

The pleasant fragrance of wood smoke drifted in the cottage from the beehive oven. Nicholas leaned back in his chair, watching her, enjoying his domestic surroundings. He caught her staring at his lips. She colored and looked away. His whole being was filled with wanting. It would be so easy.

"Samuel called them the village dragons. Molly warned me away, saying a 'a goat's business is not the sheep's concern.'"

Alexandra clapped her hands on the table and leaned toward him, her face alive and animated. "Miss Gertrude tried to take you into her confidence, but beware, she had a tongue like a rapier. In truth, both ladies were such grand practitioners of their craft that you could furnish them with some solid tales, and in no time, the gossip spread like fire through a haymow, reaching everyone in the community."

He liked how she made funny voices, mimicking the village shrews, a natural storyteller. "I'm sure you provided them with plenty of fodder."

She rose while he made his move, groped for the tinderbox on the upper shelf. "I told the Cornett sisters' the grocer had a special on pigeon's milk and to drink it would restore their youth and vigor. Can you imagine the look on the grocer's face when they asked him for pigeon's milk?"

Alexandra scraped flint against steel. Click. Click. Click. The spark took hold on the candle wick, producing a solid flame. The shadows retreated to the corners of the room, lapping there like a diminishing tide. She dropped the tinderbox and made another move that was against his earlier instruction. She'd never learn the game at this rate. She was so enthused talking about the villagers that she didn't realize how distracted she had become. He didn't have the heart to tell her she would lose. "So, the Cornett sisters were the recipients of your deeds?"

"One time I told them a prince from a foreign country was coming to the village. He was going to marry one of the village girls, but I couldn't say who."

He moved his rook. "Of course. The *who* being you."

She frowned in concentration and moved her castle, taking one of his pawns. "Well...it lent to my fantasies that a prince would come and sweep me off my feet. I embellished the story, how they met when she had fallen off her horse and broken her ankle...which had happened to me months before in a neighboring village. How the prince had come at that precise moment with his coach and how they immediately fell in love."

"In no time the whole village was preened and outfitted waiting for the illustrious guest to arrive...who never came. Molly asked if I knew anything about the rumors. I couldn't lie."

"After my admission, Molly was in a terrible temper. What kind of daughter was she raising to be part of this deceit and befalling a trap of the devil? She marched me over to the Cornett sisters and made me apologize." Alexandra studied her hands in her lap.

"And?" Nicolas prompted.

He saw her glance drift over his open shirt and caress him there.

She swallowed hard and said, wistfully, "Well, there are some roads I do not need to travel. Molly regretted it the minute we left. The Cornett sisters do not forget an offense and made my life miserable."

He didn't need to ask what trouble two spiteful old harridans would cause. Despite the difficulties thrown her way, Alexandra rose above her hardships, showing no bitterness or acrimony.

Her turquoise eyes, her smile, her sweetness snared him. He didn't want to feel this way. He had so many responsibilities facing him in England. He had a lot to learn about the ducal properties and a lot to prove to his father, if his father were still alive, and if they ever got off this island. And responsibility? He shouldered a huge burden, preserving the Rutland legacy. No. He couldn't be sidetracked with an attraction to Alexandra.

But they could be there forever, and what then? What harm would there be, especially if they were never rescued. They could be fated to live out their lives together.

He reviewed her story, divulging she was a baron's daughter. Was she a con artist in addition to a thief? The simplest truth was more powerful than an elaborate lie and had easily trapped Nicholas's friend in a scam that lost him thousands of pounds. Could Alexandra weave such a web? Perhaps she was a seasoned seductress.

On the chance he did get off the island and returned to England he could make inquiries. He'd ask Lady Ursula. Yet if what Alexandra said about her history was true, Lady Ursula would lie.

Nicholas drummed his fingers on the table. But Alexandra seemed without guile, and the soul of honesty and sincerity. He remembered the words of his brother, Joshua who was wise beyond his years.

Men would rather deny a hard truth than accept it.

Nicholas fiddled with his chess piece. If she was telling the truth, she was the sort who deserved a forever kind of man, but with her unproven background, her insertion into society would be difficult. To introduce her to a lesser kind of lord bore possibilities. Alexandra in the arms of someone else? Some stuffy aristocrat, caressing the line down her back and beyond…her slim legs wrapped… A demon of jealousy rose and twisted inside him. He'd lock her up before he'd allow that.

She moved her queen into final position and her eyes met his with a force that licked through his body. Why did he have the sense he had been waltzed backward?

Alexandra had his king surrounded. "Lord Nicolas, am I playing the game correctly?" She pasted a benign expression on her face while she twirled his king.

Oh, how she loved the dawning realization on his face. With a flick of her finger, she knocked his king over. "Checkmate."

He stared her down. "I have been outflanked."

"To think I defeated the Oxford Chess Champion on my first try. I must be terribly lucky." She laughed.

"You have the presence of a hummingbird with shark's teeth. I'll never underestimate you again." Nicolas jammed the chess pieces away. "You could have let me win."

Alexandra scoffed. "You wouldn't want victory that cheaply. It would be an insult. Looks like a trip to the shore tomorrow to confirm we reside on Alexandra Island," she reminded him.

"I promise I will repay you."

"Is that so? With coconuts and mangos?"

"You do not think I will get even?"

"Does an ape flinch when a monkey throws a banana at him?" She laughed, and then the candle sputtered out, concealing them in darkness, the last red speck of the taper light glowing like a firefly. She walked outside, an unexpected ache in her heart growing from the evening concluding. She stumbled. Before she could react, Nicholas's hand closed around her upper arm to steady her. She started at his touch, his breath grazing her cheek.

He murmured an apology and released her arm.

She had not realized he was walking almost at her heels or that he had been observing her.

Alexandra glanced over her shoulder, but he was staring ahead.

His lonely hammock clung to the gloom. Behind her the cottage surrendered to a sphere of twilight.

His dark head lifted to the heavens. "There is a faint circle around the moon taking up half the sky, portending bad weather."

"Rain?" she said.

"A storm is brewing."

Beneath the glimmering of moonlight, waves moved like a contemplation attempting to arise on the fringe of consciousness, their spumes rose and tips fell away, mountains of them, already speeding forward into deep swells. She swallowed. Took a deep breath. "You must come in for the night."

She pivoted and pointed. "You can sling your hammock on the hooks anchored in the coral block. They are rusted from being exposed to salt air, yet sturdy."

The wind picked up, flapping loosened shutters, raising the hairs on the back of her neck. Storms. She hated them especially after the hurricane at sea in which they had almost perished. Nick tossed his hammock in the cottage, went back outside, closing shutters, and nailing them with spare boards.

The roar of the wind grew into a cacophony. He staggered into the house, shoved his shoulder against the door and slammed the bar in place.

"I'll need to work on the shutters. They aren't sound enough but will be better than nothing."

An enormous clap of thunder made her jump, and then another. Wind tore open one of the hinged panels. Palms were bent sideways. The sky was a crying fire—massive cobwebbed nets of jagged lightning ran horizon to horizon. Rain slashed inside, soaking everything. Nicholas yanked on the shutter and Alexandra tied it closed.

He tore off his damp shirt, drying himself with a towel, and then tossed it on a chair. He stretched a knot of his hammock to one hook and strung it across the room—right next to her bed. Heat pulsed in her cheeks. *Out of the question.*

She had slept next to him on the beach. Except he was asleep then. She lit a candle.

Nicholas's dark blue eyes smoldered. While his gaze searched hers, she felt as if she were the only woman on earth.

She glanced away, then back again. She cleared her throat.

His slow smile spread lazily across his mouth with her discomfort.

She crossed to the shelf for a quilt and placed it on his hammock. Rain pounded the roof. A lightning bolt split a tree near the house. Alexandra trembled. The candlelight flickered, went out with the wind that hissed through the shutters. Shivering, she crawled into her bed, pulling the quilt up to her chin. "As a child, I

was afraid of the fierce storms that hailed across the southern pen-
insula. Molly and Samuel would tell me stories to make my fears
go away."

She heard him climb into his hammock, his breathing next to
hers. She could smell him, an earthy scent she had grown to associate with—him.

"I'm quite comfortable during this storm. But the storms tearing across this island are not the storms of home. At Belvior, I was
sheltered under a solid roof with a thick pane of glass to keep away
the rains and snow. A fireplace stoked by servants to keep away the
chill and a bevy of kitchen staff to fill my belly with every whim,"
Nicholas said.

Her heart squeezed. He was distracting her from the storm.

"We saw the worst when the *Santanas* was torn apart,
Alexandra. We're safe. The shutters are up. The cottage is sound
and...I'm here to watch over you."

I'm here to watch over you. The snap of connection roared through
her like the crackling of a fire and a release of tension flowed from
her body. To know he'd keep her safe.

"What was life like for you growing up? At Belvoir Castle."
The air was moist, heavy, as if filled with secrets. He rested, cast
in stygian darkness. Did he think the arrangement strange? He did
not indicate his thoughts.

"My siblings and I had an ancient Jesuit tutor and despite his
age, he was extremely astute. Not many days could we get by him.
We learned a variety of subjects. Mathematics, a good smattering
of Calculus, different languages, including French, Latin, Greek
and Italian, and philosophy and the sciences. The priest, a strict

taskmaster, sharpened our debate skills on all matters of learning, nourishing an advantageous competition between us. And we did not disappoint."

"How many siblings do you have?" Flashes of light, showed the outline of his form. He was more filled out with the better diet and hard work—large and overwhelming. She could reach out and touch his shoulder, let her fingertips move down the hard planes of his chest.

"Three. There was my brother, Joshua. He's disappeared in the American wilderness, haven't heard from him in a long time and I worry what has happened to him."

"Do you think he is working with the Colonists in their Revolution? I've heard people who have gone there are influenced by their cause."

Nicholas exhaled. She could almost hear him thinking about the possibility. "Not likely. Enamored with stories of the American wilderness, Joshua travelled there on a lark to get away from home."

"And there's Anthony who's next in line from me. He's a genius. Rarely comes out of his laboratory to see the light of day."

"He is a scientist?"

"He has always tinkered with the physical world, since he was a child." Nicholas laughed. "He once formulated a sleeping potion for our tutor so we could have the day off and go to the village fair."

"What happened?"

"The tutor did not wake for a day and a night. The outraged Jesuit reported to my father at the exact time, Anthony's lab exploded. Anthony had been mixing chemicals, perfecting a new experiment and left seconds before. Both he and Abby might have been killed. We were disciplined for our misdeeds to the tune of no weekend activities for six weeks. Pure purgatory, reciting Latin phrases over and over. *Amo. Amas. Amat. Amamas.*"

She listened as he conjugated the Latin verb, *to love*. His voice had a pleasant sound that could command in such a way as to compel obedience. Oh, he would make a fine duke with that voice, his baritone possessing a quality that could woo seductively and caressingly, most of all her.

"Abby is the youngest. We were very close and I always protected her, often taking the blame for her schemes. When she was eight summers, Abby maneuvered me on a prank to fool her best friend, Lord Humphrey. Humphrey loved noodles. Abby convinced the cook to make noodles, loads of them. With the footman, we hung them all over a tree. When Humphrey came up the drive, his eyes popped wide as saucers watching us go up and down ladders, harvesting baskets of noodles. Every time he visited, he stared at the tree, waiting for noodles to sprout."

"You sound like a charming horde of imps." Her heart panged. "You are so lucky, to have brothers and sisters to share joys and camaraderie—to take away any loneliness."

His voice deepened and there was a touch of sympathy. "Were you lonely, Alexandra?"

If he knew the poverty of loneliness that inhabited her soul, would he think differently about her? Could she be honest with him? Bare her soul?

"Deconshire was so isolated and we lived so far from town. I didn't fit there. Do you know how that feels? To be caught in a world where you don't belong, feeling like a foreigner and not understanding the language."

"Molly and Samuel were wonderful and did everything they could to make me happy. But all my life, I was haunted by dreams, had visions of a handsome man bouncing me on his knee…a secret…a latch…a desk…a trap door…papers. The man would hold my face in his hands, telling me it was important.

"None of it made sense until the night I broke into my father's library. Polished wainscoting, a large desk…even the smell of leather from the many volumes collected on the shelves. Everything flooded back. This was my home. But before I could tinker with the desk, Lady Ursula discovered me.

"Samuel had said, my stepmother passed rumors my mother had cuckolded my father and I was ill-legitimate. Samuel was convinced Ursula had papers forged, showing my father had established her son as the heir and inheritor of the Sutherland Baronetcy."

"Back-up, Alexandra. Why would your stepmother go to all the trouble, spreading rumors of your illegitimacy? Why bother blackballing you, if the papers were forged to secure her son's standing? Estates will go to the closest male heir…unless—and by some rare occurrence when there is no male heir, a title would pass automatically to the female heir. I can assume Lady Ursula is hiding something and that is why she is afraid of you, and that is why she had Molly killed."

Alexandra grew silent mulling Nicholas's conclusion, the same calculations that had churned in her mind. Life was full of mysteries she'd never solve, the least of which was proving her ancestry. Oh, to rightfully claim what was hers by birthright.

She clenched her hands. "I want justice, Nicholas. I want justice for my father and Molly. Bringing Ursula and Willean before a magistrate for their crimes burns in me like a fever."

"I can help you by petitioning the Crown."

Alexandra leaned over and snorted. "The chance of wild pigs on this island, sprouting wings and flying us to England has a higher likelihood than the King bothering to hear my case. I suppose you are going to next tell me you are related to the King."

"He is my father's cousin."

Alexandra fell back on her pillow. "Never in a million years would I have guessed that possibility. But I cannot prove who I am. Molly is dead and the only witness to Ursula's crime."

"What about the night you broke in? Did a servant see you? What about on the docks? Were there any eyewitnesses?"

"None that I saw."

Nicholas said nothing. His silence spoke volumes. Tears of frustration burned the back of her throat. There was no answer to her dilemma. Even if they were rescued, her future was bleak. Never could she take her rightful place in society. Lady Ursula had made sure of that.

And then too, her life would be in danger if her stepmother discovered her whereabouts. Samuel too. Always looking over her shoulder...living in fear.

"Alexandra, I will find a way, I promised you before and I promise you now that you will get back what belongs to you, and your stepmother and brother will pay for their crimes. However, there is a condition—"

"A condition?"

"You must promise the first dance to me at the Summer's Eve Ball."

To dance with Lord Nicholas? To pretend what he said was true, even for a little while was a wonderful dream. At least she'd fantasize a little. "The Summer's Eve Ball?"

"It is the grandest display of balls that my family puts on at Belvoir on the eve of the summer solstice. No expense is spared. Indeed, the surroundings are beautiful. Lanterns hang in the gardens; a riot of roses bloom and the scent drifts everywhere. The music is soft and lilting and the smiles and chatter of all the celebrators mark the evening to be every triumph London society imagines. All eyes would be focused on you."

Her breath hitched. Her hands were stained and calloused from working in the gardens. Not a lady's hands. She fingered her linen shift, no more than a rag. Never could she afford a ball gown let alone slippers. Oh, Nicholas, you paint such a pretty picture. To step into your world for just a second. A white ball gown that shimmered as she descended a stairway. Moving into Nicolas's arms, and swaying to a waltz. She closed her eyes, surrendering to the miraculous scope of human generosity. Nicolas had given her a gift of flowers and sunshine, a castle in the sky.

The cold reality was that when they returned to England, she'd resume her life, hiding in Deconshire, always fearing Lady Ursula would attempt to get rid of her again, and Nicholas would go back to claim his responsibilities.

She clutched her chest. Her chequered past reared its vile head again. Ursula's damning defamation created negative moral judgment. Even coming from a small town, she knew how vicious the wagging tongues were. Multiply that a hundredfold by an aristocracy who sought gossip as recreation. To be associated with a woman who was considered illegitimate would put a stain on Lord Nicholas. No. She would not jeopardize him with any censorship driven by his association with her.

The terrible and absurd sting of emotions would not let her rest. The longing of the impossible lay heavy in her heart. The same longing of another soul to cling to, to watch the evolving tides, and the laughter of the rain, a body to keep her warm, to pour herself into. Just as the man lying next to her.

How long could she keep up the charade? Day by day her attraction to Nicholas grew. To pretend she did not have feelings for him was torture. How many times had she cautioned herself to stop staring at him like a lovesick fool? Would he dismiss her affection? Someone with her hazy lineage might never be elevated to his status.

Yet the intimacy of sleeping side by side had her thinking the impossible and a curl of desire grew inside her. They had brushed shoulders from time to time when working or when he held her hand to assist her up on a ledge. Other than that, they had kept their relationship familial. But it did not keep her from wishing things were different.

She stared at the ceiling, anywhere but at him, laying exhausted and doubting if she'd get a wink of sleep. Was it wrong to imagine laying her head on his chest, and feeling his heart beat beneath her fingers?

Chapter 10

*A*lexandra grabbed hold of the smooth bark of a mahogany tree and spun around it. "Jump to it, Nicholas. You are half asleep today. If we are ever to get to the beach, you'll have to quit your lagging."

Nicholas rubbed fingertips in his tangled hair, tugging the sleep from his mind. He had lain awake most of the night, with her lush body inches away. At least, when he had slept outside he had a physical distance to separate them. But the storm last night had changed that remoteness. Her smell and soft sighs while she slumbered had his body on fire.

She dashed ahead of him, her shift clinging to her rounded hips. He groaned.

"Did you say something?"

I want to throw you down in the sand and make love to you. He said nothing.

"Are you suffering from ennui, Lord Nicolas?"

Far from it. He had a lively inner world. What would she feel like, taste like? He had to change the view before the primitive force inside him demand that he reach for her and… Damn it! He pushed ahead of her.

Never had he been in such a constant state of arousal. "What else can you tell me about life in your village?"

"I cared for the Vicar's children in exchange for my education. The vicar taught me and had a library that gave me access to many books."

"So that is how you are so well-educated, knowing Paine and other theorists. I must admit, your self-learning is admirable." He glanced over his shoulder to see how she'd take his compliment.

She beamed and he took a certain pride in that fact.

"Vicar Thompson had three adorable children. I taught and cared for them. How I miss their antics and youthful zeal.

"The twins, Sylvia and Julianna were very bright and a handful, led by their nine-year old, older brother, Jay who is smart with a dash of mischievousness. He liked to hide up in a tree, in company of his sisters and toss apples on unsuspecting villagers. One of their escapades followed the sermon their father had given about Moses leaving Israel. They captured dozens of frogs and released them on the Cornett sisters' doorstep, and the sisters shrieking they'd been cursed by a Biblical plague."

Nicholas threw back his head and laughed, startling a flock mourning doves. "Of course, you made the miscreants apologize."

"Heavens no. If I'd known, I might have added a frog or two." She burst out laughing. "Overall, the vicar's children were sweet and affectionate and I never tired being with them."

So, she liked children. Suddenly, Nicholas dreamed of coming home to a comfy house, the sound of children playing and a loving wife. That loving wife merged into Alexandra's image. He wiped his damp palms on his breeches.

"What do you wish for, Alexandra?" He was tempted to take her hand in his.

"I'd love to have fried goat cheese with gooseberry sauce. It is my favorite. And to see an opera."

"No. What do you wish *for*?"

She sighed. "Children, lots of them. Running all around. Christmases, Easters and summers, late nights looking at the stars and swimming in the ocean."

"I cannot imagine having children one day, can you?" He'd have to produce an heir someday but with Lady Susannah? That notion turned him sour.

She drifted away for a moment. "I'd love to have children but it won't happen to me."

"Why not?"

When she didn't answer, he retraced his steps. She had stopped to examine a butterfly on blooming sea lavender. Her silence troubled him. Nicholas hated uncertainty, in fact, he detested it. He thrived on pure calculation and order. He weighed all pros and cons, exercising his instinct in crafting an image of the thoughts and motives of the men he dealt with in his business relations. He did not completely know Alexandra Sutherland.

"Why not?" he insisted.

"Did you ever notice how a butterfly has an endless cycle? The egg morphs into a cocoon until it finally emerges into a butterfly."

What should that have to do with her having children? What she left out said volumes. He waited.

"Well, potential beaus who came to ask me to dance—"

"Village boys asked you to dance?" Never should Alexandra been allowed to cavort with village boys. She was a lady. He picked up a coconut and threw it. It banged against a palm thirty yards away, unhitching other coconuts, and crashing them to the ground. "You never mentioned you had a beau."

"I didn't?"

"No, you didn't. I would have remembered that conversation." A snake of jealousy twisted around him again.

Her turquoise eyes widened and she skipped in front of him. "I don't know why you are so angry."

"I'm not," he shouted.

She let a palmetto fan snap back in his face. "All of them were scared off by Samuel."

Nicholas whipped the palmetto out of the way. He liked Samuel already. "What was Samuel's response?"

Alexandra exhaled. "He wasn't nice at all. In fact, he was rude."

Nicholas would bet his prize stallion, Samuel took deliberate action to make sure she didn't have any affections with commoners, believing that someday she'd take her rightful place as Lady Sutherland. Samuel may have not known how that event would have occurred, regardless, he protected Alexandra and Nicholas was thankful for his safeguarding her.

"There was the Miller's boy who was tenacious and...well, there are two things that are infinite, the universe and the Miller's boy dim-wittedness. He was the size of an oak tree and wasn't as intimidated of Samuel as the other young men in the village. The Miller boy took hold of me on our doorstep and tried to kiss me. Samuel swung wide the door, held a sword to the Miller's boy's throat and threatened to draw and quarter him."

If Nicholas had been there he would have helped Samuel hang the Miller's boy from the nearest tree. That was after he pounded him into a bloody pulp. "How'd the Miller's son take that threat?"

"I never saw anyone walk in reverse so quickly. He fell over a stump and scuttled like a crab on his back." She laughed, and then sobered. "I think Samuel had a past that I never knew about. Perhaps his reputation during his years in the Royal Navy.

"The bad part was the two Cornett sisters happened by our house at the exact time the Miller's boy had tried to kiss me. They passed terrible rumors about me, saying I was wild, disreputable, and had terrible character. For the most part, my reputation in the village was in ruins. None of the boys wanted to ask me to dance at the following socials. I was miserable."

He knew how narrow-minded and unforgiving the villagers on his ducal estate could be. Once black-balled, one was shunned.

"The Miller's son never came again. What was embarrassing, when I was in the village, he ran to the other side of the street and made the sign of the cross."

He liked the fact she was not attached. She didn't belong with the villagers. She belonged with gentry.

He drew up beside her. Alexandra's inviting lips beckoned him. "So, you've never been kissed?"

Her mouth quirked. "Plenty of times."

Nicholas raised a brow and it teased a smile from her face.

"Samuel and Molly kissed me every night before I went to bed. A ritual, you know."

Alexandra stumbled and floundering, she grabbed his hips to break her fall. His temperature shot up, spiked several degrees.

"I missed that palm frond."

He righted her, took her hands from his heated skin and their gazes locked in the morning light. He opened his mouth to say something, but he couldn't speak—her scent entwined him, his nostrils flared from primal instinct, the proximity of her body, and the sultry look in her eyes drugged his mind. That latent attraction erupted with a force that made him lean down. He yearned to seize her mouth with hard, demanding hunger, to devour her sweetness. Her lips parted, and his body went rigid with desire. A pulse beat at the base of her throat. His tongue could explore that area down to the soft tips of her breasts and beyond.

The cries of gulls jerked him to reality. With Herculean effort, Nicholas pulled back. *Keep your hands off her. She saved your life. She deserves better.*

He was beginning to abhor her spontaneity and unaffected-ness, like a sea nymph free and comfortable in her skin.

The beach swung in a long, lazy crescent, heavily fringed by massive palms, bent away from the water for it was the windward side of the island. The sand was soft and glistening beneath her feet. Small waves raced upon the shore with a foaming curl and a hissing sound. She cooled her toes in the lapping surf.

He had almost kissed her. She couldn't let that happen. It wouldn't be fair to Nicholas.

She had slipped, almost revealing that most painful part of her past. Oh, to have children—to sing, to laugh, to love. That dream was beyond her grasp.

Images of that fateful day taunted her, a childhood accident… The doctor confirming she'd never be able to bear children. She swiped at a tear.

Nicholas passed her, tearing off his shirt and diving in the ocean. He swam in swift relaxed strokes, and then stood waist deep, his forehead swept clear by the wind that caressed him. Curious about his body, she stared at lean rippled stomach muscles. She could never get enough, admiring his male beauty, his body lean from years as a boxer.

Staving off the quick unaccustomed tingling in the pit of her stomach grew impossible. He called to her. She bent over and picked up an empty conch shell, pretending not to hear.

"Alexandra?"

How quickly he had come up on her. She gasped when he took hold of her braid, running its silky length through his fingers. "Your braid is bound so tightly. You should leave it down. It draws the eye like a river of gold."

His face was harsh, his eyes a penetrating blue. He caught her hand before she could take flight, his flesh warm against hers…and a vague, sensuous light passed between them.

Her wariness stood no chance against his allure. With some carnal fascination, he drew and captured her awareness, until the sea, the sky, the world itself, faded around them. His hand glided up and down her arm, her body felt heavy and warm, and her heartbeat raced at the mere impact of his gentle touch.

"What is bothering you, Alexandra?"

His nearness made her senses spin. His gaze roved over her in lazy regard, appraising her, and leaving her exposed. What if they were stranded here forever? What harm could there be to find solace in each other's arms. Reason warred with caution—such an attraction was impossible. She drew an uneven breath. She had to stay positive. They would be rescued.

"Do you question my word?"

She shook her head. "You don't understand. Her pulses leapt with excitement. She could feel the heat from his body—so close. It wasn't him. She was ashamed of her barrenness. "I can't explain." She tugged. Tears grew in her eyes.

"Alexandra—"

"No." She jerked her arm away and bolted in a flat out run, hearing him pound the sand behind her. "Go away, Nicholas. Leave me alone." He wanted an answer, but he raised so many fears and uncertainties—a warmth…a wanting.

Leaping through a stand of bristly Casuarinas, she landed in the next cove, her heels making divots in the beach. She stopped. From the storm the night before, numerous casks and flotsam had been cast ashore. Nicholas jumped down beside her.

"What do you think is in the barrels?" she said.

Nicholas ran ahead. He knelt in the sand, digging with his hands and plying the barrels free. For an hour, they freed the casks and rolled them above the tideline.

"We'll find out later. Be thankful for our bounty," he said tersely.

He wanted an answer as to why she ran from him, why she avoided him. She balled her hands into fists. She was under no obligation to tell him she could not have children, yet Nicholas was the type of man who didn't let things go.

He pulled a sword out of the sand, held it up. The blade glinted in the sun, throwing sharp sunlight everywhere. He tied the sword about his waist, and strode down the beach, hands behind his back, the sword flapping against his thigh.

Pleased for the moment, he allowed a temporary withdrawal from their discussion. Alexandra scanned the horizon. "Do you think we will find more? Do you think there are any survivors?

A long ridge of sandbars, like uneven humps, ran a space. Beyond that, the waterspout of a whale rose violently as if to give a greeting. At any other time, she would have been excited over such a sight.

She picked up a stone and examined it. "You've told me little about your Uncle Cornelius who was so important in your life."

"He had a hard life. His mother produced an heir and as far as she was concerned, she had done her job. She didn't want any part of Cornelius. His father spent his time on extramarital affairs, and was hard and demanding of Cornelius, spending no time with him at all."

Alexandra raised her eyebrows with that knowledge. Cornelius's relationship with his father mirrored Nicholas's.

"Cornelius was my father's closest friend through their school years. And then entered Lucretia Hansford. She was kind, gentle, fun, loving…everything Cornelius's mother was not. He fell in love with her."

"What was the problem?"

"The problem being, Lucretia was in love with Richard Rutland, my father."

Three sea hawks flying overhead shadowed Alexandra. "So, Lucretia is your mother."

"Yes, and she and my father became engaged. Cornelius felt betrayed by my father. Cornelius possessed a mad obsession for my mother, kidnapped her, and took her to Gretna Green where he could get a special license and force her to marry him."

Alexandra widened her eyes. "What happened?"

"My father heard about the debacle and found them in an inn just before Cornelius was to compromise her. I don't know all the details but there was a sword fight between the two men with Cornelius blinded in one eye."

"The Duke of Westbrook, Cornelius's father was so enraged, he banished his son from England and refused him his inheritance. Years passed, the old duke on his deathbed, having second thoughts of his legacy, bid his son to return and all was pardoned. The duke died shortly thereafter and Cornelius assumed his role as the Duke of Westbrook. Cornelius came to my father and begged forgiveness for his rash deed in the past. Ever since, he's been wonderful to our family treating the Rutland children, as his own."

"An extraordinary story." She stumbled over a plank sticking out of the sand and sank to her knees, clearing away seaweed. "We can put the milled piece to good use."

She clutched her chest. "*Santanas.* This is the stern of the *Santanas.*" She rose and moved farther down the beach. "I do not want anything to remind me of that voyage."

His stride longer, Nicholas overtook her. He stopped at a craggy outcropping of limestone, grabbed a hold of a Sapodilla limb, and heaved himself atop. He peered over the edge. "Don't come any closer, Alexandra."

Too late. She already hauled-up beside him. "Oh, dear God."

Bloated half-eaten corpses, littered the shore. Crabs covered the bodies, competing with vultures, devouring what sharks had left of the *Santanas* crew.

Chapter 11

His hopes high, Nicholas swung his telescope over a galleon armed with fifty cannon and a lesser hulk with twenty-four cannon. Spanish flags flew from their masts. His heart sank. No need to light the signal fire.

Since discovering the remains of the *Santanas* two weeks before, polite civility had erupted between them, each working independent of the other, a silent acknowledgement of keeping a kindred relationship.

Once when he had dared to take her in his arms, she put up her hand.

"No."

"Alexandra, I keep thinking what if we are on this island forever.

"There's the conundrum. What if we are rescued?"

Nicholas exhaled. "I'm attracted to you. I want to——"

"As I am to you. But one of us has to think with a clear head."

"I have complete respect for you, Alexandra, and—if your wish is to be left alone then I will honor it."

"Besides, I'm not worthy of your status."

"I don't give a damn about it."

"Then I'll have a care for you. If you respect me, then do not go against my wishes."

It had been difficult curbing his desire for Alexandra. She had grown distant, building walls of an impenetrable fortress, and damn if he hadn't grown aloof, holding fast to the bulwarks of his pride.

Life was pure hell.

Nicholas had carried the casks of flour, wine and other food-stuffs up to the house, storing the barrels in the lean-to. Half of their gains had to be thrown out, spoiled from saltwater immersion. He fished, dove for lobster and conch to supplement their diet. While diving, he had discovered oysters, yielding one huge pearl, the iridescent quality of immeasurable worth. He had thought about giving it to Alexandra and maybe he'd still give it to her.

Now he cut bamboo, joining ends with a flexible material that leaked from a rubber plant and served as a water tight glue. He had two scores of bamboo rods left to fit to complete his secret project. The undertaking had been a monumental task he couldn't wait to test out. It relieved them of many hours of grueling labor. With his limited skills, even he was impressed and couldn't wait to show his invention to Alexandra.

"Nicholas," Alexandra shouted.

The sun had practically set, leaving streaks of red, mauve and indigo in its trail. He wiped his brow and vaulted over a pile of bamboo.

He arrived at the doorway and she stood on a chair and waved a book, her eyes sparkling. "I was dusting and slipped my hand into a hole carved in the beam."

"A book?" What was so exciting about a book? He was hungry.

She stepped down from the chair and placed two platters of bread, roasted fish and a spicy bowl of conch stew on the table. He seated her.

"Not just any book. A diary left by the owner of this house. His name was John Sharp and he was a sea captain. His story is penned in these pages. I have just begun to read how he came here. But where he has gone, I do not know. His tale is so sad… he loved her."

Nicholas spooned some chowder into his mouth. "Her?"

"Yes, he was madly in love with a lady of quality. Their love was mutual but he was of low birth, and it was forbidden."

Nicholas sipped the wine from the casks of the *Santanas*. "What happened? Why was he here?"

He could see Alexandra was ready to jump from her skin she was so excited. She thumbed through the pages, and commenced reading.

> *June 1762 "Every experimental philosopher knows the steel and the magnate, when brought within striking distance, cannot be kept apart and so our love evolved. That there is only one person you meet in your life who can turn your life around and that was you, my dearest Jane."*

Alexandra sighed and read more.

> *July 1762 "There is a tie more binding than humanity, and stronger than friendship that binds us. That*

we shared an emotional affinity and unconditional trust that knew no bounds… I dream of you, lovely dreams but when I wake, my life is a nightmare for I do not have you in my arms.

August 1762 "I told you things I never shared with another soul and you listened with every breath you took. How we shared our future hopes and dreams that alas, never will come true. Never will I share in your excitement, or share your feelings.

September 1762 You have a good kind heart Jane, always building me up, knowing when I was hurting and making me feel like a king. You had that splendid quality to make me feel special, a wonderful calm that surrounded you. I could be myself in your company. And you loved me for myself despite my wretched circumstances."

Placing a hand over her heart, Alexandra looked up from her reading. "His wretched circumstances differentiated him as a lowly sea captain." She continued.

"The irrelevant became of consequence—a note, a song, a walk in the woods befell treasures to be cherished. Your laughter, like a thousand angels, brought joy. The colors of the world danced sunnier and more dazzling when you smiled."

Nicholas put his tankard down and she refilled it with wine. As Alexandra read, her voice, velvet smooth, ran over him like the wine that settled through his veins.

January 1763 "I think of you every day, Jane. We didn't need continuous conversation. We contented ourselves in silent communion."

June 1764 "How I remember our picnic in the meadow. The bluest of sky, a gentle wind and fair weather clouds. The day you put your arms around me and told me how much you loved me and could never be separated from me. The day you gave yourself to me in body and soul."

Alexandra snapped the book closed and Nicholas liked the rush of color in her cheeks.

"I hadn't read that far..."

"Who is Jane?"

Alexandra widened her eyes. "You are so impatient. She is Lady Jane Winthrop Dabney. Do you know her?"

"I do. She was at my sister's betrothal party. I feel sorry for her because Sir Dabney, her husband is the worst kind of scoundrel, a born profligate, gambler and drunk. Lady Jane Winthrop would have been better off with the sea captain." He cursed the aristocracy's propensity for marriages of convenience. People should marry whom they love and damn the contract.

He tossed down the contents of his flagon, thinking of his father, so like Sir Winthrop. "The Winthrop's were a good family but her father was stern. If he perceived a growing fascination between Lady Jane and Captain Sharp, he'd marry her off and put a stop to the attraction. Her family was wealthy. Sir Dabney possessed an old and noble title and a selling point."

The wine rolled sour over Nick's tongue. Part of him did not desire to hear anymore. Like Alexandra, the mysterious existence of their benefactor called to him. Why was Captain Sharp alone on the island? So many questions unanswered.

"I had one more voyage. A voyage beyond all voyages."

Nicholas put his fork down. "What does that mean?"

Her food untouched, Alexandra shrugged and turned the page.

"I set sail with your promises to wait for me. You gave me your locket to remember you and I never took it off. I hated leaving you, but you deserved the world at your feet and I would make it happen."

"What happened?"

Alexandra flipped through pages to where she remembered reading the information.

"No sooner had I sailed into the Atlantic, we were attacked by Barbary Pirates. With my ship seized, I faced unspeakable brutality by my captors. How I survived the privations was a miracle when many of my crew did not. My future lay dim, journeying to Algiers to be sold into bondage, my Muslim inheritors, promising a fate worst then death. My only thoughts were that I'd never see you again."

Alexandra pressed her hand to her forehead. "That could have been our fate in the Brazils."

Nicholas nodded, understanding how similar their destinies were entwined.

> *"Mid-route, a fortuitous attack by a Danish ship saved us from the ruthless hands of the Corsairs. With my ship freed, and my crew restored, I moved forward on my expedition. Because of our delay, we were caught in several storms that plagued the Caribbean at that time of year. Blown off course several times, meant weeks of travel to make up the distance lost, and more agonizing time from you."*

"What was on the island that he would risk life and limb?" Alexandra said.

Nicholas picked up his chair and dropped it next to hers. "Only one thing would drive a man to such extraordinary measures."

She turned her face to his, so close. A smattering of delightful freckles covered her nose and the rings around her turquoise eyes grew darker with her question.

"Read on," ordered Nicholas, his shoulder pressed to hers.

> *"At a remote island, I ordered the men to drop anchor. While they drew fresh water, and gained respite, I set about the island. You may have guessed by now, my love, I had a map in my possession given to me by a friend on his deathbed. I had once saved him from financial ruin and disgrace. He never forgot that charity. How he came*

into possession of such a prize, I do not know, but he
promised riches of inestimable wealth."

Alexandra's face lit with excitement. "A treasure, Nicholas." She
popped a piece of mango in her mouth and turned the page, grip-
ping the book with her long fingers.

*"While my crew cavorted, and played on the island, tak-
ing needed sustenance, I searched the island. I did find
what I came for, hauling and secreting my prize aboard
my ship beneath the noses of my crew."*

Alexandra slapped down the book. "If he had treasure, then why
didn't he and Lady Jane reconnect?"

Nicholas combed his fingers through his hair. Was the sea captain prone to fancy? Loneliness coupled with tedium on an island
could lead to the possibility.

She reopened the book and thumbed to the last page read.

He regarded her quizzically. "Who is impatient now?"

She made a tiny growl in the back of her throat that he found
diverting.

*"I made the shores of England. You had been married
and were celebrating the birth of your son. My world
lay shattered. To find you had abandoned me was
incomprehensible."*

Alexandra shook her head. "I can't imagine."

"The treasure?" Nick leaned back on the two legs of his chair.

She flapped a hand in dismissal. "Is that all you think about?"

> *"To have come so far and through many trials was more than my heart could bear. I left England, sailing to this unmarked island, built this house and survived my days knowing the love of my life belonged to another."*

"What about the treasure?"

"You are so anxious." She blew out a breath, scanning through the entries in the diary.

No need to point out she was just as keen as he was.

> *"Loneliness is abundant and wreaks dreadful suffering. The island and I is all there is. In the deep still silence, I can feel your beating heart."*
>
> *"Today I came to a lagoon and thought of you, my darling. I would trade all the treasure in the world to hear your voice, to see your smile one more time."*

"With certainty, he's daft." Nick dropped his chair to all fours. He rose, poured a flagon of rum and Alexandra lifted a brow. "I've had enough of lunatic ravings." He headed out the door.

"He's in love," she shouted at him.

He liked the passion she put into the story, better yet, he liked the fact she followed him with book and candle in hand, reading as she went.

He flopped in his hammock. She sat beside him and he smelled her scent and the jasmine flowers she placed in her braid. There was no remedy for the persuasive power of her scent. He breathed her into his lungs. Not one single cure to eradicate her scent.

> *"A dreadful storm has hit the island for three days and I'm marooned inside. How I wish your son were mine. Jane, how could you have abandoned me? I deviate from anger to crushing despair. I never told you why I left without saying a word to you. I accepted the fact that you married Sir Dabney because your heart changed. I loved you so that I wanted only your happiness. I sacrificed my own happiness for you."*

"About the, treasure Nicholas, I was wondering…"

"You are a woman who does a lot of wondering. Not a bad fault." He smiled and swallowed his rum in one gulp. "Nothing like a tot of rum under my belt."

"You are starting to sound like a pirate."

He spread his hands. "I'm on a tropical island, no treasure map to follow…what else do I need?" He imagined her next to him in his hammock, laying her head on his chest, his arms around her. And he realized how desperately lonely he'd become.

She cleared her throat to get him to pay attention and he lay entranced by the pulse that beat in the hollow of her neck.

> *"My only wish is that despite your changed feelings toward me, that our friendship will be infinite. For the*

moon never beams without bringing you as part of my dreams. Each tender caress of yours will never die of weariness, of withering, of errors or betrayals, of illness and wounds. For me, our love was eternal."

The candle flame desperately sputtered, the flame sinking into the melted wax and dying away. A cloud obscured the moon. A wind rose, and a light capping of the sea could be seen below. Alexandra closed the diary and held it close to her chest, so involved with Captain Sharp and Lady Dabney's tragic story.

Nicholas grew quiet, too. Of course, he had drunk a lot.

"Are you awake?" she asked

"Yes."

He folded an arm behind his head. Stars poked bright holes in the blackness overhead. The moon, a silver crescent in the west, emerged from the cloud that shrouded it, only to be crowded out by the immensity of stars and planets and the universe unfurling its enormous arms above them.

"I never see a sky like this back home. I finally understand why the ancients worshipped the sky and named their gods after the wanderer's overhead that seem so close you can touch them with your hands." The stars, the rum, the hopelessness of not seeing home again, washed over him with a weariness.

She tilted her face to the heavens. "Look over there. The Tarantula sprawls across the north as Orion's belt and Orion's dagger, pursuing each other over the Milky Way. They are like old friends, these stars and planets that grace the darkness, dancing with the waxing and waning of the moon. You can see the hot and fiery Venus unfurl against the horizon and touch the moods of Mars, so cold and red."

Her enthusiasm faded from him. Locked in his own world, he fought a battle no one knew about. Suddenly he wanted out.

He dropped his tankard, the heavy pewter crashed on a rock. She bent to pick it up and he stayed her hand.

"I killed a man."

He was glad for the darkness—to not see the condemnation in her face, yet the night would not cloak the censure in her voice. She would either be the death of him or the one who brought him back to life.

"I know."

She had heard the rumors in her remote village? Of course, news like that traveled. No wailing or denunciation of him came from her. She sat quietly waiting for him to continue.

"I must tell you what happened."

"I'm not here to judge you, Nicholas. I'm sure what you did was honorable."

His fiancée had been less forgiving. Lady Susannah Tomkins… her claws unsheathed…the explosive ugliness of her face…her outrage.

Sustained by Alexandra's empathy, he treaded through his murky history. "I box for sport. The physical activity gives me satisfaction and keeps me in shape. I sparred with the tenants on my father's estate, massive farm boys built from hard work, eager to take on the duke's son with no regard for my position. The fighting was dirty, and I liked it that way. In London, I learned speed and footwork, honing my crude skills to become the best."

Nicholas exhaled. "You still do not judge me?"

"I would not be sitting here if you had not been good at what you do. If you had not defeated Damiano, we would have drowned on the *Santanas*."

He fingered the pearl in his pocket, felt her gaze on him.

"Wallowing in the muck is not a way to come clean. Out with it, Nicholas."

He nodded reluctantly. "A few years ago, I was at a social gathering in London, and walked into the gardens. A serving girl was assaulted and because she was helpless, I defended her. The scoundrel aimed his gun at me...I hit him with a left. It was his last breath. Because of his rank in the House of Lords and family's influence, the girl was frightened and changed her story to benefit her assailant. Due to my notoriety as a champion, my fists were treated as weapons. I was besieged by an army of gossips, unfair press and the man's family who wanted me prosecuted for the murder of an unarmed man. There were no other witnesses. My father had to use every ounce of his influence to keep me free of prison."

"Never-ending remorse is an undesirable sentiment, Nicholas. You were defending yourself. You should not feel guilt."

Her absolution was powerful—the promise of rebirth, the removal of past transgressions.

To breathe again.

Except for his parents and close friends, he felt the whole world was against him. How the words of one sweet, beautiful woman exonerated him from wrongdoing and humbled him with her compassion.

He jumped out of his hammock and hauled her up toe to toe with him. She gasped. Her hair was drawn back in that abominable braid, and her chin was both determined and inviting. He put his left hand under it and slowly brought it up to his. There was enough moonlight for him to see her eyes, and he was captivated by their calm assurance, so that for some moments, they studied each other. And wasn't his heart falling in love with Alexandra a little more day by day, taking him with it?

He couldn't stop it.

His mouth came down on hers. He was hurting with wanting her; fueled with anger toward a world where he struggled for vengeance and survival…and for desiring her. Then his senses fled him, but inside he knew he couldn't…wouldn't…do any more than kiss her.

He brought his own experience to bear, coaxing, gently persuading, enticing her lips to open, and when they did, he swooped in and claimed her sweetness. Her stiffness relaxed, and she melted into him, holding on to him for support, her soft full breasts flattened against his chest. Nicholas took full control, reaching down and pulling her tight against him, thrusting his tongue deeper, to wield her passion. He breathed her, tasted the sweet mango in her mouth and savored her. His mouth gentle at first became brutal on hers, twisting, bruising, rousing, his tongue thrusting through her like a brand, searing her, having her.

Oh, how Nicholas towered over her, his fingers cupping in the back of her head and his other hand hauling her bottom to him so she couldn't move. He gripped her hair in a savage grasp so she couldn't avoid the ravenous onslaught of his mouth. She melted against him, her body wanton and willing.

Alexandra drowned in his scent, the taste of rum mixed with wine, and the heady strength of his body emphasized her vulnerability to him. Breathing was near impossible and she felt she would expire from suffocation. Her hands were splayed across his chest, firm healthy male flesh tingled beneath her fingertips. Her dreams had stoked desire and now, to touch him everywhere, to explore every part of him... She brushed her fingers over muscle, heat, moisture then slid her arms around his neck, sighing.

She lifted her hands to his hair, running her fingers between the silky strands as she held him close... and firm, terrified he'd move his mouth from hers if she released her hold.

He outlined the tips of her breasts with his fingers and her nipples grew taut. His other hand splayed across the small of her back and Alexandra gasped, felt his hardness through their clothes. He cupped her breast in his hand and kissed her eyes, nose, and the hollows of her neck and down...

How could such kisses tighten the muscles in her stomach, weaken her limbs and flood a warmth between her thighs? The world grew vague, unaffected by any color, yet spinning all her senses into a pool of pleasure. Like quicksilver, lust raced through her veins and a wealth of feelings leaped from her, blossoming, exploding.

A sound struggled to escape her, a release of emotion such as she'd never imagined.

He drew away from her, his chest heaving. The gap between them gave way to a chill. Alexandra managed to gulp in sweet air, her heart hammering in her chest, his head rested against hers. She was glad he had stopped and pushed away from him. He took a step toward her and she turned, unable to talk anymore she ran into the cottage, her secret, silent and stony locked in a cheerless place, wearying her of its tyranny and forbidding any relationship.

Chapter 12

Alexandra wove palm fronds into a hat, thinking about Nicholas's confession. Nicholas was a proud man. Despite the murder publicized in all the papers, and at risk to her scorn, he had humbled himself to her. He had been released from the tragedy that surrounded his life.

To admit her own secret, to say the shame of not being able to bear children aloud was like saying she wasn't a woman.

She wanted Nicholas. How she dared to dream. Yet the vagaries of life were as wide as they were severe, leaving her with no choices. Like continents they were, undiscovered, and sitting apart, with oceans of uncertainty between them.

His kiss was the kiss to end all kisses, but never could she cross that line again. Yet how could she stop from falling desperately in love with him?

He had fired a latent primitive force inside her, making her yearn for what was forbidden. Her longings were a young girl's fantasies, a fool's dream, causing a choking bitterness to rise, for the very thing she wanted the most and could not have—Nicholas. He need only to look at her—really look at her, to let his eyes fall on hers, deeply blue and penetrating, to see her soul laid bare.

The wind blew, flipping the pages of the diary, touting the unfortunate lives of Captain Sharp and Lady Jane. Alexandra's heart ached for the sea captain and his lover, their bond wider than the plains of England. If they were ever to get off this island, she'd give the diary to Lady Jane.

Her hands worked quickly weaving the fronds, in and out, up and down, over and back. Parrots chattered in the treetops and she lifted her head. Two of them perched side by side, one leaning into the other for support, their bright colors gleaming in the sun. She smoothed a hand over her weaving and sighed. How their lives were entwined, she and Nicholas so like Captain Sharp and Lady Jane, a mirror image of their own difficulties.

She dropped the hat and picked up the journal, loosened the straps that bound it together and flipped open the corroded metal latch. A tightness in her chest held her rigid, held her in suspense. The book spine was worn from the binder. She held it up to the sun and a sliver of light protruded. A paper was stuffed in the tiny space. With care, she grasped the end of a parchment and pulled.

Her mouth went dry. A treasure map? Had Captain Sharp hid a map in the spine? With trembling fingers, she unfolded the paper.

*"If anyone should read this diary, please give it to Lady Jane Dabney of London, England and tell her that I will always Treasure her in these terms, **L**ovely, **O**nly, **V**aluable and **E**nthralling and that all the riches of my heart I hold for her, are on this island."*

How strange. No map and the sentence was not like the prose written on the former pages. Disjointed. She had to find Nicholas.

Prohibited to see what he was working on, she strode through the gardens to the tree line. His dark head was bent over an odd bamboo contraption, his calloused hands, fitting and gluing segments together.

When her shadow crossed his, he looked up and beamed. "You were not supposed to come until I called you, but since you ae here, what do you think?"

"What is it?"

Before she could protest, he grabbed the book from her hand and placed it on a stump. "Come," he ordered, impulsively grabbing her hand. They ran along the path, following a line of bamboo. She was breathless when he stopped at the river.

"Let me demonstrate." He tilted a bamboo segment to catch the descending waters. Water gurgled and gushed down the bamboo pipes. He grabbed her hand again, racing with the flow, and ending up where they had started, a clear stream of water pouring from the end piece.

Her laughter bubbled over and she clapped her hands. "You are absolutely wonderful."

Shoulders back, chin—up, he exaggerated the puffed-up arrogance of an academic, and waved a hand over his invention. "Channeling water down a bamboo tube from the river to the house will solve the many hours of backbreaking hauling. Our plants can be watered and washing can be done at the house with minimal effort."

She picked up the frayed hems of her shift and curtseyed her approval. "I am in the august company of a scientific genius."

He leaned into her and for one frightening moment she thought he was going to kiss her again. She skirted away and said, "Nicholas I've something important to tell you. I have made a discovery. I believe Captain Sharp's treasure is here. She presented him with the note tucked in the spine. Nicholas sat on the stump.

She read the phrase aloud over his shoulder. "Note how Captain Sharp capitalizes the first initials of Lovely, Only, Valuable and Enthralling. He even goes so far and to run his pen over the letters twice to give accent. In case the diary fell into Lady Jane's hands, he wanted to make her aware."

Nicholas nodded. "Definitely code. The T is capitalized in treasure to draw the eye. Well done, Alexandra except what does the emphasis on the other letters mean?"

"*LOVE*. I believe the set of initials represents a code for something else. We must convert the letters and discover Captain Sharp's intended meaning. L could stand for anything as well as O, V, and E. Think Nicholas, what on this island would be characteristic to serve as symbols?"

Nicholas shrugged. "L might stand for London Tower."

She smacked an insect on her thigh and slanted him a knowing look. "We are not in England. We must think of the secret meaning and how it relates to our present environment. Lookout or lake come to mind except there is no lake."

She tapped her finger on her lip. "You are not helping much. You can step in with an idea anytime you want."

Nicholas ran his fingers through his dark hair. "Captain Sharp did mention lagoon in his writings. "O" could be for oranges but more likely ocean which won't help us much because we are surrounded by the ocean and that is a big area to narrow down."

Alexandra walked around him. "V means what?"

"I can't think of a thing. 'E' could stand for escarpment. We have explored that part at the island's summit."

"Brilliant logic, Nicholas."

He stood and walked to the house.

Alexandra hurried after him. "Where are you going?"

"I'm going to fill the gourds with water. If we are to hunt treasure, we will need hydration."

Chapter 13

*N*icholas readjusted the gourds slung over his shoulder. "We are on a fool's errand, governed by the ravings of a man gone mad in his isolation."

Alexandra leaned on a gumbo limbo to catch her breath. "I think you are frustrated. Let's go to the summit again. Maybe we can glean an idea standing on the escarpment."

"No. It is a stupid idea. I'm not going to try one more insane notion doomed from the start." He reached in his sack, pulled out a piece of smoked pork and ripped it with his teeth.

"Clearly, I have overstepped my bounds," she said, unapologetic and undaunted by his anger.

"For days, we have traversed the island looking for treasure, coming up with nothing. *Clearly*, you have been wrong about a treasure."

She brought up her chin. "Being right all the time must be a burden."

"You have dragged me to the north, south, west and east on this island with no results." He turned her toward the cottage. "I want rum."

She stopped dead in her tracks. "I refuse to listen to your cantankerous outbursts. We will keep looking."

He propelled her onto the path again.

"And I refuse to be bullied, Lord Rutland."

How he hated her sarcastic inflection when she resorted to calling him, *Lord Rutland*.

As the smoked pork took the edge off his appetite, he felt himself afflicted with hunger of another sort. The curves of her lovely *derriere* rendered nicely by the fall of her shift, presented a delectable picture. Ever since he kissed her, he had been unable to deal with the sweetness of her lips and the tightening in his loins. He was ready to upend trees and toss them into the ocean.

A cold edge cracked in his voice. "Alexandra, I'm sick to death of your common platitudes. You lived with coarse, unrefined commoners all your life and you have become one."

Her eyes flashed, dipping to the pork he chewed. "I'm sorry, I'm not a refined, polished, sophisticated aristocrat. Hail the pitiful, Lord Rutland, caught in his superiority and trapped in his arrogance." She stabbed a finger in his chest. "What an ungrateful creature you are. I am the one that saved your miserable life. I'm the one who has taught you how to survive."

He towered over her. She was the most beautiful, enraged angel of retribution, her chest rising and falling with fury as she confronted him. Suddenly, she pivoted and ran.

Nicholas raked his fingers through his hair. What an ass he'd been. He had deliberately picked a fight, taking his anger out on her for being stuck on this God-forsaken patch of earth. He called for her. No answer.

He threw a few punches into a tree, and then laughed aloud. That wasn't the entire reason. Every night he resisted the urge to pull back her quilt and gaze at her slender white body. Every night he'd suppressed the almost overpowering desire to take her in his arms and let go inside of her.

He pushed through the undergrowth.

At times, Nicholas could feel her watching him and he'd look up. She'd cast him a modest sidelong glance, a morsel to tempt him, to leave him panting like a hound of summer on the scent of deer.

Blast it, where had she gone? She was a thorn in his side. He crisscrossed the lagoon, river and cottage. Nowhere. Another part nagged him. Every time he got close, she skittered away, made-up excuses. She was hiding something. He slapped several palmetto branches away. With all the time they spent together, why didn't she trust him?

For the same reason, he hadn't told her about Lady Susannah Tomkins. Alexandra deserved the truth.

He made his way down to the shoreline. When she didn't answer his shouts, his apprehension gave way to alarm. Had she fallen? Was she hurt? Unable to answer? A nauseating wave hit his stomach.

Hopping over fallen trees, he pushed through palmettoes and thick undergrowth to get to the beach. Sweat poured down his back. He stopped to catch his breath, wiped the moisture from his head and blinked. Footprints. Her footprints. He followed her trail up to a rocky cliff. Of course, her favorite place to watch the sea.

Soberly, Nicholas looked at Alexandra, sitting beneath a bright green sea grape tree. Sea lavender rippling around her knees, the land sloped upward behind her. The thong holding her braid had been torn, and her hair hung wild about her shoulders and down her back. The sun, shining through the leaves, caught the gold in bits and pieces, exposing her as the siren she really was.

"Will you come down?" he asked in a more pleasant tone.

"What for?"

He couldn't think of a thing. A moment later he blurted, "I want you to go for a walk with me."

"You will have to do better than that," she sniffed.

"I want you to go for a walk with me, and…I'm sorry."

"What's the second part?"

"I'm sorry."

"It's more than that. I'm not common. I'm tremendously exceptional."

"You are exceptional. Now come down from there and go for a walk with me."

She stared at his proffered hand and dammed if she didn't look down her nose at him like a queen, acknowledging an undesirable serf. "I'm a brute, Alexandra. I blamed you for my misfortunes."

"I know."

The woman had uncanny discernment, always divining his moods.

"I find myself with no purpose here. So it's hard to shake off the intentions of my life at home where my day's brim with helping tenants, buying horses. The island makes my time filled with not-doing. And then, there is the looming threat the island will become my sepulcher."

Alexandra dropped his hand and faced him. "Not doing? Since we have been incredibly busy with the purpose of trying to survive a kidnapping, potential slavery, farming, hunting, fishing, hauling water, curing our food, and surviving the elements. Our lives have been chaotic. But sometimes chaos is the very thing that deliberately shakes up our neatly ordered world to get us out of our neatly ordered ruts that keep us stuck."

Nicholas blew out a breath. She had the ability to lash him with *common* wisdom.

"Is it also the helplessness of not getting off the island and the vengeance you seek?"

She cut him a sharp look that dared him to argue with her. He gritted his teeth. "Yes. Now do you forgive me?"

"I have similar emotions since I would do anything to avenge the wrongs done to me by my stepmother, and seek justice for Molly's death." Alexandra picked up stones and pitched them into the sea. "You know I forgive you."

His melancholy started to evaporate as he watched a half-dozen sandpipers skitter up the beach, his foul mood of the morning fading like the darkness before the dawn. "Alexandra, what do you want?"

She gave a half-hearted shrug, intent on pitching stones in the surf. "You'd think I was silly."

"Nothing about you is silly," he challenged.

Silence as thick as wet sand oozed between them. Alexandra pitched stones into the sea with greater rapidity.

"When I was a girl, I saw a lady get married in a neighboring village. She had a beautiful bridal gown, so regal and fine, and roses and lilies in her bouquet. There was a pretty coach pulled by two dancing white horses. To have a fairy tale wedding." A wistful expression of longing covered her lovely face.

"Why?" He had always loathed such affairs as nothing but pomp and circumstance. Yet he hated the despair etched in her voice when all he wanted to do was pull her into his arms and soothe her. Hands at his sides, he stood, patiently listening while watching her eyes gloss over with moisture. To speak could break the fragile hold she had on her emotions.

She shrugged. "I suppose it is every girl's dream but mine is more important."

"Why is that?"

She stopped throwing stones, dropping them one by one to the ground. "Remember the Cornett sisters? My name is smeared. Just for once, I'd like to be someone special."

His hands fisted with anger at what had happened to her in her village. To be an outcast. He'd do anything to eradicate the cruel ghosts of her past.

"There is something I want more than anything else in the world."

She continued to surprise him. Just when he thought he knew all there was to know, she revealed another layer yet to be peeled away. What else had happened beyond the guilt she suffered from the loss of her surrogate mother, Molly?

"So many words get lost. They stay in my throat and lose their courage, wandering aimlessly until they are swept away like dead seaweed on an outgoing tide. I wish to ignore it, but how can I hide from something that will never go away?" She gave him a tremulous smile. "As a child, I loved to climb trees."

Trees? What did climbing trees have to do with anything?

"I was nine summers, it was such a fine day. The sun was glori-ous. I climbed higher and higher, immune to danger as children so frequently are, just to get a bird's eye view. The view at the top was like a heady aphrodisiac, the tree so alive I could feel it breath, the winds scented with coming rain swished and swayed the branches. I was so mesmerized, I barely heard the branches crack....and then...falling. And darkness."

Alexandra scrubbed her hands over her face. "I drifted in and out of consciousness, as if in a dream. Molly crying. Samuel wringing his hat. The doctor shaking his head. Molly had labored for three days, despairing if I'd survive, her expert nursing skills, bringing me back. I survived, but I learned I'd never be able to have children."

She turned her gaze on him, would know instantly he'd see differently. He'd see her not as a fertile woman who could bear children, but as a...spinster. When he didn't speak for full minute, tears pricked at the corner of her eyes.

"I'm sorry," he said, his voice a little hoarse.

I'm sorry. Numbness overcame her. Her knees buckled and she sank into the sand. She covered her face with her hands, unable to see the look in his eyes. She was sorry, too, but that didn't change the facts. "I-I know what it means, so don't feel sorry for me. I don't need anyone's pity.

He pulled her up and into his arms and she tilted her chin upward, unable to discern the darkness in his eyes. More than anything she wanted to melt into the warm comfort of him, wanted to be all the things she knew she would never be. She could never be the woman he needed.

"Do you pity me?"

She pulled back. "Of course not."

Good. Because your injury was the result of an accident and out of your control...as was my punch that killed my adversary."

Her heart melted with his words. Just looking at him made her tremble, making her yearn for things only a husband had the right to offer. His large hand held her face and gently, his calloused fingers brushed the wetness away, his touch almost unbearable in its tenderness. His hands slipped into her hair and brought her closer.

"I have wanted to confide in someone, but the stigma——"

"Never could I think less of you, Alexandra."

Nicholas's mouth descended on hers and her body started at the first brush of his warm lips.

"I was so ashamed."

"You are very brave to have shared with me."

Her body came alive as his lips pressed against hers. The heat. It was not just her cheeks that burned. She was sipping liquid fire. It flowed over her tongue and down her throat and spread through her entire body. She leaned into him.

"For so long, I have carried that burd——

He groaned into her mouth. "Your gravest error was to despair. You should have told me sooner."

She leaned into him, her hands slid up his arms and linked around his neck. "You do not judge me?" she asked, some part of her still unable to believe what was happening.

Nicholas took a ragged breath. "No more than you have judged me. It is your faith in me I find admirable. I wish I was as strong as you."

"But you are strong. The strongest man I've ever known."

Breathing hard, he stopped. And suddenly, he took her arms from his neck. He broke away, leaned against a palm across from her. Casual but not casual.

She straightened. "Forgive me, Nicholas. I have forgotten myself." She turned to leave, wanted to be alone, anywhere away from the mortification she was drowning in.

"Don't leave." He rasped, stooped on his heels, picked up a piece of driftwood and drew circles in the sand. "Can I ask you something?"

"Ask away."

"How do you know we will be rescued? What makes you so sure?"

Mystified, she wiped the tears from her face, stared at him. Had saying he was strong have something to do with his mercurial change? "I'm not sure."

"My life before...I was so sure of the world. And now it feels so remote. What is it you're looking for?"

Instead of the warmth she felt in his arms a moment ago, she saw his detachment. She turned her gaze on the palms lining the beach, and then to where pelicans were dive-bombing the stretched surface of the sea far out from the shore. *I want you, Nicholas.* She returned her gaze to him. Silent.

"Did you ever ask yourself why we survived out of a whole ship of sailors? We could have drowned, yet we're here."

He gave her a lop-sided smile.

"One thing I had when I was back in England was structure. I knew my place. And then I had my family provided me a circle of strength. I'm away from England, from them. I just want to wake up and be whole again. To realize my life."

With certainty, he was stalling. *There's something else. Something he can't seem to get out.*

The horizon was edged with a silver tint and a cormorant flew into the place where the sun and the water converged. His wings were a blur of motion and he soon faded from sight. She knelt in the sand. "I wish my heredity were proven, I wish to have Molly back, I wish to have children, but it is impossible. All I want is to not look forward or back. I just want to be in the moment I'm in."

He concentrated on digging in the sand, and then looked at her. Agony lined his handsome face.

"Alexandra, there's a woman back home. Lady Susannah Tomkins."

"A woman?"

He took a deep breath. "If I get home, Lady Susannah and I are getting married."

A dry sob burned her throat. She drew back, felt the blood drain from her face. Of course, he'd have—a wife. He was to be a Duke. Duke's had to produce heirs.

Her head spun. Of course. How stupid she'd been. So why did she feel so betrayed...as if he'd delivered a knife to her heart. "Oh...well."

"I shouldn't have kissed you, Alexandra. I can't make commitments. I have a duty. I have a life waiting for me. I'm sorry."

Her stomach rolled. Suddenly nauseous, she stood, her legs wobbly. "Of course."

"She is waiting for me. We had announced our betrothal a month before I was kidnapped. I've made promises."

Anger and grief bled from his voice.

"She's a perfect match and she pleases my father."

Stupid. God, she'd been so stupid, believing her own fantasies. Bile rose in her throat. She turned...and ran...before she vomited, before she made a further fool of herself.

Alexandra ran and ran, tears flowing, arms thrashing at the air and the invisible visions of a life that would always be just out of her reach. It was her fault for having dared to dream. If she'd known, she'd never have revealed her darkest secret. To be that susceptible, that vulnerable to a man who never cared.

"Alexandra."

He followed. Why? Why couldn't he just let her alone to deal with her pain and misery?

"Alexandra."

She stopped in her tracks, feet digging into the soft sand. She turned. Faced him. Opened her mouth to tell him to go away, but the words clogged in her throat.

Why are you here, Nicholas?

He stepped closer. "Please listen, Alexandra."

She pressed her lips together to keep the tears and a sudden rush of anger at bay. "Why? So you can unburden yourself again and not feel guilty?"

"No. Because I have something to say to you. Only to you."

She crossed her arms. Waited.

"I've been doing everything my whole life to please my father, to be the best duke he wanted me to be. Pretending my whole life..."

He took another step toward her. She held up her hand. *You've made it clear, you don't want me. Fine. Now leave me alone.*

"I am to marry the perfect woman, a well-connected woman who will add value to the Rutland's prestige in assets and power," he said, each word slashing like a knotted whip. "My life is built on it and it's a good life and it's always been the life I wanted."

And she was a nobody who could not give him an heir.

She blinked back another rush of tears. She would not shed another. She would not let Nicholas have the satisfaction he so needed. Ridding himself of guilt at her expense wasn't a road she wanted to travel. Not again. She'd fooled herself when she knew full-well what could never be.

"Then I arrived here and I got a glimpse of a freedom on this island. I don't have to pretend a life in which I can be truly alive." He took a step closer. "How can I go back to pretending when I know what this feels like?"

Nicholas bridged the gap between them, grasped her face in his hands. "I want you, Alexandra. *Only you.*"

Tears coursed down her cheeks. She couldn't be certain of anything other than the searing pain in her heart and her raw fear of the immense power in this man, a potency he tried hard to keep leashed.

"We were meant to be together. We can no more stop it than the sunrise."

She shook her head, the tears she'd so valiantly held in suddenly erupting like a geyser. Giant sobs came from somewhere deep inside.

He closed the space between them, gently wiping away her tears as they fell. "Alexandra, love," he whispered tenderly. "The longest journey is taken a step at a time. My love can wait, but it will neither yield nor change."

"I do not want to love you, Nicholas. I cannot love you. I cannot bear your children."

"You think that matters to me? My courageous, wonderful Alexandra. You fill my whole world. And then he hauled her into his arms. He drew her up to him, holding her tight in his embrace, as if shielding her with his body against all the torments, the fears and loneliness.

Cocooned within Nicholas's arms, Alexandra closed her eyes and drank it all in—the man, the millions of ways he moved her. He lifted her ever so gently and carried her beneath the shade of palms, reverently laying her on the sand. She buried her face against his throat, so conscious of where his warm flesh touched hers.

He brushed her hair with his calloused fingertips. "Your hair ripples and shines like a cascade of golden waters."

The air lay thick with the heat of day. She dared to glide her hands down his shoulders, chest, and midsection.

He grabbed her hands. "Slowly," he warned her, watching her with hunger.

"Are you sure this is what you want?" He locked his eyes with hers, commanding her complete attention. He was giving her a way out. A choice to stop. But how did she tell him to stop?

Alexandra swallowed. Who knew how long they would be on this island. Perhaps an eternity. But what if they were rescued... she didn't want to think...to go back to southern England, to an endless void of lonely days. The reaffirmation of all she knew to be true and cruel about life, about her own existence, destined for precious little happiness. "I want you, Nicholas."

She sensed his vulnerability and reached up to stroke his cheek, awed by the splendor of the moment, yearning for so much more.

Alexandra remained silent as he lay beside her. She thought she could speak, that there would be many more words to share. But there were no more words. Nicholas reached out to her, the heat and passion forged in his body, so great she trembled, for she really did not know what to do.

He pressed his lips to her mouth, more than kissing it. She quivered at the sweet tenderness of his kiss. Then he pulled apart for a moment and probed her eyes. She dropped her hands. Had she done something wrong?

"Do you trust me?"

"She nodded. "I'm scared. I have never——"

Nicholas smiled his boyish smile, obviously trying to relax her, an expression of satisfaction glowing in his eyes. "We are man and woman and made to fit."

She lay with her arms at her sides as Nicholas's long thick fingers clutched her shoulders, finding an incredible consolation in the gentleness of his grasp and undeniable look in his eyes. The stroking of his fingers sent pleasant jolts through hers. His hands slipped to the hem of her shift, pressing down on the soft material, from her thighs, searing a path over hips, up her abdomen and over her head. *Naked*.

"Alexandra." He caressed and teased her flesh until her breasts budded full and heavy against his warm hand.

Like quicksilver his palm moved, the gentle massage sending currents, spreading like embers on a newly turned fire, spiraling down her stomach and lower, eliciting a trembling between her thighs. Her body craved his hand, his mouth upon her lips, and distinct warmth flooded the area between her legs.

"Nicholas."

His tongue traced the soft fullness of her lips, his hands glided over her shoulders then down, exploring the hollows of her back, pressing her length into the solid contours of his muscled body and hard thighs. Dragging her mouth from his, she followed his lead, imitating what he had done to her and with shaking hands, ran her fingers over his chest, tracing his nipples. His jaw clenched involuntarily as she moved her hands up and over his shoulders. They stared in mute silence, sharing an intense physical awareness of each other while latticed sunlight poured hotly on them through the palm fronds above.

Alexandra licked her lips as Nicholas shrugged out of his breeches, fully exposed, her eyes widened, riveted on his manhood, impressive and frightening.

"I will be tender with you," he promised, taking her into his arms, pillowing his head in the veil of her hair.

His gentleness was her undoing. "What we are doing is a promise, a time for loving and once given will never disappear."

His mouth grazed her neck, her earlobe, and then swooped to capture her lips. Coaxing them open, his tongue explored the recesses of her mouth, firm, demanding. She groaned.

He smelled wonderful, strong, healthy male, of sea and sweat. His arms encircled her, his hand splayed at the bottom of her spine holding her in intimate contact. She gasped as her bare breasts crushed against the firmness of his chest and the hard, intimate contact of his arousal against her stomach. Suddenly his hands were everywhere, her body aching for more.

Outlining the tips of her breasts with his fingers, Nicholas brought their tips to crested peaks. Slowly, languorously, his hands moved downward, skimming either side of her body to her thighs. He explored her thighs then plunged down again searching the warmth that lay hidden intimately between.

"Let me ready you, Alexandra." His deep voice slid along her veins like warm honey.

His mouth came down on hers, sapping all her strength, making her boneless while he plied her intimately with his finger, withdrawing and sinking, pushing her over some unnamed edge. She writhed beneath, her body arching toward the power of his ever-present fingers. She could not get enough of him; her impatience grew to explosive proportions, his expert touch driving her to higher levels of ecstasy. She cried out in release, exploding in a downpour of fiery sensations.

Dazed, she opened her eyes to meet his blue gaze, dark as lapis…and poised above her… the Duke of Rutland. A man who had the lethal power to kill a man with his hands, who had fought off Damiano. Yet all he had yielded to her was an aching tenderness and fierce desire.

"Oh, Nicholas." She lay there in a gasping heap, her arm still trapped beneath his weight.

He laughed. "That is just a measure to prepare you." The vow he'd made not to touch her had disintegrated like a sandcastle in the wind. She lay there soft…yielding, all for the taking, a fulfillment of every waking dream that had tormented him since the first time he clapped eyes on her on the beach. To think that aboard the *Santanas,* he had thought her an old crone who robbed people. She'd been so dirty he hadn't realized her beauty until she had cleaned up on the island.

Her full ripe breasts thrust impudently like dark rose buds. Her trim waist melded down over rounded hips, revealing the dark triangle of her womanhood where his hand explored. He swallowed, imagining a hundred wicked things from her. He wanted to kiss her there, to taste the sweet saltiness of her skin, to tease his tongue down the soft curvature of her spine.

Her fingers touched his bare chest, circling his breast. Nicholas closed his eyes, torturous thoughts of long, slow love making aroused him to a fevered pitch.

He nudged her legs apart and with incredible constraint, entered her. He paused when he felt the barrier of her virginity. She was tight and so damp. Barely hanging on to his control, Nicholas bowed his head, his breathing ragged next to her ear.

"It will only hurt a little bit."

She clenched his shoulders, expectant.

He shifted his hold on her, continued his probing, perspiration beading his brow. To bury himself in her hot, moist warmth. The last remnants of his control failed.

Grabbing her hips, he plunged hard with one solid, powerful thrust.

She pushed at him, scrambling in the sand to get away. He had hurt her. He stopped, his mouth came down on hers, and he whispered into her mouth, reassuring her.

"No more." She pounded his shoulders, but he held her in place.

Nicholas stayed rock still inside her, waiting for her to adjust before he started moving again. "My love, the worst is over." He hated hurting her. But she felt so damned good.

In reply, her arms entwined his neck in an aching tenderness that tore at his heart.

He began to move, slowly at first, a whisper of a caress, his manhood deep inside her. He groaned as the dormant sexuality of her lush body burst into full bloom. His control shattered like a million shards of glass, nights of restraint he had harnessed, now unleashed, his ardor mounted as she rose to meet his scorching need.

Nicholas matched her movements, thrusting his fingers into the silkiness of her hair and lifting her hips to meet his rhythmic thrusts. Her fingers dug into his shoulders and he buried his face on the side of her neck, the pressure building inside of him unlike anything he had ever experienced. Exquisite. She abandoned herself to him, and with every forceful thrust, he claimed her in a raw act of total possession, mindless of everything except the indulgence of granting them both complete satisfaction.

She arched, and her body vibrated with liquid fire. Nicholas taut above her, emptied his seed into her. Breathing hard, he rolled to the side, keeping her intimately joined to him, and reveling in the sensation of her wet warmth, and the brush of her lips against his neck. He cradled her in his arms, his hand drifting up and down her spine as she leaned her soft cheek against his chest. His chin nestled upon her head and his fingers buried in the golden waves of her hair. For a moment, he abandoned all the fears of the past and future, basking upon the wonder of the intimacy they had just shared.

She ran a fingernail across his abdomen. "Nicholas…did I?" She was too shy to ask if she pleased him.

He exhaled a long sigh of contentment, basking in male arrogance that she was shaken as much as he. He kissed her head, the scent of jasmine mixed with the musky scent of their lovemaking permeated the air.

"Perfect," he said.

"I can't imagine such fulfillment. Is it like that for everyone their first time?"

She was whirling through a haze of new feelings and desire, and she wanted him to explain what she was experiencing. "Seldom."

"Will it always be like this?" She squirmed closer to him. Her innocent movements and conversation put provocative thoughts into his head. No woman he'd known had ever kindled this overwhelming surge of lust. Despite his wild desire for her again, he seemed to revel in her struggle with future anticipations of which he had no doubt.

"Better."

She drew his hand to her lips and kissed the hard, lean knuckles. "Then I wager a game of chess and the winner demands the prize."

Nicholas chuckled. "I shall not let you distract me. You will find a worthy foe in the future."

"Is that a threat?" Her eyes were wide and dared to taunt him.

"No, Alexandra my love," he whispered. "Only a vow."

In the last months, he'd been kidnapped, imprisoned, set to be sold into slavery, endured a hurricane and survived on an island, and met an enchantress. Yet England, a distant, cloying shadow, called him to return. They would get off this island. She gave him confidence in that notion. And she was his. He would face his father and damn the consequences. For now, he was rooted. He rolled her over onto her back and made swift violent love to her, more hopeful, more demanding than before.

Chapter 14

*N*ight lent an intimacy to the cottage and his body warmed with the remembrance of long, slow lovemaking, and then falling asleep with her in his arms. His love burned for Alexandra, not just for this moment but stretched out before him in a million lifetimes.

Now with the birth of morning, Nicholas nuzzled his chin in her silky hair. How marvelously beautiful those few hours of storms that swept down from the heights, rain sluicing over the sides of the cottage, and unfolding a mantle of benevolence, cleansing the land and adding a dazzling sparkle to all things green.

Without a doubt, it was the very way she loved him. Turning his darkness into light. Playfully dismissing his pessimism. Mocking his doubt with her enthusiasm. Bucking her passion against his stubborn nature. Making him feel strong and confident. And all the while, her steadfast heart remained there for him.

Except for his family and close-knit friends, he'd been a loner and he could think of no one else he wanted at his side. Never would Alexandra doubt his abilities like Lady Susannah Tomkins. He grimaced. How could he have ever thought of marrying that shrew?

He brushed the glossy strands of Alexandra's unplaited hair from her face. Under Alexandra's guidance, he'd softened, found her laughter infectious. She was dependable, encouraging his dreams and aspirations. She had endured the most horrid of conditions, yet never gave up, looking at every hurdle as an adventure and opportunity.

While everyone in England yielded to his title, she had never been impressed. Oh yes, she had sarcastic wit, enough to skewer the best of naysayers, which exasperatingly enough, could rile his normally cool state of mind and snap his temper. He needed a woman who would challenge him.

Alexandra listened. She was non-judgmental when he had confessed to her he had killed a man, even aware of the tragedy beforehand. Her integrity, her spontaneity made him look forward to the magic of every day. She trusted him.

He crawled out of bed while she slept, shrugged on his breeches and retrieved the black pearl from his pocket. With twine, he weaved hitch-knots to fashion a band, perplexed by her humility. How she downplayed her beauty, dismissed her intelligence, and selflessness to the point of exhaustion. She avoided self-pity like the plague, her generous, intuitive, and unassuming nature making her dear to him.

Nicholas dropped the homemade pearl ring between her breasts. She lifted her eyelids and sat up.

"Oh, Nicholas. It is beautiful. Wherever did you find it?"

He sat on the bed. "I found it among oysters, lining the rocks along the shore. I believe it to be of considerable value."

She placed the ring on her finger, admiring the iridescence. "I shall treasure this ring always."

"Which leads me to a demand."

She fell back onto the pillow. "Any more demands, and I'll be laid to waste."

He chuckled, taking delight with the color forming in her cheeks. With a mischievous smile, she traced a finger across his chest. He hauled her from the bed, before other things that came to mind were set into motion and placed her shift over her head. "We're getting married. I want to do this right."

Alexandra put her arms around his neck, and tilted her head up for a kiss.

"I'm serious, Alexandra. I demand that we marry."

"There is a shortage of preachers on this island in case you haven't noticed." The vixen moved her hands seductively down his chest around to his hips. He grabbed her hands

"We are getting married and that's it. You are going to be by my side for the rest of our lives."

She kissed his chest and neck.

"Control yourself." Before she could do anything more to distract him, he strode to the shelf, jerked orchids out of the vase, handed them to her, and then grabbed the Bible. "This won't be the fairytale wedding you dreamed about, but it is the closest to a real ceremony I can think of."

Alexandra sobered. Nicholas's moods were like the tides, ever shifting from amusement to irritation. Did he view her as another duty to oversee, an unaccountable desire to be responsible for her? "You don't have to do this."

"I command it. Put your hand on the Bible. We will swear before God."

Of course he'd command the nuptials, yet it wasn't the author-itative side of his nature, she struggled with, but the import and relative consequences of what they were about to share. She was a nobody. She could not give him an heir. His father wanted a tried and true aristocrat with perfect breeding. He was betrothed.

What if they were never rescued? Weeks had turned into months and only two ships had passed. The probability grew every day that their lives were eternally bound on these shores. Alexandra made a silent vow. However long they lived on this island, she would pledge herself to Nicholas.

His smile drew her gaze. Unable to resist, her eyes met his, and the world faded. The palms ceased to move. The swish of the surf vanished, and despite the lack of church or vicar, her heart flut-tered with the sincerity in his eyes, the vow he was about to speak. The look of resolute and unwavering resolve manifested on his face assured a rare kind of promise, coupled with an indomitable will to succeed.

Shaking, she placed her hand on the Bible.

"I, Nicholas Richard Rutland, heir to the fourth Duke of Rutland, take you, Alexandra Sutherland, to be my wife. I prom-ise to be true to you in good times and in bad, in sickness and in health. I will love you and honor you all the days of my life."

"I, Alexandra Sutherland, take you, Nicholas Richard Rutland, to be my husband. I promise to be faithful to you in good times and bad, in sickness and in health, to love you and to honor you."

Nicholas took her hand and placed the ring upon her finger. "What we have just done is forever, Alexandra. I will love you in word and deed. To do the hard work of making now into always. To laugh with you, to cry with you, to grow with you."

"Oh, Nicholas. I love you unconditionally and without hesitation. All that I am, all that I shall ever be will be yours."

"And all I want in this world is only you."

His powerful arms swept around her, and she drowned in languid warmth, a contentment and peace drained all her thoughts and fears of the future.

She was shaken at her own fervent reaction and slipped her arms around his neck. Nicholas pulled off her shift, laying her on the bed and she opened herself to his lovemaking. Her heart flooded with aching tenderness, holding fast, the time for things meant to be, the last instance where after everything else, this would remain as what really mattered.

Sated, they lay entwined, Alexandra secure in his arms. Under extraordinary circumstances they had been brought together and promised an oath to each other as strong and binding as any sacred vow uttered in a church. She committed to memory every line and plane of his face. Marriage was to be long and enduring, yet the unspoken reality between them expressed volumes.

Alexandra took a deep breath. Yesterday was gone. Tomorrow had not yet come. She had only the present moment and she would cherish these days with no misgivings, only sad regrets that if rescued, it was to end.

Chapter 15

*M*onths blurred into a year and no ship had been seen. Getting home seemed nonexistent. Despite moments of nostalgia, Nicholas had never been happier, enamored with Alexandra, his *wife*, in every way a man could be in love with a woman.

He hummed a tune, picturing Alexandra entering the ballroom at Belvoir in satin with scintillating diamonds, and then contrasted her garb on the island, the veil-like shift she had patched. He had to admit there was no greater beauty and he remained a bit selfish, preferring to see her that way, reluctant to reveal the cloth in the box in the lean-to.

Everything about Alexandra was honey-gold and warm, as if he were the focal point of her whole world. Her passionate nature had taught him to love. It was a new feeling for Nicholas. A feeling he embraced.

Even the natural and unassuming way she took his hand in hers, soothing, and washing away the resentment toward his father's mandates that had been roiling in him for so long. Yet fracturing his peace were the choices he made and the subsequent consequences. Tearing him apart was the likelihood of disinheritance.

He would not be duke, a role he was born to.

Yet a life without Alexandra would be no life at all. If the worst scenario occurred, he would start new in the Colonies.

A butterfly sipped nectar from a scarlet hibiscus, and he stood stock still, charmed by nature's loveliness. Like falling under Alexandra's enchantment, yet aware of the transforming hardships her life presented and the final triumph of her splendor.

He swung the shutter back and forth, satisfied with his repair, thinking how her turquoise eyes, without speaking, revealed the thoughts of her heart.

Alexandra leaned through the window and surprised him with a kiss.

"That's a dangerous thing to do. You shouldn't kiss a man like that unless—"

"Unless what?" Her eyes challenged him. Her lips lifted in a mirthful smile.

He leaped through the window, picked her up and placed her on the bed. "I lose count how many times we make love a day. In no time, you will be with child—"

Her face paled. Dammit. *Too late.* "I'm sorry. I'd do anything to take back that boorish remark."

She looked away. "I would love to give you children, Nicholas, but fate has denied me. How can I describe the feel of a tiny hand that by no means will ever be held?"

Nicholas held a greater sorrow, and a unique pain it was, making a place in his heart for a child to never come. That once he died, he'd be erased from the world for lack of that certifiable stamp on his lineage.

Nicholas saw the tears in her eyes, the heartbreaking realization that hung like a lodestone around her neck.

She sobbed. "I adore children. To know, that I will never be able to hold my own babies in my arms, to laugh and play with my children."

What an ass he'd been to make that blunder. The stab in her heart, speared his own. Her feelings came first. "I love you, and all that I want, is you."

He kissed her but she moved out from beneath him. "You must be hungry."

"You'll make a fine duchess, Alexandra."

"I can't be your duchess." She rose, crossed the small room. "While we are on the island, we can pretend—

"What nonsense. You will always be at my side."

At the table with her back to him she peeled a mango. "I would fail at being a duchess. I do not even know how to dance let alone what silverware to use."

Coming up behind her, he rested a gentle hand on hers, eased the knife and mango out of her hands, and placed them on the table. He motioned for her to follow him outside. "We will begin your first dance lesson. A waltz."

"What?" Her eyes widened in question when he held out his hand.

"I cannot dance alone, Lady Rutland," he said, leaning down to take her hand.

"Really, I haven't danced much, only a few village dances."

"Then you have not been living."

She shook her head, but Nicholas bowed and took her in his arms, holding her close and started counting.

They had no orchestra, glittering chandeliers or polished dance floor, but whirling her around beneath the palms was better than any dance he had ever experienced.

"How am I doing?" She laughed aloud.

He had his Alexandra back. "You are a rare jewel and outshine any woman I've ever known."

Chapter 16

*I*n the corner of the garden, Alexandra performed the onerous task of preparing a new area of land for planting. She lifted her face to the sun and swallowed hard. Nicholas's slip the day before rested heavy. He pretended having children was not important and his denial confirmed to her more than ever, she would release him from his vows if rescued.

She tugged at a mass of vines, yanked them free and tossed them behind her. Although the afternoon wind had fallen, a slight breeze off the ocean lifted her hair and cooled her heated neck from the glare of the tropical sun.

The patch was dense from years of neglect and the roots held fast to the soil. She pulled away an elephant ear leaf. Two long thin bones were stretched out across the ground. She inhaled, forcing her fingers to clench around more stalks and ripped away. A skeleton reclined against a tree. Bony legs led-up to a spine and rib section, and a skull leaned sideways, its eye sockets staring off to sea. Suspended from the neck and resting over the ribcage where his heart would be was a gold locket.

"Nicholas." Her knees buckled and she sank to the ground. Hands shaking, she opened the locket. Gazing back at her was the miniature of a pretty woman. No doubt, the gold locket Lady

Jane Winthrop Dabney had given to Captain John Sharp, and with it, his dream of a life with her extinguished. Alexandra's gaze drifted over the sad remains of the sea captain. To think he had died alone.

Nicholas approached from behind. After a moment of silence, he said, "I'll bury him. There can't be happy endings all of the time, Alexandra."

Like Nicholas and her.

She stood and unclasped the locket from Captain Sharp. "Maybe someday we can return Lady Jane's locket and the diary to her. It is the decent thing to do." Tears burned her cheeks with their heat and quiet power. Nicholas turned her around and she put her arms around his neck, sobbing into his chest. She cried for the darling sea captain and for Nicholas, the man she'd have to leave behind if they ever reached the shores of England.

With his machete, Nicholas hacked through the brush, an endless task for wherever he cut, the growth reappeared. To erase the tragedy of Captain Sharp and his own indiscretion about children, Nicholas diverted her attention with an outing. He pulled Alexandra up on a high craggy cliff overlooking the beach that lay like a shepherd's hook of gold. "My senses are heightened on this island. I see that which is far off with but a glance, I hear the crack of stone or branch on high protecting myself from falling branches and rocks. I smell the coming of the storms while they are still days away. The soup you make tastes as fine as any I've ever eaten back in civilization."

Nicholas swept up his cocked hat and jammed it beneath one arm. His nose twitched, the air was pregnant with the smell of salt. "The folly of looking for treasure is an exercise in uselessness, Alexandra." They had been talking about his sister, Abby. How he missed her, how he worried about her. "She is probably dead by now."

"Like you, Nicholas, she survived. You must count on that, live with that thought."

His eternal optimist. "How do you know?"

"I don't. But if there is a just God, then she is safe."

He took a swig of water from the calabash and offered it to her. "How can you treat your life like that?" So far, he'd survived, but if his father or siblings hadn't...that yoke of guilt would be the price he'd have to bear.

She shrugged. "We can't control the wind, but we can adjust our sails."

She was right.

He took a deep breath. If his family did survive, what did they think happened to him the night of his abduction? Would there have been any witnesses? He was certain if there was a trail, they'd be looking for him.

"My intuition says the treasure is here. Captain Sharp did not come all this way and not have his treasure with him. I can use that money to get justice for Molly and my father."

She wanted justice as much as he wanted vengeance. If they got off this island, he'd do everything in his power to have her stepmother prosecuted for her crimes. But without witnesses, the charge would be impossible. Molly was dead. How convenient for her stepmother. And to prove Alexandra's heritage? Like blowing thistledown against a hurricane. Yet maybe a Sutherland servant would know.

"Just tell me why, and I'm not talking about the treasure. For what purpose have we had to go through this struggle?"

"Sometimes trials are to make us stronger, to act as a bridge to another part of our life. Samuel always said, 'Birth is the day molded into a sculpture, happenstance is an oil painting and experience is a mosaic of them all.'"

They came to an end of an animal path with a cliff a quarter mile straight up. They would have to climb. "Are you ready for a new experience?"

She grasped thick strangler vines and Nicholas followed behind her. "I have to say the view from here is fantastic."

"Leave it to you, Nicholas to point that out," she laughed and hitched herself over the top of a ridge.

She lay there panting when Nicholas heaved himself up beside her. Her scent beckoned him. His mouth was bone dry, sweat ran between his shoulder blades like warm rain. Temptation lay one foot away. He looked down on the ocean where waves slammed against rocks in a surge of spray.

Alexandra shielded her eyes from the sun and looked at him. "Who else could have plotted against your family?"

"There could be any number of persons. An angry tenant."

She tossed a stone off the cliff. "An angry tenant would not have money."

"Lord Eaton, the father whose son I killed in self-defense. He definitely has the financial means."

"And the motivation," she added.

She picked up another stone and examined it. "Have you ever had a hint of enmity from Duke Cornelius?" Alexandra said.

"Nicholas shook his head. "Never have I seen any animosity, only kindness, bestowing us with gifts and all the things he did for me are countless."

"Yet he never married? Doesn't that trouble you?"

Nicholas shrugged. "Why should it?"

"Do you think that in a twisted way, since he didn't have your mother, he substituted the Rutland children as his own? That there might be subterfuge and patience to get back at your father? Samuel always told me to look at my closest friends before my distant enemies. The Duke would have the resources to pull off such a scheme to destroy your family."

Nicholas stopped to ponder. "That is the most absurd notion I've heard to date. I'm also thinking of a fellow in the House of Lords. My father has gone up against those pushing the war in the Colonies because it is bankrupting England. He has many war-mongering enemies who stand to profit from contracts and have the funds to seek his demise. I would start there."

"You are probably right." Alexandra stood and dusted her bottom. "Look, Nicholas, an 'E' is carved into the rock, probably by Captain Sharp. We have not climbed this high before. Remember his diary. *Lovely*, *Only*, *Valuable* and *Enthralling*. If we take the first letters of each word—"

"Not too hard of a clue to figure out. His love for Lady Jane."

She whooped loudly. "Yes, but you've missed Captain Sharp's point. As we speculated before, he used the first letters of each coordinate, and then applied each letter to a landform. Lagoon, Ocean, Valley, Escarpment."

Nicholas snorted. "And?"

She pointed to the rocky ground, and then to the 'E.' We stand on the escarpment which is to the west of the other land features. The ocean is down there to the east. South is the lagoon and the valley is to the north."

The sea crashed on the sand below, seagulls soared and cried overhead. She waited for Nicholas to see her point.

The emergence of recognition flooded his face. "The cottage was built where the four coordinates merge."

Chapter 17

They tore up floorboards. Nothing. They searched the beams. Nothing. They started on the lean-to. Alexandra climbed up in the rafters and opened a box before Nicholas could stop her. He folded his arms in front of him, waiting to weather the storm.

"Nicholas! You were aware of this fabric all the time and let me gallivant around with nothing on. How dare you."

He surveyed her from head to toe. "I like the way you look."

She burst out laughing and held a blue cotton up in front of her, smoothing it with her hands. "You are incorrigible, Lord Nicholas. I should rain a hundred curses on your head. I'll get even. To think, I will make all kinds of dresses for myself and be covered from head to toe."

He grimaced, clearly not liking the idea.

She huffed and carried the box into the cottage. "Would serve you right for lying to me."

He followed her. "I didn't lie. You asked me if there was a *chest* of fabric. The material was in a box."

She lifted several of the fabrics up for close examination, and then narrowed her eyes, looking him up and down. "Your breeches are in tatters. For misleading me with your dance of words, you will be tailoring your own pants."

He grabbed her from behind and tossed her on the bed. "How about we walk around like Adam and Eve?"

She put a hand on his chest. "What about the treasure?"

"To hell with the treasure. You enticed me that whole climb up the cliff."

"I didn't think you noticed."

He didn't answer and hungrily crushed his mouth to hers, his gut ablaze with need. He suckled her breast through her shift and she groaned, circling his arousal with her hand. He cupped a hand beneath her bottom, tilted her hips and buried himself inside her, as deeply as he could and let go of his seed. He pulled her into his arms and kissed her. She brushed a sweaty curl from his brow, the treasure hunt forgotten for the time being as they lay side by side.

A moon, grown to half, hopscotched over fast-moving grey clouds. He rubbed his eyes with his knuckles, weariness enclosing him like a vice. He tried not to think of the endless problems they faced ahead. It was good she couldn't get pregnant. Childbirth brought complications, even death. He could not imagine a life without her. Rain pattered against the roof and he closed the shutters he had restored. The wind was already picking up.

Every day, they watered the gardens and everything grew rich and fine under Alexandra's administrations. Nicholas leaned toward her until his mouth was a hairsbreadth from her. "Do you desire my kiss, Alexandra Rutland?"

To his amazement, she shook her head. "No."

He grinned, understanding he had the ability to befuddle her when he wanted to get out of work.

"Liar," he said, rubbing his lower lip against hers.

Alexandra huffed. "I know exactly what you are doing. We have to finish the watering."

The tip of his tongue emerged, and with a feather light lick, he tasted her lips. Salty and sweet. "No?"

"Certainly not."

He nipped her lower lip with his teeth and she shivered.

"Nicholas." She pushed him away, and in that light of crystallized time, her face brightened with sudden and striking excitement. "I know where the treasure is."

"Not again. I'm not spending my whole life digging in the dirt. That lunatic, Sharp, has his treasure buried in the sands of time, far from our reach...that's if it really exists."

She grabbed a shovel from the shed and reached the corner of the garden. "This is where Captain Sharp died, Nicholas. He could have died in the comfort of his bed. No. He chose to die here because it was where he buried his treasure."

Nicholas scoffed and took the shovel from her. He stabbed the dirt, spooning the soil in a heap. "Dead men tell no tales," he muttered.

After ten minutes of digging, the shovel clanged and it wasn't rock he'd hit. Alexandra dropped to her knees, and eagerly swept away the earth with her hands.

"Dig. This is the treasure."

They scooped and scraped, a pile of loam growing high from their efforts. A trunk was cleared and Nicholas hauled it from a hole. She reached to open it.

"Wait," said Nicholas. "There is another trunk."

Alexandra squealed. She scrambled down into the hole and helped Nicholas pry it free. He heaved the trunk next to the other.

"A third." Alexandra clapped her hands and climbed back down in the hole.

"Don't be disappointed if there is nothing valuable inside." Nicholas brushed the sweat from his brow and dirt smeared across his face.

She bit her lip, the quest of the unknown and at last unearthing what they had been searching for.

"Don't open them yet. Let me haul them in the cottage."

Inside the cottage he blew out a breath and laid a hand on her shoulder. "Again, Alexandra, don't be disheartened if we have been duped by Captain Sharp."

"Hurry, Nicholas."

With a pick, he cracked open the lock on the first trunk and swung back the lid. "Indeed."

She stared wide-eyed for a full two seconds. Gold doubloons, brilliant ingots, winking jewels, silver coins, dazzling pearls, gold plates and goblets. "My God, this is more than the King's treasury."

"Definitely gains from a Spanish haul. But they can't all be full of such treasure, can they?"

Nicholas cracked open the remaining two trunks and threw back the lids.

In a twinkling of the eye, pure energy boomed around the cottage. Alexandra whirled, her arms extended from her sides, and Nicholas's laughter became the sunbeam of her soul. He picked her up and twirled her around.

Out of breath, he put her down. "You were right about every-thing."

He scooped up strings of pearls and placed them around her neck.

She reached for a crown and steadied it on his head. "Hail, King Nicholas."

He tumbled her onto the bed. "Your faith and persistence paid off."

She placed her palm on his chest and pushed him back. "It isn't right. None of this. We cannot keep the treasure. It belongs to Lady Jane."

"Lady Jane gets it all, now let's attend to more important things." His crown fell over his brow, she lifted it off and tossed it into the chest. He was hot, hard and ready when she scrambled on top of him, her pearls teasing his chest and her hair veiling them when she leaned over for a kiss.

Nicholas eyed her with the slightest hint of a smile. "A bold wench, I have."

A signal cannon boomed in the distance. She scrambled off him. Heart thumping, Nicholas crossed the room, picked up the telescope and focused on the horizon. "A schooner. And a British flag."

Nicholas dropped the scope where it clattered on the table and grabbed for the tinderbox. Books crashed off the shelves to the floor.

"Run, Alexandra."

She was already sprinting down the mountain. He passed her, leaping over vines and fallen palm logs. He tripped on a root, som-ersaulted mid-air, landed on his feet and kept running.

"I can't believe this," said Alexandra. "Hurry, Nicholas, get the signal fire lighted before they leave."

Nicholas skidded in front of the pile of gathered driftwood. He pulled out the protected coconut husk fibers and struck the tinderbox.

Alexandra joined him. Breathless she knelt beside him. "Hurry, Nicholas."

He struck the tinderbox several times. In the breeze sparks darted around the fibers.

"Damn."

Alexandra cupped her trembling hands around the tinder. He struck the flint to metal again and again. The sparks caught to the fibers. He breathed onto the embers, adding small tinder and glancing over his shoulder at the ship.

"Dear God, will the ship leave before it sees our signal?"

Sweating, Nicholas placed more dry wood on the fire careful not to put it out. "There is no way I will allow that ship to leave without us."

The fire roared to life. Alexandra placed dry leaves on the inferno. "The smoke will be more visible to the ship."

Nicholas and Alexandra waved their arms and shouted to get the ship's attention. The ship blast her cannon in acknowledgement, the reply reverberated up the coast.

Nicholas picked Alexandra up and twirled her around. "We have been saved."

Toes in the lapping surf, they waited for a small boat to be rowed ashore. Nicholas caught hold of the bow. Dressed in a navy frockcoat with gold trim, the captain stepped from the boat.

"I am Lord Nicholas Rutland. We have been cast ashore for a year."

The British captain stood thunderstruck. Extraordinary. I can't believe the miracle of fate that drags me from the scouring the Caribbean and puts me in your presence. Truly extraordinary."

"At your service," Nicholas bowed.

"I am Captain Charles Sawyer and charged with finding you. Months ago, we discovered flotsam from the *Santanas* and assumed you perished with the ship. But your father, Duke Rutland said not to give up."

"My father is alive?" His heart stopped. Had he heard Captain Sawyer right?

"Yes, very alive and well. He ordered a complete search of the islands for you. After that terrible debacle at Belvoir where the laboratory blew up with the intent to kill your brother and his Lordship, a kidnapper's note was found, saying you were sent to Brazil. There was an eyewitness to your abduction on the docks of London. We traced you to flotsam discovered in the Greater Antilles never believing we would find you. Lo and behold, here you are."

"My father is alive?"

"Yes, Lord Rutland. He never gave up hope of finding you."

"My brother, Anthony? Any news on my sister?"

"Your brother is alive and well. Your sister is another matter. The Governor-General of Nassau informed me that as far as he knew, Lady Abigail Rutland, was alive. She had been a guest of his but kidnapped by barbaric American Colonials during an invasion of his city. He surmised there would be an exchange for her since England was at war with the Colonies."

Nicholas made a mental note, impatient to get home to secure the exchange.

Grinning from ear to ear, Nicholas clapped Captain Sawyer on the back, shaking his hand.

The captain cleared his throat, his eyes scrutinizing behind Nicholas.

Nicholas turned. Alexandra's lack of attire had come under the inspection of Captain Sawyer and the crew that had rowed him to shore. Alexandra blushed. He shoved her behind him.

"This is Alexandra, another English subject who was kidnapped with me and has suffered terrible deprivations. If you could give us safe passage back to England…"

"I would be most happy to accommodate you and Miss Alexandra, but your father gave express orders that if you were found to take you to Nassau, Bahamas where you will be escorted home by a flotilla of His Majesty's ships. You will have better protection."

Suddenly realizing that this was the end of their sojourn on the island, Alexandra dragged her feet to the cottage. She slammed down the trunk lids and secured them so not one of the crew would know the contents. Who knew the avarice of men?

She swept the cottage, made the bed, and washed the dishes which Nicholas said was a waste of time. She wanted the memories that warmed her up inside, yet those same memories now tore her apart. The oversized wool gown Captain Sawyer had procured scratched at the neck and overheated her skin. Would she ever get used to wearing clothes again?

After packing shells and other trivial memorabilia collected on the island, she closed the shutters and the door. She had come to the island with little and would leave with little. The rest of the contents were to be left behind in case some other unfortunate soul was castaway.

She was halfway down the mountain when she remembered Captain Sharp's diary and locket. Running back, she glanced around the cottage for a last look, touching the table where they ate their meals, running her fingers along the bookshelves and chess set, and smoothing the quilt over their bed. For Alexandra, the tides of change reminded her that life was an unknown path marked with twists and turns.

Part Two

Chapter 18

From the initial cannon blast that had snapped across the island, their lives had been a whirlwind. The heady rush to light the signal fire, and then packing everything, including the treasure, to boarding Captain Sawyer's schooner. They sailed to Nassau, Bahamas, a Colonial extension of the King's realm. From there, Nicholas had sent a hurried message to his father, rowed out to a departing packet. He had apologized to Alexandra later for not sending word to Samuel but she had been resting at the Colonial Inn and he didn't have time to get the address from her. Passage was booked on a larger merchant ship, the *Achilles*, and escorted by one His Majesty's man o' wars to England.

Nicholas held her to his side, his arm tightened around her.

The wind was freshening now and the *Achilles* heeled under stretched sails and the bow thrust against the water with a hissing sound as they entered, and then skimmed along the Thames River to London Harbor.

For Alexandra, whatever they'd promised, the vows they had spoken, belonged to the island. Nicholas had vowed nothing would change his feelings for her, but if he persisted in his belief, he would lose everything he held dear. She couldn't let him do that. Because no matter how he fought it, he would come to hate her in the end.

She yielded to Nicholas's happiness, reuniting with his family, yet her shoulders sagged with the weight of it. She sighed, then wrinkled her nose as the smell of floating garbage welled-up from the river. Ahead, dingy, decrepit warehouses, huddled on land of flat and slimy mud. A depository lay charred and blackened.

"I must confer with the captain," he said, smiling down on her.

She swallowed hard and nodded. "I am going below to freshen up a bit."

His eyes misted as he kissed her forehead and disappeared in the melee of sailors. Alone at the rail, she steadied herself against the craft's rolling motion, experiencing a moment of vertigo. Strange, all the months at sea and she never became dizzy. The wooziness halted and she fixed her gaze on the thronged sunlit dock below where pandemonium and discord ruled.

Sea gulls screeched over bales of cotton and tobacco, hogsheads of rum, bags of grain, piles of timber, and crates of tea. Men with barrels hefted on their shoulders pushed through the mob. Boys hawked meat pies. Dock hands shouted orders. Shrill laughter emanated from doxies hailing sailors to their trade. People waved and squealed greetings, while deckhands tied ropes to secure the vessel.

So far from the island where the wind's lullaby flowed through the palms.

Alexandra passed her gaze over the crowd. With certainty, Nicholas's family would come to greet him. Just as she thought it, a black coach with a golden crest pulled up and a dark-haired man alighted—a facsimile of Nicholas in his senior years. With his dark hair greying at the temples, the man stood straight and tall. Handsome. Regal and imposing. And as forbidding and ducal as—Nicholas.

Another man, taller than Nicholas, and similar in appearance, swung from the coach—his brother, Anthony, who turned and held his hand out to help a gorgeous auburn-haired woman alight. Alexandra did not miss the beaming expression between the two.

Suddenly an open carriage with harnesses jangling on four white horses clattered through the crowd, sending young and old alike running and screaming, nearly crushed by the pounding hooves. Like the fairest of flowers, a woman of impeccable beauty, reclined, impervious to any destruction she might have wrought, and relishing her staged tableau to impress any onlookers. Including Alexandra.

As if ordered to do so, the clouds opened and sky-piercing light haloed the woman. Her gown was white, her hair piled high and powdered, added to the woman's radiance. Alexandra frowned. Was the woman deliberately wearing a dress to match the color of her horses and the white livery of her grooms?

Alexandra's heart leaped. No doubt, this was Lady Susannah Tomkins, Nicholas's fiancée. Blood drained to her toes. She couldn't move. She simply stood there, immobile...paralyzed. A prism through which her sorrow splintered into a never-ending spectrum.

She ran a hand over the nubby cotton texture of her own gown, one of two, hastily made by dressmakers in Nassau. The month at sea and salt-spray had damaged her gowns. She gripped the rail, suddenly acutely aware of her work-roughened hands and sun-bronzed skin; far from the delicate, porcelain complexion of the lady who possessed a beauty to inspire artists and poets. There was nothing to do about her wild appearance.

Her vision blurred. She pushed back tendrils of her windblown hair and went below deck.

In her cabin, she flung herself on the bed where she'd made love with Nicholas on nights he'd stole in from his cabin, and drawing from him a memory to last her a lifetime. Her shoulders quaked as she put on her cape, and then placed a letter that she'd written earlier on the table for Nicholas explaining her departure. She picked up her valise containing her other dress, shells from the island, and Captain Sharp's diary.

She reached into the pocket of her dress, fingers brushing over the small amount of gold coins sewn and concealed in the material. She'd taken no more than what she required for travel expenses home. She kissed the black pearl ring Nicholas had given her on the island, and laid it on the table. Taking a step away, she stopped, closed her eyes for a moment, turned, snatched the ring, and then closed the door behind her.

Two gangplanks had been placed. Crowds rushed the stern, and she saw Nicholas hugging his father and brother. Alexandra pulled her hood over her head and departed at the opposite end in the bow. No one noticed. On the street, she shouldered through the melee, pausing at a tavern on the corner just in time to see the fair flower in white, Lady Susannah, throwing herself into Nicholas's arms.

Nicholas would have his perfect life. His perfect wife.

Chapter 19

"*W*here is she?" Nicholas raked his fingers through his hair.

"Who are you talking about?" said the Duke.

The captain hurried down the gangplank and handed a Nicholas a letter. "This was left in her cabin and addressed to you, Lord Rutland."

He ripped open the note and forced his eyes to the missive. Alexandra's elegant scrawl confirmed the worst of his suspicions. "She's left. The fool woman deserted me."

"What woman?" Lady Susannah huffed.

Nicholas spun around, scanned the crowded port. "She was kidnapped with me."

Lady Susannah narrowed her eyes. "You mean to tell me you were alone on an island with a woman. When were you going to inform me?"

Nicholas pushed aside the driver, scrambled on top of the Rutland coach, his blood pounding, eyes darting. She had just been there. She couldn't have gone far. But...why? He curled his hands into fists. Why did she leave him? "Alexandra, come back. Right now."

Lady Susannah gasped. "Nicholas stop shouting and come down. People will think you're a lunatic."

Nicholas jumped to the ground. Wide-eyed, the Duke stared. Anthony raised an eyebrow. His wife, Rachel smiled.

"Your behavior is appalling," Lady Susannah said through her teeth. "Nicholas, think of the scandal you may create…yelling and screaming on the docks, acting like an ape from that wilderness where you were stuck for so long."

She was right. No doubt they all thought he was mad.

He grabbed his brother's arm. "Anthony, help me. It is too dangerous for her on the docks. Who knows what unsavory hands she may fall into?"

The Duke tipped his hat back. "Nicholas, slow down. Give me her description. I will have my men comb the docks."

"She's golden-haired, blue eyes, the most beautiful woman in the world. I'm not leaving until I find her."

"You must look for her," Lady Rachel Rutland concurred.

Lady Susannah glared at her, turned on her heels and steamed toward her carriage.

"Alexandra," Nicholas shouted, bumping aside one person and then another as he pushed through the throngs, his brother and father keeping up directly behind him. If he wasn't so frightened for her well-being, he would have thought it absurd his behavior, and the fact his father and brother broke decorum, following him was equally absurd.

After several hours of searching the docks and nearby streets, darkness fell and his father convinced him to go to the townhouse.

In the library, Anthony and Rachel sat opposite him, silent.

"Oh, no." Nicholas shot to his feet. "Abby. I almost forgot. We must arrange a prisoner exchange for her. The Governor-General in the Bahamas said she was kidnapped by the dangerous privateer, Captain Jacob Thorne during an invasion by the Colonials. We must free her of those cruel ruffians."

Rachel laughed.

He glared at her. "I don't see what is so funny. I can only imagine what Abigail has suffered at the hands of those uncivilized savages. I will kill Captain Thorne if he touches her."

"There will be no killing, and all is well with your sister," said the Duke.

"Is she back in England? I must see her."

Anthony winked at his wife. "I take exception to you calling my wife an uncivilized savage. Rachel is a Colonial and Captain Jacob Thorne's cousin."

"What madness is this?"

His father placed a hand on Nicholas's shoulder. "Although I don't know the full story, Abigail was saved by Captain Thorne. That terrible night when both of you were abducted from Belvoir and Anthony's lab exploded, she was put aboard a ship where she suffered at the hands of a cruel English slaver until Captain Thorne rescued her. I am indebted to him."

"Where is she?" Nicholas demanded.

Lady Rachel Rutland smiled. "She is living in Boston and happily married to the uncivilized savage, Captain Thorne. Did I mention you are an uncle?"

His father told him of the eyewitness on the docks the night of his abduction. How he'd recognized Nicholas and gave the names of the ships they sailed on. How his father had ships sent out to search for them.

Nicholas dropped into the chair, astounded by the extraordinary course of events.

Alexandra had told him Abigail was alive. That his father and brother were alive.

She had always given him hope.

Like you, Nicholas, she survived. You must count on that, live with that thought. Alexandra's prediction and faith came true. His eternal optimist.

He held his head in his hands. Without Alexandra, London would never be home again, no place would be. He remembered her smell, her laugh, and gentle mocking to rouse him out of his moods. Everything about her was perfect and without her, his soul withered and scarred.

"Nicholas, someone must have seen Alexandra leave. There must be a trail. I've given her description to runners to pursue her. We will find her. What village does she come from?"

Nicholas fell back into the settee. "I don't know. All she ever told me was southern England."

"We could search for her father by name," said the Duke.

"Elwins. Samuel Elwins, a sea captain. But he is not her real father."

"Go on," said the Duke.

Nicholas looked right at his father. "She is Lady Alexandra Sutherland and she saved my life."

"Oh." Everyone said in unison.

"Did you say Alexandra Sutherland? I thought she was dead," said Anthony.

"She is not. Lady Alexandra is alive, spirited away by the Elwins when Lady Ursula Sutherland murdered her husband, Baron Sutherland and planned to do away with his daughter."

Lady Rachel Rutland gasped.

Anthony jerked his head back and his father nodded, taking it all in. "Baron Sutherland was a great friend of mine and I always thought it strange he died when in vigorous health."

Nicholas further recanted the rest of Alexandra's story, explaining her unfortunate life, including her stepmother, Ursula, and how she had taught him to survive on the island.

"I'd like a private moment to talk," said the Duke.

Anthony handed Rachel up. At the door, Rachel peered at Nicholas over her shoulder and said, "Keep your hopes up, Nicholas. I can tell this woman is very special to you."

Nicholas was just getting to know Anthony's new wife who he hadn't met until a few short hours ago. He liked her. She was far from Anthony's selfish first wife.

The door closed with a light snap. Alone now, Nicholas waited, dreading his father's new demands. "Don't tell me—

His father raised his hand. "I'm not going to tell you what to do, Nicholas, ever again. You cannot imagine the dreadful hurt and pain of not knowing if you were alive or dead. Time became tenuous, and cruelly oppressive, thinking of your fate."

Nicholas slumped in the chair and rubbed a hand over his unshaven face. "I want to become a great duke, but you cannot tie my hands anymore. I can't be the person you want me to be. I want to bring progress to the estates. I cannot go back to the stagnant—"

"I'm a different man now, son. I admit after your mother's death, I became detached and morose. It is no excuse and I hope you can find forgiveness in your heart for my distance. I have not been a good father, but from now on, I will be at your side. You can do anything you desire to do with the estates. I give you free rein." His father poured a brandy and handed it to Nicholas.

"I don't want to marry Lady Tomkins. She is ill-suited for me."

The Duke smiled. "With you turning London upside down and...after a year on an island with a certain Lady Sutherland, I gathered nixing your relationship with Lady Tomkins might be in your future."

"To think Alexandra wanted me to be free of her. That daft woman. When I find her, I'll drag her back to London and chain her to me."

The Duke swirled the amber liquid of his brandy. "Despite what she said in her letter of not wanting you, Alexandra Elwins, or Lady Sutherland is in love with you, Nicholas. Looks to me like she sacrificed her happiness for what she believed you wanted most."

"And how do you know so much?" Nicholas retorted. He was tired and touchy as a bear.

"Your mother was the same."

Nicholas took a deep swallow. "I made the mistake of expecting children. She left because she could not produce an heir due to a childhood injury and any of your protesting about producing an heir, I will not hear. I want Alexandra."

"I am not protesting at all. I told you, I'm a different man, Nicholas. Anthony can produce the heir."

Nicholas exhaled. "I must be delusional."

"You are not."

"I expected you to object, to disinherit me."

"No, son."

Nicholas was silent for a few minutes locked in disbelief. This couldn't be happening. All this time he'd believed what his father had wanted and it caused Alexandra to leave. Now, just like that his need for an heir was gone. The fear that cut him was eradicated. Gone. But in its place, and even worse fear because Alexandra...for no good reason...was gone. If anything happened to her...

The danger Alexandra had mentioned, her stepmother's desire to have her killed, meant her life could be in danger at this very minute.

Or what if dockworkers grabbed her or a nefarious highwayman. She was vulnerable on the streets alone. He had to get to her. *Now.*

Nicholas raked his hand through his hair. Never had he been so scared in his life. If anything happened to her, he'd never forgive himself.

"I want you to ask the King to help her get back her title and lands and whatever is owed to her. And we must find a way to ferret out Lady Ursula and Willean and have them punished for their crimes."

The Duke went around his desk and sat. Picking up a quill and dipping it in ink, he said, "I will do it immediately. In addition, I keep a sensitive finger on the pulse of London. I want you to go over everything again about her past. Her connections. The people who moved her away from the stepmother. Any detail you can give me to trace Lady Sutherland. We will find her."

Chapter 20

*A*lexandra reread the paper from four weeks earlier, heralding the miracle of Lord Nicholas Rutland's return from the Portuguese slaver, the *Santanas*—and with a mysterious lady by the name of Alexandra Elwins who had vanished. She sniffed and then wiped at her nose. If that wasn't enough sensationalism, the next day's paper trumpeted the upcoming nuptials between Lord Nicholas and Lady Susannah Tomkins, long separated and finally reunited. The article detailed the wedding arrangements with all the grandeur and splendor to accompany the happy event.

She sniffed. "It certainly didn't take you long to forget me, did it, Nicholas?"

"What did you say?" said Samuel.

"Nothing," she mumbled, numb from crying. She had fallen into her adoptive father's arms upon returning to Deconshire, and begged his forgiveness for running away and not telling him where she had gone. But his cheerfulness at having her back couldn't change the enduring misery. Without Nicholas, Deconshire became a prison.

The people of Deconshire had read the papers, assuming the worst. The Cornett sisters had a holiday of their own, spreading their vicious gossip and accusations.

What if Nicholas because of some misplaced reason or guilt used his resources to find her? Guilt had a strange effect on some people, but then why would he risk his future wife finding about her...about their life on the island. No, it was a stupid to think that. And even if there were a remote chance, she'd never mentioned the name of her town, but she had told him Samuel's surname and his rank as sea captain. She shook her head. There couldn't be any records that would lead him to Deconshire, could there?

Chills ran up her spine. Lady Ursula must have read the papers. Thank heaven, the journalists didn't know where she and Samuel lived. But Lady Sutherland had passed Molly on the streets in London and had her followed to her hotel where she was murdered. What if Lady Sutherland followed Alexandra's journey from London to Deconshire? If anything happened to Samuel...

With that thought, her stomach rolled. She blew out a breath to make the nausea go away, an affliction she had possessed for many weeks. No doubt, an illness she contracted at sea.

She dropped the paper and took a sip of her tea. The familiar cottage she'd grown up in wrapped around her like a warm quilt. Shiny copper pots hung from the ceiling, a slab of smoked bacon suspended from a hook on the stone wall, her hat, and coat hung next to the door, and a savory beef stew she had made earlier, simmered on the stove. She rubbed the heel of her palm against her chest. Everything spoke of Molly.

"Enough," said Samuel. "Let's go out and get a spot of air."

Visiting Molly's grave had been a daily event, an excuse to forget Nicholas. She didn't blame him for restarting his life and didn't hold him to the promises he made on the island. To leave had been her decision. Lady Susannah Tomkins. She wanted Nicholas to be happy. But knowing Nicholas as she did, she doubted that he'd be happy with Lady Tomkins. He'd have the perfect life, but would he really be happy?

Alexandra had told Samuel about her abduction and life on the island but remained vague about Nicholas. If Samuel understood what really had occurred between the two of them, he would have demanded that Nicholas marry her. Neither did she want Samuel to know how humiliated she was when replaced, once they'd reached the shores of England.

Although she had left so Nicholas could pursue his former life by fulfilling his promise to marry Lady Susannah, she should have not been surprised that the woman he was supposed to walk down the aisle with would show up. It was just that Alexandra didn't really expect him to act so quickly. She folded her arms around her, holding herself. To assume anything else to occur that would include her was dust in the wind.

At the graveside, Alexandra knelt and lay flowers. How she missed Molly. Samuel said nothing. With a ragged sigh, she rose and looked over her shoulder. Two men, leaned against a stone wall that edged the cemetery. One smoked a pipe and the other looked at his nails, a rake and shovel laying at their feet, probably new graveyard workers, waiting for them to leave.

She laid a hand on Samuel's shoulder. "I want to be alone so, I'm going to hike to the cliffs. I haven't been there since I've returned."

He nodded. He liked to have private time to talk to Molly. Her heart heavy, she left using the opposite gate.

Pewter clouds hung low beneath a sunless sky and dense gray fog cloaked several thatched-roof cottages. Alexandra crossed an ancient stone stile and followed a pony trail northward to her favorite place. Moisture beaded on her from the somber mist and she buttoned up her cape to ward off the late spring chill. The path, a rather dubious and uncertain one, led her along the high bluffs of blood-red sandstone that bordered the darkened sea far below.

She'd never been skittish about the narrow path before, but why the sudden wave of dizziness? Her foot slipped on the grassy path and she bent, clutching her knees until the light-headedness passed. Rising, she noticed the two men from the graveyard coming toward her. "I'm fine," she said, waving them off. She wanted to be alone.

But the men didn't turn back. they kept on coming.

Never would he have searched in this tail-end of the world, traveling for three days over impossible roads, reaching the southern coast of England. He pushed his horse hard, leaving the Rutland Coach that broke an axle, and his guards, his father had insisted on far behind.

Weeks had eclipsed and the runners in London had come up with nothing. His father had suggested the maritime offices. Night and day, clerks searched records of sea captains. Nothing. Then Nicholas remembered Alexandra telling him, Samuel served in the Royal Navy. At the admiralty's offices, a clerk produced an address for Samuel Elwins, to where his pension check was to be delivered located in a village named Deconshire.

Nerves rattled up his spine. Alexandra was in danger. He had read the papers, and with certainty, so had Lady Ursula Sutherland, recognizing the ship, *Santanas* she had paid to take Alexandra away.

If he could find where Alexandra lived then so could Lady Ursula. He had to get to Alexandra first.

Deconshire was a sleepy little harbor village dotted with a row of stone, thatched roof cottages. He inquired of a village man who directed him to the Elwins home at the end of town. Dusty from his travels, he leaped off his horse, met an older man, bowlegged from years at sea and setting his pipe between his teeth.

"Captain Elwins?"

He looked Nicholas up from toe to head. From anyone else, Nicholas would have been insulted, but he surmised the old salt knew who he was. "Aye. And what business do you have?"

"I'm Lord Rutland."

"And?"

Nicholas gritted his teeth. The sooner he got to Alexandra and shook some sense into her... "I wish to speak to Alexandra."

The old man let him squirm. "Depends."

Nicholas's hands curled into fists. For four weeks, he had pushed himself beyond human endurance to find Alexandra. No one was going to stop him. "Excuse me."

"Depends on what your intentions are."

It dawned on Nicholas, Captain Elwins read the papers too and had read about his betrothal to Lady Tomkins. Had the sea captain incorrectly surmised, Nicholas was there to ask Alexandra to be his mistress?

"Captain Elwins, my request is honorable. I'm asking for Alexandra's hand in marriage. I've torn up half of England and won't take no for an answer."

Captain Elwins adjusted his pipe. "I have my pension delivered to an address in London and a friend forwards the allowance to me from there. When I saw how bereaved Alexandra was on her return, I had a hunch there was more to her story. I had my pension delivered to Deconshire…just in case you wanted to find her. Took you long enough."

"Where is she?"

He pointed the stem of his pipe. "You'll find her up the line along the cliffs."

Nicholas sped down the path for a mile with no one in sight, and then Alexandra's screams ripped through him. He dug his heels in the path, sweating into a full out run. Two roughs wrestled with her. She clawed at them, slipping inches from the cliff's edge. Two hundred feet down waves thundered against sharp rocks. Nicholas pitched his full weight into the first man, his inertia and force, pushing the trio away from the rim.

A pistol fired, the ball aimless in the air. A gun sailed over the cliff.

Alexandra scrambled from her captors. Good. Nicholas sprang upon the first one he came to, hit the gaping thug in the mouth. Teeth went flying. The thug crumpled into the grass.

He'd been looking for a fight. He focused on his prey. The other man came at him, eyes wild, launching a right. Nicholas ducked, the buzz swept over his head. The thug's momentum carried him in a curve, his kidney exposed for the taking. Easy enough, a question of force.

Nicholas hit a short right, a colossal blow, one that would have cracked an oak rafter. The thug stumbled and bent viciously backward from the force of the blow, the breath whooshing out of him. No doubt, the shock hit the back of his lungs like a million tiny needles, heated red-hot in a fire. The man tottered, and his right leg went stiff. He grew brave, swung around on his good leg, plowing at Nicholas like an ox, slamming him in the jaw. Stunned, Nicholas shook his head.

He wanted to finish this.

He hit the man with a right. All the way up from his planted feet, as hard as he could and felt his fist drive right through and beyond it. The thug's head jerked backward and he flopped into the grass.

Breathing heavy, Nicholas wiped the blood from his mouth. He cleared his head and tipped his toe against the big man's body. "He'll be out for a while. I'll have my men tie them up and take them back to London for questioning."

Nicholas folded his arms in front of him. "Alexandra, you have some questions to answer. Why did you leave me?"

Head down, she refused to look at him. "What are you doing here, Nicholas? Here...with me...and then you saved my life."

Her voice came in tearful breaks and he wanted to take her in his arms, but he wanted to hear from her lips that she didn't want him. Pain like a white-hot bolt of agony ripped through him with the possibility.

"Those two thugs, probably sent by Lady Sutherland...you could have been killed, Alexandra."

She looked at the unconscious men and clutched her throat. "How-how did you find me?"

Nicholas folded his arms in front of him, refusing to cross the divide. "Took me a month. You had never mentioned where in southern England you lived, but I was willing to tear apart the countryside to find you. Then I remembered you had mentioned your father was in the Royal Navy, the *HMS Victory*. My father used his connections with the admiralty and traced where Samuel's pension was delivered. You have led me on a fine chase and now, I want answers as to why you left me."

"I am ill-suited for you, Nicholas. London is filled with beautiful ladies who would be eager to flirt with a duke."

He let out a loud breath. "Not good enough. I was born to meet you, Alexandra."

She drew a line in the gravel with her toe. "And then there is the fact of Lady Susannah Tomkins, your fiancée and your upcoming wedding. She offers you everything."

"Wrong. There is no Lady Susannah."

"What? I saw her when we disembarked the ship. I read the wedding announcement in the *London Chronicle*."

"That was all orchestrated by Susannah. She was overeager to strike-up the alignment with the existing engagement. I called the wedding off."

"Oh?" She lifted her head.

They stood in silence for a while, half a lifetime in the space between them.

"When you disappeared, I was as fresh and raw as meat being put on a hook. I couldn't sleep. I couldn't eat. I was so afraid I'd never find you."

Tears came down her face. "You need someone with a perfect pedigree and you need an heir. I cannot provide either."

He took a step toward her, wanted to wipe every tear from her face. Like his father had said, Alexandra was completely self-sacrificing. She left because she didn't feel worthy. She left him because she felt *he* needed someone better for him. He shook his head. Never had he met a woman so noble.

"It's time to end this." He took a step closer, felt her yearning. "You have to come half-way. It's all in your power. Take my hand. Do it. Come to me."

With the roar of the ocean drumming below, she stared off over the horizon.

Nicholas caressed Alexandra's arm and turned her face to him, making her look in to his eyes to see the import of his words. "You see color. I see shades of gray and all the negatives. I need you to see color and bring out all the positives."

"It won't work, Nicholas. I don't want you. And here you are when I was trying so hard to get over you."

He pulled her into his crushing embrace. "Prove it."

He slanted his mouth over hers, her lips, silky and moist. His entire body hummed as she melted into him. For days, he hungered for a taste of her, worried he'd never find her again, afraid the whims of life would punish him.

"How I've missed you." She moaned into his mouth, kissed him back, and he felt a potent mix of desires and longing from her.

He dragged his mouth from hers and leaned his forehead against hers. "Alexandra, your worth is beyond a million treasures. As the sun and the moon rise and fall, we are meant to be together, have endured insurmountable odds. We cannot stop it. I love you wholly and unconditionally and will never stop loving you. Promise me, you'll never leave me again."

"I promise, on one condition."

"What's that?"

"That you'll keep on kissing me like that for the rest of our lives."

Nicholas kissed her again, a long soulful kiss, and then stopped. "Before I begin something on this bluff, we need to stop." With his arm tight around her, he escorted Alexandra to her cottage where they met an anxious Samuel. The ducal coach rambled to a stop with Nicholas's men.

"You both are in danger," Nicholas said. "I'm taking you to London where you will be under the Duke of Rutland's protection. Pack what you will. My footman and guards will help you. I have a few things to attend to and will be right back."

Nicholas turned. "Guards, bind and collect the two vagrants out on the cliff. I want them taken to London. After I get done questioning them, I'll turn them over to the magistrate."

The Rutland coach stopped at a small rustic stone church near the center of Deconshire. Nicholas leapt out. With vigorous purposeful strides, he followed a flagstone path to the vicarage. A sharp bonk on the top of his head made him stop. Damn. He rubbed his head and saw an apple rolling down the pathway. He looked up, just as another apple dropped. He covered his head. And then another apple dropped. He roared, ready to climb the tree. Hidden in the boughs of the oak was a round-faced boy with dark hair. "You must be Jay."

On a branch to the left sat two identical little girls, swinging their legs back and forth.

"And you must be Sylvia and Julianna," he addressed the twin girls, their stockings torn and dresses smudged with dirt.

"How did you know?" They pouted, disappointed he knew their names and their invisibility was uncloaked.

"The same reason I know you will be coming to a wedding soon."

The door of the cottage opened and a man in a frockcoat stepped out. "A wedding?"

Nicholas held out his hand. "You must be Vicar Thompson. I am Lord Nicholas Rutland. I'm marrying a dear friend of yours, and would be honored if you and your children would attend."

"Who is the lucky bride?"

"Alexandra Elwins."

Vicar Thompson's mouth dropped open. "Our Alexandra?"

The girls squealed. Jay dropped the rest of his apples. Nicholas stepped aside to dodge the raining missiles.

Jay pursed his lips as if weighing the most important question of the century. "Will you have cake?"

"The biggest cake in all England. That's if I don't get killed by a falling apple first."

"I apologize for my children's behavior, Lord Rutland," said the Vicar.

"I have a favor, Vicar Thompson. Could you direct me to the home of the Cornett sisters?"

"You aren't going to invite the witches, are you?" asked Jay.

"They're witches?" shrilled the girls.

"For out of the abundance of the heart, the mouth speaketh," the Vicar reprimanded his children, and then raised an eyebrow to Nicholas. "They are not home. I just saw them in the village store. Alexandra has been through a lot, and forgive my opinion, but the Cornett sisters could learn a lesson in humility. I hope you do me proud, Lord Rutland."

"When I get done with them, you'll have so much pride, you'll be choking from the sin."

With four outriders, the Rutland coach pulled up in the center of the village common. Nicholas waited ten seconds, so onlookers could see the elaborate gilt detail of the coach, with the Rutland ducal crest emblazoned in gold on the door panel. No doubt, the remote town of Deconshire rarely saw nobility. He'd use that to his advantage. Normally, he'd never condescend to such an act, but defending Alexandra from the small-minded meanness of two spiteful crones was the right thing to do. With the decorum of a king, he made his exit and grimaced.

The store seemed to collapse in on itself like a cake taken from the oven too soon, and, boasted one large front window. His footman raced to open the door to the establishment, and Nicholas entered, passing his gaze over a collection of old gawking men, idlers who, with certainty spent their day loafing. The storeowner ceased sweeping. Dust motes flew across the brightness. Two women stood at the counter, examining bolts of fabric, their backs to Nicholas. With certainty, these two henwits were the infamous Cornett sisters.

"Mr. Grimes, would you stop that infernal sweeping and attend us," demanded one of the sisters. *Hortense.* On the island, he had assumed Alexandra's description of Hortense was hyperbole, but nothing in God's creation could mimic the shrubs of hair curling from her ears.

The store clerk pointed his broom handle at the sisters. "I've attended you six times today and you still can't make up your minds. I have to get my store swept."

"Of all the nerve, my sister and I shall take our business elsewhere," threatened Hortense over her shoulder.

"Be my guest, nearest town is twenty-five miles away." The store clerk rested his chin on top of his broom and then remembered to bow. "What do I owe the honor of your lordship?"

At the word, *Lordship*, both women turned, sinking into curtsies, nearly toppling to the floor.

Gertrude, the sister with a million yawning cracks in her face, grabbed hold of the counter and heaved her bulk up, batting her eyelashes at him. "Your lordship, what do we owe the honor?"

Nicholas loathed using the haughty presence of the highborn to kindle a sense of inferiority in the two women, but their malicious gossip-mongering toward Alexandra stuck in his mind. "I'm the Duke of Rutland and have traveled far. I'm looking for Lady Alexandra Sutherland."

Hortense combed the hair from her ears with her fingers. "I assure your lordship there is no lady in our village by that name except for Alexandra Elwins who is of no consequence and a woman of ill standing."

Gertrude smirked. At least he thought it was a smirk because a crack opened into a crevice. "She has a reputation that precedes her."

Nicholas inspected the two twittering Cornett sisters with a condescending glare. "She is the same woman. I take exception to you besmirching my future *wife*."

Their mouths worked up and down like beached salmon. "Alexandra Elwins?"

Nicholas slapped his gloves on his hand. "I hope there is not any negative conversation against my betrothed or there will be heavy consequences."

Gertrude's eyes bulged. Hortense hyperventilated. "Consequences?"

Nicholas stood silent for a full minute as if he were examining the worst of possibilities. *Thumbscrews? Submerging them in ice water? Dropping apples on them?*

"Draw and quarter them," yelled one of the old men.

Nicholas wasn't that bloodthirsty. But the effect from the man's comments was beneficial. Gertrude clawed her face. Hortense let go of her ears and clutched her heart.

"No, sir. I mean, no, your lordship. Never would you hear anything disapproving from our mouths," said the sisters in unison, breaking into full body tremors. "Alexandra is the nicest girl in Deconshire."

"That is what I thought and in the future, I better not hear otherwise."

The old men burst into applause.

Smiling, the storekeeper pointed north with his broomstick. "She lives in the stone cottage at the end of the lane."

"Then I shall take my leave. Good day." Nicholas pivoted and the storekeeper tripped over his broom to open the door for him.

Nicolas vaulted in his coach. From the corner of his eye, he noted every person in the store had their noses pressed up against the windows. He laughed. His act was enough to get the tongues in southern England a 'wagging.

He tapped the roof, in a hurry to get back to Alexandra and pack her and her father up to London before there was more danger and before she changed her mind.

Chapter 21

They traveled overland for better part of a week, arriving at the Rutland Townhouse in London. Fronted by a three-sided courtyard stood a red-brick mansion with an impressive Doric colonnade situated at the north end of Piccadilly. Her hand fluttered up to her throat and then slid over her pounding heart. She peered at her father and he nodded reassuringly. Nothing had prepared her for this.

She glanced at the dress Nicholas had bought for her, dirty from her travels, and then wistfully at the steps.

Nicholas looked her over. "You are perfect as you are and my family will love you. I'll take care of your wardrobe posthaste."

Nicholas helped her disembark and laughed when she widened her eyes at the edifice. "Imposing, isn't it."

An aura of carefully restrained power, of forcefulness, emanated from him. Nicholas was all that a duke would be.

"Come along. I have someone I want you to meet."

He guided her to the top of the stairs. Rigidly proper, and attired in dark maroon livery, a tall, beak-nosed, and silver haired man stood, his grey eyes speculative beneath thick bushy brows. Chest out, shoulders back, bearing stiff as new canvas, he gave the impression that if he hunched for the slightest moment it would be a slur to himself and to his King and country.

"Welcome home, Lord Rutland."

Nicholas chuckled. "Thank you, Sebastian. May I introduce you to Lady Sutherland? I have convinced her I will make a tolerable husband. And this is her adoptive father, Captain Elwins."

Except for a singular twitch of Sebastian's dense brows, the butler's face remained expressionless, though his warm brown eyes twinkled. "Indeed, my lord."

"My lady, and Captain Elwins, this my family's butler, and my dear friend, Sebastian. I've known him since I was in my nappies, and he's helped me out of plenty of scrapes. Haven't you, Sebastian?" Nicholas winked at his butler, and then he gave Alexandra a lopsided grin so endearing, the knot in her stomach eased a degree.

The butler cleared his throat. Humor danced in the eyes of an otherwise stoic face. "You were always a perfect gentleman, your lordship."

Bowing formally, Sebastian intoned, "Welcome to London, my lady and Captain Elwins."

Alexandra smiled. She liked him already. "Thank you, Sebastian."

Sebastian gestured inside with his hand. "His Grace, Lord and Lady Rutland await your presence."

Alexandra's gaze roamed the large, opulent entry. At one end of the entry was a helloidial staircase that spiraled up to a fourth floor. White marble floors glistened beneath a crystal chandelier and paintings of colorful landscapes hung on the walls. Several carved doors graced the sidewalls. Sebastian skirted ahead and opened one of them.

She fought the urge to turn and bolt. Nicholas's family would take one look at her, put Nicholas in an asylum and send her packing.

White-knuckled, she gripped Nicholas's arm and he looked down on her.

He patted her hand and smiled. "O ye of little faith."

"Lord Rutland and Lady Sutherland have arrived, your Grace."

She was stunned the butler had spoken her unproven title, but Nicholas had introduced her as such and Sebastian had taken his lead. Nicholas propelled her forward. The room had clusters of sofas and chairs scattered about and a massive fireplace with pictures of ancestors on the walls beneath elegant moldings trimmed in gold.

Everyone stood when they entered. Nicholas's father, Duke Richard Rutland, his brother, Anthony, an elderly woman, and the beautiful woman she had spied on the London docks the day of their arrival.

Silence. Maybe her presence was not the rosy picture Nicholas had painted. Her stomach started to cramp. She wanted to run from the room.

Nicholas's father strode toward her, his face serious. She licked her lips. Was he going to throw her out?

He took her completely by surprise, broke decorum and hugged her. "Thank you for saving my son's life. I am indebted to you."

Her breath hitched. Nicholas's father acknowledged her. Of course his family would be grateful because she saved Nicholas's life but accepting her into the family would be another matter.

The auburn-haired woman rushed forward and hugged her, too.

"I'm Rachel and welcome, Alexandra."

Her accent was different. Alexandra frowned.

"My accent confuses people. I'm from the Colonies." Rachel laughed. "We have heard so many wonderful things about you. And this is my husband, Anthony, Nicholas's brother."

Anthony shook her hand and Samuel's. "I understand you had a bit of trouble in Deconshire."

Nicholas shrugged negligently. "I took care of it, convincing them of their lack of respect for Alexandra."

"It was more than what Lord Rutland modestly allows," said Samuel. "Thugs tried to kill Alexandra and Lord Rutland took care of them in the first order."

"He's handy with his fists." Anthony grinned. "Been awhile since we've had a serious bout, brother. Are you still in shape?"

Nicholas snorted. "Try me."

Samuel spoke up. "I can confirm the condition of those two thugs if you're worried about his competence. I was grieving in the cemetery and did not notice the two toughs following Alexandra. Lord Nicholas's arrival at that time was by pure providence or she would have been cast over the cliff."

"When I get done questioning them, I will release them to the magistrate. But enough of that controversy for now. This is Alexandra's introduction to the family and I don't want to spoil the occasion," Nicholas said, his undisguised pride showing in his dark gaze.

"How did you survive that horrid Portuguese slaver? Hurricane? What did you eat?"

Amid the firestorm of questions, Rachel asked, "Tell us about your adventures." Everyone quieted, awaiting her response.

Alexandra answered to the best of her ability, leaving out certain details. They were spellbound as she described how Nicholas had saved her from Damiano and how he hunted on the island for food and piped in water so they wouldn't have to carry the water so far.

Alexandra glanced to the elderly woman unfolding from her chair and hobbling forward on her cane. "You are far too modest, Lady Sutherland, reciting what Nicholas has accomplished."

She took Alexandra's elbow and ushered her to a settee. "Am I the only one with civility? Sit and rest from your journey." The old woman skewered Anthony. "Where's Samuel's chair?"

"This is Aunt Margaret," Nicholas put in, placing a kiss on the elderly woman's cheek as she sat next to Alexandra. "Don't let her kindly manner deceive you. She is a hawk among canaries."

Aunt Margaret brushed him aside. "Lady Sutherland, I want to hear about how you dove into the ocean in the middle of a hurricane and cut Nicholas away from the sinking rigging. How you had fed Nicholas through the hole in the wall. How you grew your food? Made medicine?"

Alexandra smiled at Nicholas. He had cast her in a positive light.

"Slow down, you are making her dizzy, Aunt Margaret. Alexandra is the true hero. Without her, I would not be here."

Alexandra protested. "Nicholas is far too humble. Without him, I would not have survived." She abbreviated answers to many of Aunt Margaret's questions.

"So, when are the nuptials?" Aunt Margaret directed her steely gaze toward Nicholas.

He cleared his throat. "We married each other on the island and as far as I'm concerned, it is a real marriage."

Alexandra dug the toe of her slipper into the soft Aubusson, waiting for scandalous gasps of disproval. To dive beneath the carpet and hide for the next decade had merit. She glanced about. There was no censure from anyone about the occurrences on the island other than Samuel's loud 'ahem' that spoke volumes. When she had returned to Deconshire, she had kept the wedding part and its implications from her father.

Nicholas planted his feet in a wide stance. "None the less, I want it legal. We will be married as soon as a special license is procured and preparations are made. We'll have the nuptials take place at the church in Bottesford and a wedding celebration at Belvoir. I don't want to take any longer than necessary."

"Done," said his father.

Aunt Margaret stamped her cane on the floor. "You must court her in a short coming out. It is only proper."

Duke Richard walked to an ornate liquor cabinet. "Aunt Margaret is right."

"I take that as a compliment, Richard," said Aunt Margaret.

Duke Richard poured himself a drink, swirled his glass. "I must have said it wrong."

Rachel clapped her hands together. "So, romantic. But we must have a formal wedding. And... we must have Alexandra outfitted."

Aunt Margaret turned to face Duke Richard. "And don't forget the gowns for all the social engagements she'll be invited to. Of course, Duke Richard, *you* will secure the invites?"

"Of course, Aunt Margaret," The Duke said, bowing. "My secretary has already made the arrangements and ordered the dressmakers."

Aunt Margaret glanced sideways at the room's occupants. "Did I have any doubt?"

"Any more commands, Aunt Margaret?" The Duke raised his chin.

Alexandra covered her smile with her hand. Samuel coughed. Rachel giggled.

Aunt Margaret fluttered her fingers through the air. "To think you are as resourceful as that George Washington fellow in the Colonies with his revolution."

"I thank you for the compliment, Aunt Margaret."

"It wasn't meant to compliment. That rascal has maneuvered the most powerful country in the world to licking his dust."

Aunt Margaret leaned over and patted Alexandra on the knee. "I think that God, in creating man, somewhat overrated His ability. In your married life, you will understand why God invented women to make sure things are in order."

Sudden tears hovered on Alexandra's eyelashes, and she couldn't seem to hold them back. Nicholas's family accepted her.

Chapter 22

$\mathcal{S}$oaking in the deliciously rose scented water and frothy
bubbles up to her neck, Alexandra sighed. The remains of
a scrumptious meal sat on the table by the vanity. Never had hot
rolls dripping with cinnamon and butter or sweet cherries smothered in a liqueur tasted so wonderful. The eggs had been poached
perfectly with a creamy béarnaise sauce, the sausages browned to
perfection, and the tea steaming hot. She ate well, unused to such
fine fare.

Nicholas had truly missed her, had gone nearly crazy hunting
her, and that thought made her feel treasured. Her gaze roved over
the stately room, taking in the blue, gold and pink rose themed
wallpaper, the damask royal blue silken draperies, and the ornate
rosewood furnishings.

Persian rugs in the same hues as the walls adorned the floors,
and six matching embroidered pillows were strewn across a love
seat that overlooked a side garden. It was a lovely room, and her
mind whirled with enlightened and joyful emotions that tumbled
chaotically over and around one another.

The thugs who had attempted to throw her off the cliffs. She
dropped her sponge and pulled her knees up tight, willing the
shaking to go away. She was safe now. Nicholas would protect her.

A knock at the door broke her out of her reverie. Rachel sailed into the room, followed by a maid with a stack of gowns in her arms. "I'm guessing we are about the same size. I've chosen gowns from my wardrobe until your gowns are made." She asked the maid to hang the dresses in a massive armoire.

Rachel plucked a blue linen gown from the pile and held it up in front of her. "I think the coloring of this would look lovely on you. Scandalous, but a new style started by Queen Marie Antoinette. The chemise a' la' reine is incredibly light and simple, consisting of layers of blue, thin muslin with a low-laced bodice, belted at the waist and no panniers. Comfortable for when I'm working in the laboratory with Anthony, but scandalous."

Alexandra smiled. What would Rachel think of her attire on the island where she gallivanted in nothing but her chemise and no undergarments?

"When we arrive at Belvior, I want to show you the bathtub I invented."

"Invented? How does it work?" The woman was a wonder.

"Nicholas's father was very generous in allowing me to tinker with my project. Water is heated and stored in a cistern behind the fireplace in the kitchen, and then pumped by pumps I had installed to a second-floor chamber. The apparatus cuts down on the need to haul buckets of water up and down the stairs."

"You are a fascinating woman, Rachel. I can't wait to see your bathing chamber."

Rachel held up a towel. "No more than you, Alexandra. To survive what you did...why, you are extraordinary. You must dry off. The dressmakers are downstairs and ready to measure you."

Alexandra stood abruptly, sloshing water over the floor. "So soon?"

"The Rutland men work quickly and demand service in a fastidious manner. There is the matter of having a dress ready for the opera this evening."

Alexandra wrapped the towel around her. "Opera! I've always wanted to attend an opera."

"That is what Nicholas said. I told him to wait, that you needed your rest from your travels. He has ordered carte blanche on your new wardrobe and we must not disappoint."

Like a swarm of locusts, a team of seamstresses flooded into the room. Inspecting Alexandra, the head dressmaker made clucking sounds with her tongue, inserting a *"oui"* intermittently to demonstrate her approval. Alexandra stood on a stool while a rich array of silks, satins and brocades were ushered forward for her perusal.

Overemphasizing her French accent, the dressmaker postured. Not because she was French but because it was deemed fashionable and no doubt more profitable. "I will make magnificent clothing. Your figure and coloring are glorious." She clapped her hands and a seamstress handed her a tape measure.

The pin-sticking dressmaker draped fabric over her, measuring and re-measuring. Laces, bombazines, undergarments, silk stockings, were flashed before her and decided upon, everything to outfit a queen. The dressmaker fussed and her seamstresses nodded in agreement. Alexandra started to protest the expense but Rachel shook her head.

Rachel sampled a pastry from a tea tray a maid had brought in. "I can't resist anything but temptation, including cream puffs." She licked the cream from her lips. "Most importantly, I am tempted to share proud news…my husband, Lord Anthony has been invited to be a member to the Royal Society of Science for a discovery he made."

Alexandra's eyes widened. Nicholas had informed her that his brother had a scientific passion and the Royal Society of Science was greatly esteemed. "What did he discover?"

"He has developed a battery that retains electricity longer than normal."

"I would love to see his device."

"I'm sure he'd love to show you for the sole reason he'd use any excuse to be back in his laboratory. Only the fact that his brother was alive and returning on a ship were we able to tear him away. I enjoy the entertainments London has to offer so it is going to be a splendid time showing you around."

Hours passed. A sudden wave of vertigo befell her and she had to step down. Her stomach flip-flopped. The illness she contracted on the ship was making an untimely entrance. "I need some time to myself."

She begged Rachel with her eyes. *Now.*

Rachel sprang from her chair and clapped her hands. "Everyone out. Lady Sutherland needs her rest. You have enough measurements to go on."

The dressmaker raised an eyebrow, picked up the bolts of materials and accoutrements and huffed out, her seamstresses following in her wake.

Alexandra sagged against the mahogany bedpost as she struggled not to retch. Pressing her handkerchief to her lips, she closed her eyes and willed her unruly stomach not to rebel. Her head pounded. Never had she felt this miserable in her life.

Her eyes snapped open in distress. Rachel had miraculously produced a commode and Alexandra wrapped her arms around her abdomen and leaned forward to retch.

A few tears were squeezed from her tightly shut eyes as she bowed and retched again. The muscles in her abdomen continued to spasm until her stomach felt like a fist. A few minutes later, she straightened and flopped on the bed.

Rachel pulled a gold brocade comforter over her. "Does Nicholas know he is to be a father?"

Alexandra tightened her fingers on the bedding. *Never.* The doctor told her she could never have a baby. Could she? Her breasts were fuller and ached. She'd been so terribly ill over the last weeks, but it usually went away by the end of midmorning. She had been a bundle of nerves, blaming her emotional state leaving Nicholas.

"Your assumption is ridiculous, Lady Rutland."

"Really? My mother was the same way with my younger brother, Thomas. I have been around enough women who have suffered the same characteristic symptoms."

"Whatever do you mean? I can't get pregnant. I fell from a tree when I was a child. The doctor told me so."

"Rubbish. An illogical notion. I'm expecting, so I know the signs firsthand. My doctor comes this afternoon. I'll let him slip in and examine you."

Alexandra clasped her hands under her chin. Her greatest sorrow was her barrenness, and Rachel had pulled her from a box of darkness into light. The miraculous possibility of having a child radiated through her chest and arms and legs. And not just any child, Nicholas's child.

Her hands splayed across her abdomen. To hold her baby in her arms? It was the beginning of all things, of wonder, of hope, a dream of possibilities.

"Rachel, do you think it is possible that I could be a mother?"

Rachel slanted her head. "I assume you were not working at survival with all that time spent on the island."

Alexandra wanted to die of mortification.

Rachel smiled. "For now, we'll keep it a secret until it is confirmed."

Chapter 23

*T*he opera house was a cacophony of sound. Alexandra entered the box unable to conceal her delight. Great chandeliers hung from a vaulted ceiling, and below in the gallery, and like so many blossoms, women dressed in rainbows of color gathered in the tiers of elegant and spacious boxes.

Alexandra pulled her gaze from Nicholas and glanced around at the young dandies in their bright satin waistcoats in the mezzanine below, trying to gain the interests of the young ladies. Instead of admiring the compliments of their nearby suitors, the young ladies stared at Nicholas. Like a painting created with an eye for drama, the lighting revealed his ruggedly chiseled face, underscored by impeccably tailored midnight black attire, his air of smooth refinement, making the ladies gawk and practically swoon from their seats.

Except for one woman in the box opposite them. Alexandra reared back. The woman in the beautiful gown, surrounded by anxious suitors and staring daggers at her, was Nicholas's former fiancée. Had he noticed her?

Nicholas took Alexandra's cape from her shoulders and a slow admiring gaze swept across his features. The dressmaker had promised a marvelous creation and had produced a sensation out of a dress that had been promised to another customer but readied for Alexandra instead. She wanted to twirl around for his inspection. Her gown of emerald satin accentuated her narrow waist and clung provocatively to her full breasts, and then fell gracefully to the floor.

"I dreamed of you on the island in such a gown," he said leaning over to whisper in her ear, "…just so I could remove the garment later."

Alexandra blushed. "I did not realize the dress would produce such vice and depravity."

"Exactly." A lazy grin swept across his tanned face. "I have a fond memory of long sultry nights beneath undulating palm trees. You cannot, Lady Sutherland, begin to imagine the wickedness I'm entertaining." His voice rich and deep, so dear and familiar to her, wiped away any uncertainty she had of his feelings for his former fiancée.

"You must stop, my Lord. All the women watching you will guess your thoughts. My reputation will be in ruins," Alexandra teased in a laughter-tinged voice.

Nicholas's smile vanished. "I am jealous, Lady Sutherland. Those young bucks are staring at you, the most beautiful woman in the room."

Nicholas had paid her the highest compliment. She glanced at her audience. He was right. They were staring at her.

Alexandra smiled but Nicholas was not pleased. He passed an impassive glance over her male admirers until they were forced to look away.

"I do not agree with the coming out period nor the idea of sharing you at all," he said, bluntly. "I should dispense with this charade and haul you off to Gretna Green."

Alexandra angled her head to the melee below. "Are you telling me there is not one suitable companion?" she teased.

"Not one. And if one of those vipers has more than one dance with you at balls we are to attend, I shall heave them out on a doorstep."

His blunt answer made her laugh. He eyed her breasts with a bold, speculative gleam that left her breathless. "What a perfectly unchivalrous thing to say!"

"Chivalry is for callow youths and old men," Nicholas informed her with a serious inflection in his voice. "However, I shan't put up with this inconvenience for long. You sitting next to me will be a statement sent to all of London that you are mine."

"Don't be a boor and keep this enchanting lady all to yourself," chastised Anthony. He bowed to Alexandra, made apologies for being late, and then seated his wife. "I don't know why you dragged me here this evening, Rachel," he said over Nicholas's head. "To listen to a bunch of Italian eunuchs squawl like a bunch of cats."

Rachel shushed her husband and Alexandra placed her fan over her mouth to hide her smile. To sit through an opera must be difficult for a man with Anthony's prodigious and scientific mind.

A tall man entered their box. He possessed an unblinking eye, black as obsidian and made of glass. Alexandra did a double take and remembered Nicholas's story of his uncle that he told her on the island.

Nicholas stood and said, "Alexandra, this is my Uncle Cornelius, the Duke of Westbrook."

The man's elegant clothing fit well, his wig perfectly brushed and powdered, yet there was an expression of forced civility in his comportment.

He took Alexandra's proffered hand, bent over and kissed it. His touch owned the infiltrating cold of a serpent. She shivered. She drew her fingers back, but he held fast, scrutinizing her like she was a misplaced ghost. Countless emotions flashed across his face. Adoration? Resentment? Why? He held her overlong for what was appropriate. She tugged her hand.

At her movement, the Duke of Westbrook came to life and, eye refocusing, he released her fingers, and then turned, clapped Nicholas on the back. "Been trying to catch up with you since your return, but you've been on the run. Know that I'm always available to help you, Nicholas, and I understand there is to be a wedding."

"Yes, Sir. Alexandra has agreed to honor me as my wife, but that is not for public review yet. Not until a coming out has properly taken place."

"Well done," said the Duke of Westbrook, his gaze assessing Alexandra over from head to toe.

"I came to pay my respects to you, Nicholas, and must leave. But I do want to hear every detail of your journey."

Alexandra did not like the private nature of the innuendo, nor the fact that Cornelius kept staring at her. His voice troubled her. Almost as if she had heard it before. She fiddled with her glove and blew out a breath. Since Nicholas wasn't bothered by Cornelius's strange behavior then she should not be either.

"I wouldn't think of it," Nicholas said. "Why sit alone in your box when you can share ours?"

Alexandra fanned herself. The two men were deep in quiet conversation, but beneath veiled lids Rachel watched Cornelius. So did Nicholas's father. A whisper of unease goaded Alexandra's senses again. Memories assailed her from the island and their discussion of who might have been behind the attack on the Rutland's. As Nicholas seated her, nerves rattled down her spine, warning her she had not been wrong to suggest to Nicholas that his uncle may not have the purest of intentions.

Rachel gave Alexandra a slight nod, confirming a silent communication that Alexandra's uncertainties were not irrational.

In a flat tone of voice, Rachel said, "We must talk later..." She indicated Cornelius with a discreet nod. "...about accessories for your new gowns."

"That would be lovely," Alexandra said. "Your opinions matter to me."

As she spoke, Nicholas sat on one side of her and gestured to the Duke of Westbrook to sit on the other side of her. Sandwiched between the two men, she leaned over and peered down at the pit, anywhere she would not meet Cornelius's eyes. "Looks like we have arrived just in time since it appears the opera is about to begin," she said, lowering her voice.

"Is something wrong, Lady Sutherland?" the Duke of Westbrook whispered into her ear.

"Why do you ask, sir?" Alexandra said.

"You are tapping the blades of your fan on your knee in iambic pentameter."

Alexandra gulped. "How careless of me," she said, mortified that she was nearly flogging herself. "I offer my sincere apologies, Lord Westbrook."

"None to be given," he said, his expression filled with warmth. "Although I like your rhythm."

Alexandra cringed.

She opened her fan and stirred the air around her face. "I often have too much energy to sit idle, and I tend to dispel it in peculiar ways."

"I can empathize," Lord Westbrook said, leaning so their faces were inches apart. "When I'm distracted, I'm inclined to hum."

"Oh," she said, pretending interest.

"Badly," he added, and Alexandra laughed at him. The man was disarming.

The Duke of Westbrook whispered another humorous anecdote in her ear. His shoulder brushed hers in an intimate fashion that did not seem accidental. "Lucretia, I'm so happy you are here this evening."

Alexandra narrowed her gaze. "Pardon me?"

Cornelius pulled back. "Please, accept my apology. You look so much like Nicholas's late mother, your coloring, your eyes, your energy, that for one moment I was in another time and place."

She blinked. Was Duke Cornelius caught between hallucinating and the world of reality? He gave her the same feeling she experienced of a forest pool she had come upon in Deconshire, half-hidden by an edging of deadly nightshade and leaning prone across it at a despondent angle was a lifeless willow, strangely halted from falling into the foul waters.

Alexandra leaned into Nicholas. Had he seen the Duke of Westbrook's odd behavior? Nicholas's smile washed away her anxiety.

The rumbling D-minor cadence of the overture filled the theater, commanding silence from the spectators. Alexandra took a deep breath and switched her attention to the stage in anticipation of enjoying the opera.

Handel's *Rinaldo* was magnificent, staged with a dramatic setting of an enchanted palace with blazing battlements and with monsters spitting fire and smoke. Alexandra was so moved by the vocally elaborate long arias that were designed to display the virtuosity of the castratos. Soon, the excitement churning in her faded to the suffocating heat and oppressive smoke emitted from candles.

Everyone was watching the opera except Nicholas.

More than once, she had felt his gaze linger on her.

"Are you unwell, Alexandra?" he said.

She closed her eyes. If only she could feign sleep so she did not have to answer him. The insides of her stomach rioted a silent tattoo.

"I know you're not sleeping," he continued, pitching his voice low so he did not disturb the others. But that didn't happen and to her embarrassment, Cornelius watched her too. Nicholas stretched his leg so his boot brushed against the side of her slipper. "You haven't answered my question."

Alexandra opened her eyes, half begging him to leave her alone. If only he wouldn't pay so close attention to her. "What question?"

He muttered something under his breath. "Your pallor concerns me. I asked if you were unwell."

It was their first time in public and she didn't want to disgrace herself or Nicholas. Quiet. That was all she needed…and to lay down. Would the room ever stop rotating? "I am fine, my lord."

"Liar."

Her eyes flared at his rudeness. She ignored the small fact she was lying to him. *Let me suffer with my dignity intact.*

The muscles in her throat constricted. Alexandra clamped her hand over her mouth and ran from the box. Where could she seek privacy? A footman whirred past her. She moved down a long dark corridor. Bile rose-up her throat. Too late. She emptied the contents of her stomach in an urn. Knees shaking, she placed her hand on the wall willing the spinning to cease so she wouldn't faint dead away. A handkerchief was handed to her.

"When were you going to tell me?"

Nicholas. Oh, he had witnessed her humiliation. Dabbing her lips, she took her hand off the wall, turned, lifting her gaze to him.

Dear heavens, the tropics could be frozen beneath his narrowed cobalt eyes. Had he assumed she had kept the pregnancy from him? She wrapped her arms around herself, loathing the trembling of her limbs, and waiting until her breathing evened. "I just found out."

He crossed his arms in front of him, waiting for an explanation.

"I have been ailing for weeks, believing I had caught a ship-born malaise. This afternoon, I was ill in front of Rachel, so she arranged to have her physician examine me. He confirmed I was to be a mother, and I wanted to wait until we were alone to surprise you with the news. And now I have disgraced myself and you are angry."

She wanted to cry, to be anywhere but here. "I-I don't understand why. I thought you wanted a child."

Nicholas stood thunderstruck. "I thought you couldn't have children."

"The physician said the doctor in Deconshire was either addled or superstitious and that a fall wouldn't prevent me from having children as evidenced by my condition."

Nicholas hauled her into his arms.

"What if someone sees us?" A door opened further up the corridor and she pushed from his arms. Duke Cornelius. Thank goodness, he headed the other way.

Nicholas murmured into her ear. "To hell with everyone else. We are going to have a baby and we are going home. You must rest."

His quarrelsome bellow teased a smile from her lips. "Nicholas, I'm not dying. I'm having a baby and the doctor said I was to maintain a normal routine until I started to show."

"How long?" he demanded.

"We have seven and a half months before our child is born."

"You should be in bed."

She giggled from Nicholas' magnanimous pontification and allowed him to escort her back to the box, to make their goodbyes, happy the Duke of Westbrook had not returned.

Rachel tapped her closed fan on her lips and arched an eyebrow. "Nicholas knows?"

"You are leaving so soon?" asked Nicholas's father, standing and shooting a suspicious glance over Alexandra.

Heat rose to her face.

Anthony sat with his eyes closed, his mind immune from the opera and the commotion.

Aunt Margaret leaned forward. "Knows what?"

Oh, good Lord. If Aunt Margaret and Duke had guessed, they would think her the worst kind of woman. Hearing a whispering sound, she glanced behind her. Attention from the audience was drawn to her and not the opera. She gasped, wrung her hands together and turned away. If she were to die a thousand deaths it would not be too many.

Aunt Margaret patted her gloved fingers on Alexandra's. "There has been too much excitement for you, dear. You must go home and rest."

The Duke clapped Nicholas's back, and then smiling, bowed to Alexandra. "You are a very welcome addition to our family, Miss Sutherland."

Alexandra cringed from the unwanted attention, yet with the well-wishes, she let go a breath. Perhaps they had not suspected anything untoward.

Rachel elbowed Anthony awake.

He assessed Alexandra, and then shook Nicholas's hand. "Six hundred and nineteen divided by perimetros?"

Nicholas chuckled and Alexandra frowned, unable to grasp Anthony's cryptic message, and finding the mathematical formula odd. Nicholas placed her cape around her shoulders. She attempted to work out the formula but her mind was far too muddled.

Outside the theatre, Nicholas hailed a footman to get their coach. With his arm tightly around Alexandra, he felt her breathe in the night's damp air. A mist drew a bright sheen on the wide street beneath the lantern light and neat lines of pollarded trees, and quiet honey-colored buildings with slate roofs settled in silence. Apart from for the coaches parked down the street, people were non-existent, the opera in the third act. He used the quiet to digest the news.

They were going to have a baby. He was the happiest man on earth and nothing could dispel the wonderful feeling of becoming a father.

"What did your brother mean by six hundred and nineteen divided by perimetros?" Alexandra asked.

"He was assessing the gestation period for when a baby is born which is nine months and two days." How he loved seeing the color rise to her face and the question forming in her eyes. "My brother is a scientist. His theories are born on observations," Nicholas said.

Horses clomped over cobblestone. Full gallop. Harnesses clanged. Was it the Rutland coach? A runaway carriage? Hooves thundered.

"Look out!" yelled a footman from behind them.

The driver cracked his whip on the horses. He hurled curses. The carriage veered onto the walkway, heading straight toward them. No time. Nicholas grabbed Alexandra and rolled with her into the street, horses and carriage wheels whizzing past them, a cat's whisker breadth away.

Nicholas pulled Alexandra up and she swayed into him. "That was deliberate. We could have been killed."

Nicholas wanted to run after the ruffian but the effort would be useless, the gloom swallowing up the rig up.

The footman rushed up to them. "Are you hurt?"

"Did you see the driver?"

"No, sir. It was too dark and happened too quickly."

Nicholas's jaw hardened. He moved Alexandra inside and instructed the footman, "Go to the Rutland box and tell my family there was an attempt on our lives and to leave immediately. We will wait."

Chapter 24

"That's two attempts on your life, Alexandra. We must keep an eye out for the killers," Nicholas said the next morning. Shoulder to shoulder they moved down a splendid breakfast buffet.

"What if the killers we met last night were meant for you?" Alexandra scooped fluffy eggs on her plate, a sweet bread and black pudding. "And why didn't you wake me last night when we returned?"

Nicholas whispered huskily in her ear, "You fell asleep on the ride home and I carried you to bed. I didn't have the mind to wake you. In your condition, you need the extra rest."

Alexandra's cheeks heated and she turned from the buffet to see if anyone had heard him. Aunt Margaret smiled at one end of the table. Samuel, Anthony and Rachel were already seated and in a discussion about commerce. Nicholas's father nodded to where a servant pulled a chair out for her next to him.

Nicholas sat across from her and gestured for a servant to pour a dark, thick liquid substance in her gilded tea cup, followed by a dab of whipped cream. "You must try the drinking chocolate."

Alexandra lifted her cup and inhaled the sweet scent of chocolate and sampled the russet-colored brew. Silky smooth, heavenly bliss coated her tongue. She emitted an unladylike groan.

A servant brought a platter of golden crispy cakes oozing with melted cheese. "Fried goat cheese."

Nicholas's grin was so endearing, she instantly wished to lean across the table and kiss him. "You remembered as when I told you how I longed to see an opera."

"Of course. It will be my delight to see you savor everything for the first time, and to make-up for all the hardships you've experienced."

She cringed by being singled out. "I don't know what to say."

"I say you, enjoy," opined Aunt Margaret. Everyone laughed.

Nicholas's father, sat benignly at the head of his table, the benevolent leader of the family, dispensing charm and affection. He spoke of the days when his wife was alive, when everyone was together and no threat loomed over his family. After an hour of familial discourse and laughter, the Duke motioned for the servants to leave.

As soon as the door closed, Aunt Margaret fixed her gaze on Samuel. "Going into your history, I find it fascinating that Alexandra was not murdered nor kidnapped. You and your wife's efforts to protect Lady Alexandra Sutherland all these years were courageous. May I extend my sympathy to the loss and sacrifice of your wife."

"You can add my sentiments as well," said the Duke. "Since Alexandra is with us now, we should finish our discussion from last evening about the carriage incident at the opera, and then the occurrence in Deconshire."

"Now tell me, what new revelations have you come up with?" Aunt Margaret narrowed her gaze on Nicholas.

Nicholas cut his smoked salmon into neat even pieces. "One of the thugs we captured in Deconshire escaped and the other remains mum. I have turned him over to the magistrate and doubt if he can do any better. The best we can get him for is attempted murder. We must be careful and have full evidence before we make allegations against Lady Sutherland and her son. Those men were too scared to talk."

"It was Lady Ursula and Willean who put me aboard the *Santanas.* Isn't that enough?"

The Duke said, "Nicholas is correct. For us to clearly get Lady Sutherland and Willean we must be more cunning, and work through back doors…and that takes time."

Aunt Margaret harrumphed. "To think I came face to face with that dratted woman and her son at Kensington's soiree last week. Lady Sutherland puts on such a holier than thou presence. If I'd known what evil creatures she and her son were, I would have…I-I don't know what I would have done, but it would have turned out badly, and you'd be fetching me from the magistrate.

"What about the runaway carriage? Was it Lady Ursula's doing?" said Rachel.

Nicholas shook his head and Alexandra's heart panged for he looked tired. "Nothing. We had runners question other possible witnesses but it was too dark to identify them."

Anthony twirled his spoon, reflecting light across the table. "Perhaps the carriage incident was planned for an attack on the Rutland family and not on Alexandra."

Nicholas leaned back in his chair, clasping his hands behind his head. "Father, we've had little time to discuss affairs. Who else do you consider an enemy of the family? Have you considered Lord Eaton, having his hand in the laboratory explosion and our kidnapping?"

Alexandra stroked the pearl ring Nicholas had given her, like a touchstone that helped orient her. Lord Eaton was the father of the man Nicholas had killed in self-defense.

"Lord Eaton died of a lung ailment, a month following his son's death. I understand he'd been sick for some time and would not have had the stamina to carry out a disciplined and orchestrated plan."

Anthony helped himself to more eggs from the sideboard and returned to the table. "Cuthbert Noot had an ax to grind, and was ready to tell us who was the one responsible for trying to kill Anthony when he was shot dead. The same thing happened to Percy Devol in Boston. He was ready to kill Abigail when he, too, fell to a pistol ball. Whoever is accountable is thorough in covering up any loose ends, and he must have unrestricted assets to have had Cuthbert Noot and Percy Devol released out of Newgate to perform their vengeances."

Rachel lifted a brow at Alexandra over her tea cup. "Interesting that Lord Cornelius tired of the opera and left just before the runaway carriage affair."

Silence filled the room. Alexandra widened her eyes. Rachel's plucky spirit bred in the Colonies made her bold enough to comment on a close family friend.

Was Nicholas wary of the Duke of Westbrook's possible intrigues? He did not indicate his thoughts. She darted a glance to Nicholas's father. His hand fisted around his fork. She couldn't wait to get Rachel aside and inquire about the Duke of Westbrook.

Duke Richard smoothed butter over his sweet bread with deliberate strokes. "I'm thinking of Lord Drummond. I've fiercely opposed his policies in parliament. He stands to lose a lot if the war in the Colonies is abandoned. He has many military contracts that have made him rich and will continue to do so if the war proceeds."

Aunt Margaret stared at the Duke as he calmly took another bite of black pudding.

Nicholas's expression remained impassive. "He certainly has the means and motivation. I'd start there," he said.

The Duke brushed a thumb over his chiseled jaw. "Alexandra, per Nicholas's request, I have taken personal action on your behalf and have begun my own investigation into your heritage. Your father, Baron Stephen Sutherland, was a great friend of mine years after our time spent at Cambridge, and I knew you as a baby. When I first saw you, I knew you were a Sutherland for your eyes are unmistakable. Normally estates go to the closest living male heir, but in a private conversation with your father, he indicated he was leaving the estate to you upon his death. In no way was the Sutherland fortune to go to Lady Ursula or her son, and I'm sure Baron Sutherland being as thorough as he was, put his wishes in writing."

What? He knew her *fath*— So taken aback, Alexandra opened her mouth, but no words came. Was this true?

"You were about one and half years and already he was thinking of your future."

The sadness she'd kept long buried rose inside Alexandra. All the senseless murders. "Thank you, Your Grace. I am overwhelmed you knew my father and would take such an interest on my behalf."

The Duke scoffed. "You are to be family, and the fact remains, I'm indebted to you and I always pay my debts. I have also enlisted runners to investigate Lady Ursula's poisoning of your father as told to you by Molly, the only eyewitness. The Runners have inquired of the servants, but they are either too scared, or fear losing their jobs. Unfortunately, investigators have come up with no leads and Samuel's testimony would be considered hearsay. I am trying to find a money trail. Lady Sutherland had to pay someone to put you on the *Santanas*."

Alexandra picked at her eggs. "Calling me Lady Sutherland, will be fraudulent unless I can show clear title. To verify who I am, I must have evidence. Despite my untried youth, there is one recurring memory of my father. He would close the library door and have me trip a secret compartment in the desk into opening repeatedly. For my father to do this, meant it was important for me to know."

Aunt Margaret pulled herself up to her full height. "Nicholas, you are a very bright young man and must understand, Alexandra's right. There is a lot at stake."

Nicholas's nostrils flared. "Alexandra, I don't give a rat's ass if you are titled or not. Your belief is a childhood dream. Look where you ended up—kidnapped and to be sold into slavery. I can see where this is going and will not allow you to be anywhere near your ancestral home as long as Lady Sutherland is about."

She ran her finger on the border of her tea cup. Nicholas had reason for his outrage. Perhaps not with her, but it was human nature to blame those closest, the ones he wanted most to protect. "I am going."

Nicholas dropped his chair to all fours. "I'm not taking any chances. My job is to keep you safe."

"I cannot marry you unless my name is secured." And if he thought she was going to change her mind, he was as addled as the town drunk back in Deconshire.

"You will marry me," Nicholas stated.

"Her musing is not a childhood vision," Samuel spoke up. "Molly had seen the secret drawer. She had gone to the library to get the baby Alexandra for her nap. In fact, Molly heard Alexandra laughing and since the door was partially open, she peeked in to see what was amusing the child. Baron Stephen had Alexandra open and reopen the compartment. The week before we departed, Molly tried repeatedly to open the compartment in case there were papers that proved Alexandra's birthright. No matter how many attempts, she could never find the trip lever."

The Duke spread marmalade on his buttered bread. "I agree with Nicholas that it is too dangerous for Alexandra. You could tell someone how to do it. One of my men could break-in."

That comment drew stares from everyone except Aunt Margaret who snorted. "I would expect nothing less of you, Richard."

"It won't work," said Alexandra. "If there is any hint of activity in the library, and your man fails, Ursula will have everything in the room burned because she will realize the importance. I must be the one to locate the compartment. I'm the only one who knows the desk."

Nicholas slammed his fist on the table. The dishes jumped and so did Alexandra. "Absolutely not. I will not have you risk your life or the— Lady Ursula is on alert and probably expecting you. She will not make the same mistake twice. You will be dead."

Tears pricked the back of Alexandra's eyes. He wanted to protect her and the baby. "I was so close the last time…I have to avenge Molly's death and this is the only way…by proving who I am."

Aunt Margaret released two lumps of sugar into her tea and stirred, the spoon clanking loudly against the cup. "Your nobleness is to be admired, Nicholas, but it is not a serviceable substitute to getting things done correctly."

Rachel rebalanced her cup in the saucer. "Your Lordship, could you not have your men canvas the house to tell us when Ursula and Willean are out?"

"Yes."

Nicholas scowled. "What good will that do if it is guarded?"

Alexandra clasped and unclasped her hands. The women were circling the stubborn men and working in her favor. *Keep it up, ladies.*

Aunt Margaret drummed her fingers on the top of her cane. "We need a ruse to get Ursula and Willean out of the house."

The Duke spoke up. "Easy. I'm friends with the Somer's and will ask a personal favor to send an invitation to Lady Sutherland and Willean to his famed ball which is two days away and ample time for us to prepare."

Aunt Margaret stamped her cane on the floor with a sharp crack. "Strike Ursula at her vulnerable spot—her arrogance. She'd never decline a social occasion hosted by the Duke and Duchess of Somers. The ball is to be the crème de la crème of the season."

Nicholas narrowed his eyes on Alexandra. "I'm not happy with you involved in this idiocy at all and you know what I mean."

She paled at the innuendo. Indicating she was with child was his last trump card to gather the family against the scheme of sending a pregnant woman into danger.

Aunt Margaret huffed. "Alexandra has shown strong constitution in everything she has gone through. I'm sure she will be careful, won't you."

Bless Aunt Margaret.

Alexandra lifted her chin. "More than careful."

Nicholas's nostrils flared. "I have demands. I'm going with you on this foolishness and you are going to follow my instructions."

Alexandra didn't want Nicholas involved and was ready to protest but when she saw the storm clouds brewing, she changed her mind. *Stubborn man.* "Agreed."

Nicholas turned to his father. "For the next two days, I want your men posted near the manor for surveillance. They must remain undetected. On the night of our break-in, I want them posted around the perimeter in case there is any trouble."

"I have my own demands," said Duke Richard. "I want you armed."

Chapter 25

Anthony pulled out an ivory chess set. "Since we have two days to drive ourselves stir crazy, how about a round, dear brother? Haven't had the joy of triumph in a long time."

"Would you play against Alexandra? The game will be a distraction for her nerves."

"Where are your manners, Nicholas? To beat your fiancée would be the height of bad etiquette," Anthony joked.

Nicholas winked at Alexandra and drew out a chair for her at the table.

Alexandra smoothed her blue muslin skirts. "On the island, Nicholas introduced me to the rules, so I have a rudimentary idea of how the game is played. Am I to understand, you have never been beaten in all of England?"

"There is that," Anthony conceded. "I'll go light, even teach you a few strategies."

"Oh my, to be granted such leniency." Alexandra purposefully fluttered her hand over her heart. "Overwhelmed by your charity, I shall remain a shadow in the sun of your greater knowledge." She heard Samuel's snort come from behind the pages of the *London Chronicle*.

Nicholas poured a drink.

"Tapping the claret to celebrate my victory, brother?" Anthony needled.

"At the very least, you should allow her to go first." Nicholas leaned indolently against the fireplace mantle where he could obtain a full view of the game.

"Of course, ladies come first," Anthony said.

"Forgive me if I'm clumsy," Alexandra said, making a bold move with her castle.

"Interesting," said Anthony over the drone of conversation between Aunt Margaret and Rachel.

Anthony made his next move and on and on the game evolved. Alexandra paused overlong, making appropriate sighs and exaggerating her confusion in moving her pieces, and asking for further instruction from Anthony. She felt Nicholas smirking behind her. Indeed, Anthony was a superb player. The clock ticked in the hall and Duke Richard leaned over on the premise of procuring a book from a table. Even Nicholas's father was intrigued.

Alexandra moved another piece. Anthony frowned. Good. She had him exactly where she wanted him.

The clock struck two bells, two hours had eclipsed. Alexandra stretched, glancing around the room. Aunt Margaret ceased talking and had hobbled over to the chess table. Rachel sidled next to Aunt Margaret. Alexandra prayed Samuel would keep reading the paper and not indicate anything untoward. He'd been watching all the time.

Anthony rubbed the back of his neck. "Looks like you played quite a bit of chess on the island."

Pasting a demure expression on her face, she moved another piece in a predatory advance. "Am I satisfactory?"

He straightened in his chair. "Very."

Your brother is an apt tutor, is he not?" She managed to keep a straight face.

"Adequate," Anthony allowed.

Alexandra suppressed a laugh, sat calmly with her hands folded in her lap, totally aware of Anthony's scowl. Of course, he had his reputation, but to admit his brother was better was too difficult for his ego to swallow.

Drat. Anthony moved and it was a brilliant counter. She moved her king into play and Aunt Margaret harrumphed. Alexandra raised her head in question, finding herself under the matronly aunt's stare. She lasted five seconds before Aunt Margaret's lips twitched. Rachel nodded her head in approval.

"Nicholas, you should sit and rest," goaded his aunt. "You've stood the whole game."

"And miss the championship of a lifetime?"

"It's hard to concentrate with everyone hawking over me," complained Anthony.

Alexandra twisted her head around. With Nicholas's knowing grin, she radiated with pride. He was cheering for her. Anthony tapped his finger on the table, studying the board. With the dawning realization of the outcome, his mouth dropped open and Alexandra moved her queen in for the kill. "Checkmate."

Anthony scraped his chair backward and stood. "Impossible! I've been outfoxed. I demand a rematch. How can you play so well? I've sparred against the best in England."

Alexandra laughed. "I learned from Samuel who is a master. He played during his long journeys at sea, cultivating his game."

Samuel gestured with his pipe. "At twelve summers, Alexandra started beating me."

"To think I'm beaten by a woman. Nicholas, you knew about this? Alexandra, you are as savage as those Colonials."

"I heard that, Anthony," Rachel said. "Perhaps I'll train my skills with a bow and arrow on you."

Alexandra had heard of Rachel's skill, utilizing a crossbow in a daring escape from an attic in a burning building. Her talent as an inventor saved her and Anthony's lives.

"Typical Anthony," chortled Aunt Margaret. "He's as touchy as a beauty losing her looks."

Anthony ignored his aunt, his glare on his brother. "I'll box your ears."

Nicholas put up his fists, jabbed his brother in the arm. "Go ahead and try. You haven't bested me yet."

Even after a year of separation, Nicholas and Anthony slid into brotherly habits of baiting one another. Alexandra warmed to their camaraderie, the family relaxed enough to enjoy themselves freely. How easy to fall in love with Nicholas's family.

Nicholas took another jab at his brother. "Good for you to learn a little humility, but don't take defeat too bad. She beat me every night on the island."

Alexandra yawned and slipped between the cool sheets scented with lavender. She tugged at the lace bodice of her fine sleeping gown, luxuriating in the soft silk and laid her head on the downy pillows. No more could she attempt to keep her eyes open. The growing child inside her sapped her strength.

The door opened and Nicholas stole into the room. He slid beside her whereupon she took his face in her hands and brought it to hers.

"What about your family?"

"You escaped me once. I'm never letting you go again. I slept with you last night and you didn't even know."

Alexandra gasped. "I don't want to start off on the wrong foot with your family. They will think me a harlot if it's discovered you share my bed. I want their good opinion."

He kissed her and Alexandra automatically curled into him. "I have missed your touch so much, Nicholas."

He cupped her breasts as if feeling the weight. Against her will, her nipples hardened into peaks and she was acutely aware of a spreading ache in her breasts. "Your pregnancy has made your breasts fuller."

"Do you think you can convince me to change my mind?" she said softly.

"I am to be a duke; I see much of life like a battle to be mastered and won."

"And do you often win, my lord?"

"Almost always, my lady."

He lowered his voice until it was a deep rumble that reverberated through her. "I suppose I can't talk you out of this madness in breaking into Lady Sutherland's home?"

"My dear, Nicholas," she sighed, "What am I to do with you when you persist in being wicked?" She could feel him grinning in the darkness. "You are a scoundrel, Lord Rutland, but your efforts will not work."

Unrepentant, Nicholas did not bother to hide his appreciative groan when she reached down and touched him. "Indulge me." The hope in his voice made her smile.

"That would be unwise." Alexandra pulled away, but he snatched her back in his arms.

"Tell me why," he prodded her.

Heat flooded her body. "Because you make too much noise when we...you know."

He laughed and moved his hand over her stomach. "I can't wait to see you grow big and round with my child, Alexandra."

"With all the food you are tantalizing me with, I'll be enormous before the month is out."

"That's the idea."

The scrape of wood drew her attention. Aunt Margaret stood in the doorway in a triangle of light. Alexandra heaped the covers over Nicholas's head. The room was dark except for the light that spilled in from a candle in the hall.

"I don't mean to intrude but wish to tell you a little story about my nephew, Nicholas. When he was a boy, he possessed a penchant for getting into scrapes." She moved further into the room and Alexandra checked behind her to make sure Nicholas was concealed. "His father warned him, if there were any more mishaps, there would be repercussions. The dear boy stepped into another fight. Black eye, torn clothes, bruises. I convinced Nicholas to stay at my home while he convalesced so his father would not learn of his indiscretion. I later learned a rude boy had insulted me. Nicholas had championed me. The point I'm trying to make is Nicholas is extremely loyal and will defend and protect you. That is his character."

In the dim light, Aunt Margaret's face was silhouetted.

"If you need my help with any situation, advise me and I will help you navigate the ropes. The Rutland family is powerful, but most importantly we are devoted to one another. As for my nephew, he can be a bear at times, but he is a good man and you will make him a wonderful wife. Good night, Alexandra."

Alexandra swiped a tear, Nicholas's matronly aunt touching her heart. To be both wanted and cherished. "Good night," sniffed Alexandra.

Aunt Margaret closed the door, paused, and then stuck her head back in. "Oh…and Good night, Nicholas."

Chapter 26

Two days of waiting had paid its toll. Under darkness and through a fog laden night, Nicholas with Alexandra moved across the damp lawn of Sutherland estate and sidled up next to the house. The library was a few feet away on the first floor. *Convenient.*

Nicholas muttered, "I'm totally against this. You are with child and this goes far against my principles to protect you."

"Will you stop worrying," whispered Alexandra, and then she yelped, tripping over an unconscious, tied-up man.

His father's men were efficient.

He made a cradle out of his hands and hefted her up to the window.

"This will look great in the papers if we are caught. 'The heir to the Duke of Rutland, breaking and entering.'"

"Sh-h. Someone might hear you." The window opened with a loud screech.

"So much for a quiet, stealthy entrance." He should have had the man he hired for reconnaissance inside the house, under the guise of inspecting the chimneys to oil the window hinges. His man had learned that there were no guards posted inside, only outside which his father's men had taken care of like they did with the man Alexandra tripped over. So he allowed Alexandra this fool mission. With the baby and all, he'd never risk her safety.

Her climbing skills acquired on the island came in handy. He watched her rounded bottom disappear over the sill.

"I rather like the view and may insist you wear breeches in the future."

Alexandra stuck her head back out the window. "At a time like this?"

Nicholas heaved up and into the room. Except for the waning of the moon there was no light.

"I remember this room so well. Some of my happiest memories occurred here. I played with my blocks and dolls in front of the fireplace while my father worked. I can almost hear the scratch of his quill across paper. I can smell the burning of wax before he thumped on his seal for his finished correspondence."

Alexandra took his hand and led him to the desk. She was shaking and he longed to take her in his arms, but this task was important and they had to work fast before they were discovered.

Alexandra crawled underneath the desk, Nicholas squatting beside her, roving his hand over the smooth woodwork as if divining a drawer to magically open. "I don't feel a thing."

"I remember my father holding me on his lap, and as young as I was, saying, '*Alexandra, very important.*'"

Nicholas glanced at the door to the library, did not hear any movement from the rest of the house. *Good.* At this late hour, the servants slept. His father had come through as promised, and secured an invitation for Lady Sutherland and Willean to a soiree at the Banfield's, and then the Duke and Duchess of Somer's ball for the next night. They would be staying at the Sutherland townhouse in London for the weekend. Rutland guards were posted there to keep them updated on their movements.

He eased upward, lit a lamp and lowered it to the floor.

"Won't the light alert Ursula's guards outside?"

Nicholas patted his gun in his belt. "They will have enough headache to last them a long time. They were taken care of. I'm very thorough. I do not want to put you at any more risk than necessary."

Alexandra ran her fingers all around. Nicholas followed. Smooth, satiny moldings, flat surfaces. Not one catch. Not one depression. Not one trip-lever. "Nothing, Alexandra."

Her fingers shook. "I have come so far and refuse to leave without proof. I know it's here."

He hated hearing the pleading in her voice.

"I will not go until I've found the proof of who I am. My father and Molly will have not died in vain. This is my obligation to them."

"Enough. We have been here longer than we have allotted." He grabbed her arm.

She jerked back, and then fell to her knees, probing, poking, crying. "I cannot leave." Footsteps pounded in the outer hall.

"Hell. Had his men missed a guard posted in the house?"

As Nicholas rose, he leaned on a brass knob. Click. He stretched his hand beneath the desk. A farthing-sized button protruded. With certainty, there was a correlation with the pressure he put on the brass knob and the button. That's why no one had figured it out. He unclasped a door and a drawer slid out.

Alexandra grabbed papers, held them up to the light. "This document speaks of my inheritance. This is the evidence I've been looking for."

He stuffed the papers in his shirt, blew out the lantern. The door swung open. He jerked Alexandra to her feet, hauled her to the window. Too late. A light shone on them.

"Lady Lucy Sutherland. Is it really you...not a ghost?"

Alexandra turned and blinked. The elderly gentleman had called her by her mother's name. She remembered him. Her father's butler, Andrew Baines, older now, his cheeks furrowed and writhen like rain-washed crags. He had always been kind to her. "Bainey?"

"My God. Is it you, Lady Alexandra, all grown up?" He lifted his light and the rays spread across a portrait above the fireplace. "You have your father's eyes but you are a mirror image of your mother."

Nicholas cursed. "By God, if that isn't evidence enough."

Bainey placed the light on the desk, his mouth gaping. "I thought you had been kidnapped and died. Where have you been all these years?"

"Molly and Samuel Elwins hid me away to protect me from Ursula."

"Lady Ursula is an evil woman, mistress. I must tell you, I believe your father had suspicions of your stepmother before he died, and informed me you were the heir. Years later, your stepmother, Lady Ursula and Willean were in their cups. They were toasting each other, and she bragged how she had poisoned your father to make Willean the heir, telling him where she kept the bottle of poison in case he ever needed it."

Alexandra sobbed. "She killed Molly, too."

Bainey swore. "I overheard Lady Sutherland saying something about killing Molly. She was a good woman."

"Why didn't you come forward sooner?" Nicholas asked.

"Lady Ursula caught me eavesdropping on her poisoning the Baron. She blackmailed me, knowing I stole silver from a former employer and threatened to have me sent to Newgate. Recently I've been told by a doctor I have tumors and have months to live. I'd like to do what is right by you, Lady Sutherland, before I meet my maker."

Nicholas stepped forward. "I'm Lord Rutland. We need you to come with us to attest to Lady Ursula's crimes. You will be under my protection."

"A pleasure, milord. I've burned to see Lady Ursula pay for what she has done for a long time. What might be helpful is that I swapped a similar bottle and kept the original in safekeeping for evidence."

"Nobody's goin' anywhere because what I 'ave to say goes."

Damn. Nicholas whirled around, shoved Alexandra behind him. His stomach rolled, obviously a guard Ursula had posted inside the house. So much for his man's reconnaissance.

The man gestured with his gun to Alexandra. "'er ladyship thought you'd show up."

Definitely East Londoners. They didn't bother to pronounce their "t's" and "h's." They were large men, dressed the same, in dirty breeches and purloined frock coats. They smelled the same too. Eau de Rookeries. They both had hats. Comical. Formal top hats jammed on dirty heads. They were both bow-legged, probably from malnutrition when they were young, yet boasted an intimidating air. One had a scar down the side of his left cheek and his companion boasted a scar down his right cheek. They could have been twins.

The two men moved into the room, stopped six feet in front of him. Nicholas pulled his gun from his belt. One against two wasn't bad except he had Alexandra to protect. Not good. His father's men outside, too far to help.

Bainey froze, his hands up, a scared man, resembling an unhappy mastiff. Not much help there.

Both thugs grinned like gargoyles. "You can shoot one of us, your lordship, but you still 'ave the ot'er bloke to deal wit'."

Nicholas flexed his left shoulder, ran some muscle tension up through his back and shoulders. "Not if I dispatch both of you first."

They both laughed. The thug on his left moved closer, waved his gun. Nicholas followed to his left. A candlestick was within reach of Bainey. Would the old servant show courage? He needed a distraction. Keep talking.

"I can double Ursula's pay. No questions asked. You gentleman could set yourselves up nice in a country house. Take my deal now. You won't have regrets."

Right scar laughed. "We're doing just fine, gent."

"So, let me guess. You'll tie us up. Deliver us to Lady Sutherland, and then hide in the Colonies."

"Brilliant, yer lordship."

"I have matchless deductive powers, able to read minds, and from time to time, give patronage to idiots."

Left scar edged closer. "Ye think ye're funny."

Nicholas flexed his muscles, he itched for some hard-knuckle fighting. "I am funny." He moved a little closer to tighten up the triangle. Bainey reached for the candlestick. The ancient butler had more mettle than he thought.

Right scar lowered his gun. Nick hooked a right, thrust Right scar's arm up. The pistol fired, the round hitting the ceiling. Plaster showered over them. Right scar's only chance.

An object flew past Nicholas's ear. The crack of glass against bone. Left scar went down. Effective, whatever it was.

"He's mine," Nicholas growled and dove for Right scar. He clubbed his fist into Right scar's face, drove it through his cheek, toppling both to the floor. Right scar lay limp beneath him, out cold. Nicolas twitched his nose, lifted off Right scar's body. He brushed off plaster. The lingering odor from Right scar stayed.

Bainey fetched the two guns. Nicholas took them from the servant's shaking hands. "Two guys. Two guns. Three seconds."

Nicholas did a double-take. Black liquid pooled around Left scar's head. She had laid the wretched scum low with an ink bottle?

Alexandra threw her hands up. "What was I supposed to do? Wait until you got around to clubbing them?"

He wiped the sweat from his head, and then wrapped his arm around her. She would always be his Alexandra. "Let's go before there are any more mishaps. My carriage is beyond the tree line."

Chapter 27

$\mathcal{A}$lexandra entered the ballroom, her gaze darting, hands fidgeting at her side. Her mouth fell open at the opulence, from the painted mural of the crowned Apollo and his drawn bow, joining forces with Poseidon punishing the people of Troy. Huge chandeliers of gold and crystal flashed like tiny suns, the polished floors reflecting the candlelight. White marble columns lined-up along the walls, like soldiers reaching for the vault of heaven.

The Duke and Duchess of Somers had spared no expense and the evening was trumpeted to be the marquee event of the year. Flanked by Rachel and Aunt Margaret, and waiting to be announced, Alexandra stood at the top of the stairs looking over the lords and ladies whirling about the ballroom in a colorful array of silks and satins.

Tonight, was especially important. Nicholas and his father had been gone for the better part of the day. She had no idea what they had arranged, receiving a note at noon that she was to attend the Somer's ball with Aunt Margaret and Rachel, and that everything was in place.

Butterflies flip-flopped in her stomach.

Aunt Margaret leaned over and spoke low and confidingly. "In addition to other planned events tonight, we must remain within the boundaries of polite society. Remember, only two dances with Nicholas, no more. And only one dance per each gentleman. The subtlety conveys your coming out, and hints Nicholas is your intended, a strong statement to the rest of the world.

Alexandra was announced as Lady Alexandra Sutherland. She halted at the top of the stairs, forcing herself to step down in a graceful manner, attempting a ladylike glide toward the bottom, instead of running like she did down the mountain on the island. Was everyone in the room scrutinizing her because of her name?

"They are looking at you because you are the mystery woman who spent time on the island with Lord Nicholas," confirmed Rachel. "With the powerful Duke of Rutland's nod and Nicholas's, I predict, you will be asked to dance many times."

Alexandra resisted the urge to tug her new gown upward. "This neckline is scandalous. I must look like a courtesan."

"Look at Nicholas," Rachel angled her head. "The desired effect is devastating."

She scanned the crush for Nicholas. His dark head was bent low as he listened attentively to a portly gentleman beside him. He laughed at something the man said, but he watched her beneath hooded eyes and caught her anxious glance. A reassuring smile tugged at the corners of his mouth.

As prophesied, Alexandra danced and danced. A legion of gentlemen's faces blurred. Beneath her lashes, she studied Nicholas, leaning indolently against a marble column. Dark formfitting evening clothes hugged the lean, taut lines of his body. Pale grey breeches clung to the defined curves of his strong thighs like a besotted lover. The clothing's restrictive elegance somehow enhanced the untamed, earthy quality that radiated from him. She giggled remembering his torn breeches on the island, and then sighed, admiring everything about him, from the easy way he wore his elegant clothes to his sophisticated charm.

For a fleeting moment, the memory of the way his mouth had felt moving over hers tingled through her, causing a misstep. She begged her partner for refreshment.

Alexandra allowed the gentleman to escort her to the side. Her breath hitched. She faced Nicholas's uncle, the Duke of Westbrook. His clothes were beautifully made and fit him well, and he possessed the pale petulant look of a true aristocrat.

"Good evening, my lady." His tongue darted over his lips.

Alexandra inclined her head in acknowledgment. How he watched her like a falcon does a rabbit. Intense, single-minded, and she, like the prey grasped within a peregrine's claw, kicking and screaming to get free. She shuddered, and then gratefully accepted a dance from a flaxen-hair gentleman.

An hour passed and Alexandra grew more distracted, looking for Ursula and Willean. So far, they had not appeared. Had they returned to her ancestral home? No. Duke Richard had verified they were coming. Oh, how she wished she had been able to talk to Nicholas earlier. What had he and his father schemed?

With Aunt Margaret and Rachel, Alexandra repaired to a dressing room. An altercation of some sort preceded their arrival. A younger woman shouted and cursed an older woman. The older woman's hands covered her face, reduced to tears.

"Lady Dabney..." said the younger woman, "...everyone in the ton knows you are penniless because or your drunken, profligate husband. He has squandered away all your son's inheritance. And your husband owes my father thousands. To think your unfortunate manor is not enough to pay all your husband owes my father. Well, I guess you will be spending time in debtor's prison when your husband dies."

The hackles on Alexandra's neck went up. She had heard enough of the conversation to glean the bullying tactics of the younger woman especially when the older woman's humiliation existed from her husband's sins and out of her control.

"Excuse me," Alexandra said.

The younger woman whirled, her hands clenched in tight fists. Alexandra stared back. Lady Susannah Tomkins, Nicholas's former fiancée. Never did she expect a woman whose beauty rivaled most women would be so unkind. "What a cruel, unfortunate creature you are. How dare you?"

Lady Susannah scowled, her face contorted. "Oh, I dare. And to whom do I have the misfortune of speaking with?"

"You already know the answer to that question. You were practically falling out of your opera box, glaring daggers at me."

Lady Susannah made a little moue of her mouth. "Oh, Nicholas's whore from the island."

Rachel gasped and so did the older lady. Blood rushed to Alexandra's face. She was at a disadvantage, an unfamiliar feeling with which she was unaccustomed and did not like.

Aunt Margaret squeezed in front of her. "What is the rumor about Arthur, your stable master? And then, the gardener and onto a variety of young men around London. You are a very busy girl, Lady Susannah."

Lady Susannah paled.

Aunt Margaret didn't just shoot arrows, she hit with the full onslaught of a hundred cannons. Lady Susannah's mouth worked up and down. She poked a gloved finger at Aunt Margaret. "I'll get even with you."

"Lady Susannah, you don't even want to attempt such a feat. By the way, what happened with that circus performer last week?"

"He was an actor," Lady Susannah snapped, then slapped her hands on her face, tricked into revealing her latest indiscretion. Her face beet red and her neck veins popping, she turned on her heel and huffed from the powder room.

Rachel fanned herself. "I have to say you did right, Aunt Margaret, knowing how you hate to be wrong."

"Wrong? I wouldn't know. I'm not familiar with the phenomenon." Aunt Margaret smirked.

Alexandra laughed. "You surrounded her like General Washington did to the Hessians at Trenton. You were brilliant."

Aunt Margaret smacked her lips in distaste. "Surrounding the Hessians was an easy endeavor. All Washington had to do was play on their arrogance."

"Exactly," Rachel contended.

"I'm not arrogant. I'm confident," snorted Aunt Margaret. "As to my nephew, Nicholas, he was never smitten with Lady Susannah, nor was he blind to her faults, but he was duty bound. I never liked the girl. Plotted against her. She never had a chance. Not that I needed to scheme against her. Quite accidently, I came upon another weapon."

Rachel laughed. "And what weapon was that, Aunt Margaret?"

"Why our girl, Alexandra. She has him eating out of her hand."

Aunt Margaret wobbled to the settee and sat next to the weeping older woman. "You can live in my home, Lady Dabney. It has been vacant for some time and needs the tender company of an occupant."

Alexandra gasped. *Lady Jane.* "Did I hear, right? Are you Lady Jane Winthrop Dabney? Captain Sharp's, Lady Jane?"

Lady Jane clamped a hand to her chest. Was the old woman about to swoon?

"You know John? I mean, Captain Sharp?"

Alexandra took hold of the woman's hands. "Lady Jane, it is an honor to meet you. Please call on me tomorrow for tea. I have something very important to discuss, but I can't tell you now. Sleep well tonight. You and your son's fortunes have been changed."

Alexandra left behind a bemused Rachel and an intrigued, Aunt Margaret and returned to the ballroom. Duke Cornelius abruptly moved in front of her, and bowed. She opened her mouth to protest when he took her into his arms for a waltz. In no way did she like how he manhandled her into the dance without her permission, but was reluctant to be at odds with someone Nicholas considered family. She had to admit, his dancing was flawless as he whirled her around the ballroom.

"Would you like to visit my home?" said Duke Cornelius and Alexandra snapped her eyes to his. His invitation seemed improper. "I promise not to bite," he joked.

He was so charming that Alexandra raced through possibilities that she had been wrong about her opinion of him. Perhaps she had been unfair in judging him from the start. He had only showed kindness to Nicholas and his family and to her. But the familiarity of his voice nagged her.

"Of course, when Nicholas is free, we would love to visit."

He bestowed her with a tight smile, obviously not liking her response. No, that was ridiculous. She was imagining the worst.

"Of course, with Nicholas. I presumed——"

"Presume nothing, Lord Westbrook. I beg your pardon, but my nerves are raw tonight." She relaxed a notch.

"I understand. A young lady making a sensation on her first introduction can be allowed to have emotion."

Why did his teasing possess the same discord as a bow that slipped off the strings of a viola? And where had Nicholas disappeared to? Alexandra's shoulders dipped in disappointment. He had not claimed a single dance.

"We can discuss the Indians in the Colonies. I have a fascination for some of their customs." Duke Cornelius stared at her lips, his head hovering near her face, and for one moment she thought he meant to kiss her. "You are an intoxicating combination of beauty and grace."

She blinked not only from the rapid and bizarre change in subject manner but by the fact he had finessed her to an outer courtyard. No one was about. Inside the shell of calm, she'd closed around her was a chaos so loud, she couldn't think. "Duke Cornelius, I tire from so much dancing and wish refreshment," she whispered in warning and stepped back from him.

The duke held her fast. "I am utterly captivated with you, Lucretia."

"I am not Lucretia." She flung his arms from her. Took two steps back. He had called her Lucretia at the opera, and it was the second time he had mistaken her for Nicholas's mother.

He stood there for a moment, his imperturbable black eye studying her. The glass eye, unmovable and just as black, haunting her, and in sharp contrast to his snowy white wig. Perhaps he was one of those unfortunate souls whose mind weaved in and out of two worlds. For a long time, he was so silent, she thought he'd turned to wood.

"My apologies, Lady Alexandra. I will fetch your champagne." He turned and strode off toward the house.

The moment he walked through the archway, Alexandra's breath came out in a long rush of relief. Whirling around, she hurried to the far end of the courtyard, entering the ballroom on the opposite side.

From that point on, she was tense and jumpy, half expecting the Duke of Westbrook to accost her in the ballroom. While dancing with another swain, she spied him twice more, standing alone next to a pillar. When he vanished, she was thoroughly relieved.

She danced several more sets and allowed her last partner to escort her to Aunt Margaret and Rachel. Surrounded by a bevy of admirers plying for her attention, Alexandra laughed and allowed them to flirt outrageously, anything to divert the tension coiling in her stomach. Even Aunt Margaret and Rachel laughed from their antics.

There was no mistaking the rigid line of Nicholas's shoulders or the taut line of his jaw as he headed straight to her. *Jealous?* This was a side of Nicholas she had not seen before and a new experience for her.

"Knowing my nephew, suppressing his Neanderthal roots, watching you dance with other men is an exercise for him," said Aunt Margaret. "I'm surprised he doesn't wield a club."

When he was near, he flicked a level, impassive glance over the men standing around Alexandra, and they parted to make a place for him as if he had ordered them aside. He glanced over his shoulder at the manservant hovering near the wall, and drinks were produced without a word being spoken.

He offered his arm and maneuvered her away to the privacy of the next two columns, yet within decorum. She was happy to be alone with him.

Grinning wolfishly, he surveyed her gown.

Alexandra lifted her chin and offered, "The underskirts are soft and full as angels' wings so that when I glide past, you can hear the material sighing across the floor, or so claims the dressmaker."

His mouth quirked in a smile and his gaze dipped to touch the rounded fullness of her breasts where they pushed up against her décolletage.

Self-consciously, she ran her fingers over the clinging silk folds of her dress, her muscles, belly-low, tightened. "Your manners are outrageous, Lord Rutland. You make me feel undressed and how you manage not to choke on fumes of sulfur is a marvel."

"I hate this charade. I'm beginning to think Aunt Margaret has a twisted sense of humor and enjoys seeing me chomp at the bit with her proprietary rules. You belong to me. Not those infantile swains mooning about you."

Alexandra laughed. "I cannot be seen overly long with you. My reputation will be ruined."

"Reputation be damned. With that gown you are wearing, I'm ready for a fight…allowing these juveniles to ogle you. I have half a mind to carry you off—"

She sipped her champagne, her gaze roving over his body inch by inch, from head to foot, deliberately repaying him for the lingering glance he'd subjected her to. His nostrils flared. Her feminine side basked in the power she had over him.

His voice dipped deep and husky. "Rather bold, my lady. When we were on the island, I would have thrown you on the sand and made wicked love to you for such activity, our bodies sticking and sucking in the tropical heat."

Her nipples hardened as if he had lightly scraped his thumbs over them.

"Hell, when we are alone tonight, I will touch and taste every part of you until your body hums."

"A pulsing, throbbing desire pulsed from her center core. Damn him. He was just as adept at this game as she was. "Nicholas, you must stop. Your father approaches."

Duke Richard Rutland joined them while Alexandra tamped down the flames Nicholas had wrought. The gentleman accompanying his father was richly dressed in a green embroidered frock-coat, satin vest and matching breeches, yet his face, like a pumice stone, flaunted dissonance with his white wig. She was so glad Nicholas did not adopt the style of headdress and wore his dark hair, fashionably pulled back in a queue.

"Lady Sutherland, may I introduce you to Lord Drummond. We serve together in Parliament," said Nicholas's father.

Alexandra blinked. Was this the man responsible for what had happened to the Rutland's? What scheming had Nicholas and his father devised? Was this the product of their conspiring and what had required their attention all afternoon?

No. Nicholas and his father were trying to figure out who the Rutland enemies were and wanted her opinion.

"Lord Nicholas, always a pleasure. How was your trip on the island? Your shipboard journey with the Portuguese? I understand you were to sail onto Brazil. How horrible your fate would have been enslaved in the jungle," said Lord Drummond.

Nicholas placed his glass on a servant's passing tray, and then narrowed his eyes on the English lord. "You are well informed of my travels, Lord Drummond."

Lord Drummond's lip curled back. "It is my business to know the goings on in London."

Alexandra looked from Nicholas to Duke Richard to Lord Drummond. Hostility brewed and roiled as thick as a suffocating cloud.

"Your journey, Lady Sutherland," Lord Drummond addressed her, "must have an interesting twist as does your mysterious reappearance."

Nicholas took a step into Lord Drummond. "She is Lady Alexandra Sutherland. There is no doubt."

Her heart panged. Nicholas protected her. He did not leave room for suspicion about her heritage.

Lord Drummond put up his hands. "I bow to your greater knowledge. No need for an altercation and I certainly do not desire a calling out." He turned to Alexandra. "My apologies, if there is any offense, *Lady Sutherland*."

"None whatsoever." Alexandra placed her hand on Nicholas's arm, his muscles flexed beneath his coat. She angled her head to the gathering stares. "A spectacle would be momentous."

"You have profited well with the warfare in the Colonies," Duke Richard accused.

Alexandra raised an eyebrow to Nicholas's father's baiting of Lord Drummond.

"Keeps me heavy in the pockets," Lord Drummond said.

Deep, rough-edged with deadly calm, Lord Richard Rutland said, "You care nothing for your country, but wish only to suck her inmost vitals, to feast on her entrails, and finally glut your devouring maws on her lifeless corpse. Your kind are a scourge to England."

When Drummond smiled, he reminded Alexandra of a vulgar caricature she had seen of a corpulent man, his lips drawn back, his broad teeth displayed like the white keys of a pianoforte and gorging on a whole ox.

"It would be healthier for you, Lord Rutland to oblige the current policies."

"Is that a threat?" said Duke Richard. "I hope not."

A muscle ticked in Nicholas's jaw. "You will save yourself pain and trouble by admitting your *mistakes.*"

"Mistakes? I never make the same mistake twice." Lord Drummond was cryptic.

Nicholas and Duke Richard's provocation was deliberate. Alexandra widened her eyes. The Duke of Westbrook joined them.

Nicholas curved his hands into fists. "Be aware, I'll not be a fool nor will I allow lenience to stand in my way, to exercise what is proper revenge."

"How dare you threaten me," said Drummond.

"Perhaps you would indulge me and make a scene...or...we can go outside."

"Now see here." And then a sudden realization dawned on Lord Drummond as he interpreted the real bone of contention. His face grew mottled with rage. "How dare you accuse me of misdeeds done to you and your family. I claim nothing about it, nor will I continue this conversation." He pivoted and left.

"He is lying," said Cornelius. "There should be serious consequences for what he has done to your family."

Nicholas lips were pressed together in a thin line as he watched Lord Drummond cross the ballroom, and then he glared at the Duke of Westbrook. Alexandra let out a breath. Nicholas, all powerful and lean grace, hauled her onto the dance floor.

She stepped on Nicholas's foot, apologized. "I believe Lord Drummond is telling the truth. Greed is his only master, not conspiracy."

"Stop being nervous. Didn't I tell you everything is going to work out perfectly?"

"You have told me nothing. I have just witnessed an altercation with Lord Drummond and your family and wasn't told beforehand. I'm upset because you have left me in the dark all day."

"The exchange with Lord Drummond was a calculated provocation and he passed with flying colors. Yet, what you should be feeling is embarrassment for me."

She choked. "How is that?"

"You left me impotent by knocking out the wretch with the scar with an ink bottle. If word got around—"

Alexandra laughed. "By the way, I've invited a surprise guest tomorrow for tea."

"Who?"

"Lady Jane Dabney Winthrop." Alexandra summarized the confrontation in the dressing room. A swift revelation occurred to her. Eyes widening, she said, "Leave it to you, Nicholas to make me laugh and distract me."

"I'd like to distract you other ways, but we have other more important issues to address." Nicholas angled his head to the top of the stairs. "Your stepmother and Willean have arrived."

On cue, Duke Richard Rutland bowed to Lady Ursula Sutherland. He guided her and her son, Willean to the far corner of the ballroom where a drape covered an exit. A footman held back the drape and opened the door so they could enter Lord and Lady Somer's private quarters. Nicholas's father was solicitous and flattering. Ursula could not refuse, and enamored with the Duke of Rutland's sole attention.

Patting Alexandra's hand, Nicholas steered her into the room and toward the trio. To finally face Ursula and Willean. So many years, so many emotions. She stopped.

Nicholas whispered in her ear. "You never told me about the enormous black mole on your stepmother's cheek. Looks like a hairy spider sunk its fangs into her skin permanently, planting itself there."

"I know what you are doing, Nicholas."

"You can do it, Alexandra. I'm behind you. My father has arrangements in play. Trust me. She cannot hurt you anymore." He propelled her forward.

When Alexandra entered, Lady Ursula's face went through a myriad of changes from shock, to hatred, to glaring. "So here is the thief who broke into my home. I will have you arrested for robbing me."

"Really?" said Alexandra, reassured by Nicholas's strong presence as he moved beside her.

"What about your kidnapping of Alexandra Sutherland?" said Nicholas.

Lady Ursula's voice held a rasp of acidity. "Lord Rutland. What would ever give you such thoughts?"

Willean cursed. "This woman is a liar and an imposter."

"An imposter? What motivated you to put me on a Portuguese slaver, Lady Ursula?" said Alexandra.

"I do not know anything about what you speak of, whoever you claim to be," said Ursula.

"To reinforce any skepticism, I am Lady Alexandra Sutherland as proven by documents taken from my own home, and true heiress to the Sutherland holdings that you stole from me as a child."

Ursula snorted, looked rabidly about. "You are an imposter, parading around, impersonating a child who died years ago. Those documents are worthless. You'd never be able to prove it."

"You killed Molly and you poisoned my father," Alexandra said through angry tears.

Ursula's laugher trilled across the room. "Stephen's bones have been cold for seventeen years. All you have is the ramblings of a madwoman. No one in their right mind would ever listen to a beggared fortune hunter and her tales."

A disturbance came from the opposite side of the room. Doors opened. Soldiers filed in, and then the King appeared, followed by her father's butler, Andrew Baines. Lady Ursula's face flashed horror. Shocked, Alexandra fell into a deep curtsy as well as everyone else. "Your Majesty."

Willean bowed, and started shaking.

"You are an evil woman, Lady Ursula, and the whole world will know it," said Alexandra emboldened by the presence of the King. "There was one eye witness to your crime, Andrew Baines.

283

He also heard you bragging about what you did to Molly. He even produced the bottle of poison that you used to kill my father."

"Take them to the magistrate," ordered the King.

Willean stepped backward, threw off his guards and ran to the door. Nicholas stuck out his leg, tripping him and he sprawled on the floor. "I've done nothing——" He pounded his fists on the parquet, screaming until the guards lifted him.

"You were an accessory, and it was your idea to sell me into slavery," said Alexandra.

Lady Ursula attempted to shake off her guards, her voice dripping with venom. "I should have had you killed, Alexandra, but foolish Willean had a soft heart."

"Enough," snapped the King. "I've heard evidence from Andrew Baines and Lord Rutland, and I don't want my evening spoiled more than it has already."

The King turned to Alexandra. "Lady Sutherland, your father was a good friend of mine. I was saddened at the time of his passing and enraged when I learned of the machinations of Lady Ursula and her son.

"Now to the matter of the Sutherland lands. Lord Richard petitioned me in your favor and as it is known that some titles are distinctive and pass onto female heirs. My secretary has read your papers as dictated by your father's hand, and it is my pleasure to inform, that you will be bequeathed the Sutherland lands and do not need to go any further with officialdom. I waive all constraints as to what is duly yours."

"Thank you, your Majesty." Alexandra pressed a hand to her chest. The presence of the King and his support left her dazed. So, this was the big secret Nicholas and his father and conspired all afternoon.

All the sacrifice, struggle and suffering triumphed in justice. With certainty, her father and Molly were smiling down on her. Just then the room began to move. Dizzy, sweat beaded on her forehead. Oh dear, was she going to swoon?

"I look forward to your upcoming nuptials," said the King, winking at Nicholas. "I assume I'll be invited."

Nicholas bowed and Alexandra saw a pleased sparkle in his eyes as she curtseyed again. "Yes, Your Majesty."

The King clapped his hand on Duke Richard's shoulder. "Cousin, I'd like a good game of chess and lack for decent competitors. It has been too long."

Duke Richard laughed as he walked away with King George and his retinue. "In the future, I will produce an opponent, in fact, my new daughter-in-law to be who has surprising aptitude."

Chapter 28

*I*n the south salon of the Duke of Rutland's townhouse, Sebastian, the butler announced Lady Jane Winthrop Dabney. Alexandra smiled and motioned Lady Jane to a brocade settee. Nicholas had volunteered to take her son, John for a tour of the gardens.

Alexandra poured tea, having dismissed all the servants for the privacy of the occasion. Lady Jane looked at the grandeur, clasped and unclasped her hands. "I'm overwhelmed by your attention, Lady Sutherland, and for Lord Rutland to take an interest in my son, giving him a tour of the gardens, but I am unable for the life of me to understand why?"

Alexandra placed her hand on the older woman to quell her shaking. "You are in good company, Lady Jane. You do not need to be worried."

"May I ask how you made the acquaintance of Captain Sharp? Is he alive?"

Alexandra shook her head sadly, allowing the truth to sink in.

Lady Jane began to cry.

"I want you to know, your Captain Sharp, in a way, saved our lives."

She frowned. "Saved your lives?"

Alexandra nodded and gave her a summary of events, how they found the cottage and supplies that helped them survive. Finally, she presented the locket and well-thumbed book. "This is Captain Sharp's diary. He died with the locket you gave him over his heart. He never stopped loving you."

Lady Jane took the locket, clenching the gold heart-shaped piece in her fist. "This is my locket. I remember giving it to him before he left. When he didn't return—"

"—You thought he had died. But he lived." Alexandra tapped the book. "In his diary, you will learn that he had returned to England, discovered you were married and expecting your first child. In no way did he desire to upset your life. Heartbroken, he quietly moved away to a deserted island and lived out his days alone."

Lady Dabney placed her palm on her chest. "If I only knew, I would have sailed away with him. I loved John more than life itself."

She started crying, full drenching sobs. "I waited and waited for him. I found myself with John's child. My father was a strict man and would have thrown me out on the streets. My only recourse was to accept Sir Dabney's proposal. I never loved him."

"Sir Dabney," Alexandra said.

Lady Jane nodded. "I had to protect my child. I loathed Sir Albert Dabney. He was a charlatan, and I soon learned he was a womanizer, drinker and had gambled away my dowry. When my father died, and left me his estate Albert wasted the entirety. Now he has left us with tremendous liabilities and terrible poverty. Every day I fend off creditors. Sir Dabney is to die soon. The doctors say he has two to six months. His profligate lifestyle caught up to him.

At least he will be in a better place while I face the looming threat of debtor's prison. Oh, how I had high hopes for my son. He is very intelligent and I wanted him to continue his education, but..."

Alexandra gave her a handkerchief. Her son, John, was Captain Sharp's child? Alexandra imagined the terrible paradox Lady Dabney found herself in. Unmarried and pregnant? Captain Sharp's delays fueled her desperation. "We all make mistakes, have struggles and regrets. But you are not your mistakes."

Alexandra moved to the door, and opened it a crack. "Lord Rutland."

Nicholas and John Dabney entered. John's dark hair and good looks at sixteen years, were probably from his father. He sat on the settee and put his arm around his mother. "I have had the most wonderful time with Lord Rutland. Mother, have you been crying?"

Six footmen entered and deposited three heavy chests. At Nicholas's nod, they departed He locked the door.

If Lady Dabney or her son thought his behavior odd, they did not indicate.

Alexandra stood next to the chests. "What I'm about to reveal, will give you the power to shape both you and your son's futures."

"I-I don't understand," said Lady Dabney.

"Captain Sharp's last wish was for you to have this gift," said Alexandra.

Alexandra and Nicholas popped open the trunks. Gold coins, pearls, and gemstones glittered and gleamed.

Lady Dabney' jaw dropped open.

John Dabney was thunderstruck. "Mother, I demand to know who is Captain Sharp and why would he give us his treasure?"

Alexandra lifted some gold pieces and dropped them into Lady Dabney's hands. "This is why he left you, but unfortunate circumstances, meaning storms, and then being enslaved by Barbary pirates, prevented him from returning to you on time.

Lady Dabney broke into sobs again, and hugged her son. "Captain Sharp was your father. You are named after him. When we get home, we will have a talk."

"I recommend you keep your treasure in our care until your husband dies," said Nicholas. "That way, you can keep it from dishonest creditors."

Nicholas put his arm around a beaming Alexandra. "I have one request, Lady Dabney. I expect you and your son to attend our wedding."

Chapter 29

*W*eeks of socials, balls, soirees, fittings, presented a whirlwind of activity and had drained Alexandra of energy. On top of that came the new responsibilities of her ancestral estate. She and Nicholas had visited often, putting Andrew Baines and Samuel in charge. Lady Sutherland and Willean were set to go on trial and had been placed in Marshalsea Prison, far away from causing any more harm.

Thankfully, Nicholas had seen Alexandra's momentum waning and insisted on moving everyone to Belvoir Castle where she would have more privacy and rest.

Awestruck, Alexandra was speechless at her first glimpse of Belvoir, the Rutland ancestral home. Stately English oak trees lined the road with a glimpse of a stone edifice far up above. Truly having no idea of Nicholas's wealth or the size of his estate, she could only stare. Manicured lawns, formal gardens, mazes, and a lake dotted with snowy white swans. Further across the green valley, were vineyards, fields of young grain and verdant pastures that looked like crushed velvet. Sheep grazed on a distant high slope, enhancing the pastoral landscape. Taking in the spectacular scenery, Alexandra clapped her hands to her face.

How she itched to explore Belvoir's grounds, so unlike the coastal village where she had grown up in, and a far different topography of the Caribbean island she and Nicholas had lived on. The coach lumbered up the mile-long, convoluted lane, her breath caught when the grandiose stone edifice materialized on the horizon.

"My goodness, Nicholas, it's a castle. Are those turrets?" She gaped, entranced by the castle's enormity.

"Indeed," he murmured.

She shot him a glance. His gaze was fastened on the horizon, and a smile curved his lips. Unreserved pride shone in his eyes as he observed his ancestral home.

He loves Belvoir.

Alexandra smiled again and focused her attention to the carriage window once more. At least a hundred beveled windows caught the afternoon sun, dazzlingly refracting the golden rays. The castle glowed as if it were alive, a living breathing entity. She inhaled, overcome with the splendor of the magnificent castle and grounds.

How was she to be mistress of such a majestic estate? Nothing in her life had prepared her to run such a vast household. Did Nicholas have any notion how ill-prepared she was for such an over-whelming task?

Before the carriage rolled to a stop, two liveried servants descended the manor's granite steps. She clasped her skirts, press-ing her fingers into her new brocade gown. At least this time she was properly attired before meeting the servants. Alighting, Nicholas then handed Alexandra down. She was aware of the covert, curious stares sent her way by the footmen and line of servants. Smiling, she shook everyone's hand, and then Nicholas whisked her away into the castle. She passed a double stairway that climbed infinitely upward, and hosted rows of ancestral paintings.

She was out of breath. "Nicholas, where are you leading me?"

He pulled her down a deep corridor where a burst of light glowed at the end. A conservatory with large glazed windows on the sides and, sloping glass at the top, rounded up to an artful cupola. The minute they entered, heat and humidity swelled. Surrounded by tropical plants and rich vibrant tropical flowers, she extended her arms and twirled with warm memories. "Oh, it is just like the island. How I miss our sojourn there and wish we could turn back the time."

She skipped under a bower, following along a path, delighting in brightly colored crotons, scorching bromeliads, and brilliant orchids. She turned and Nicholas was gone. Where was he?

She found him leaning against a smooth glass door, the light illuminating his fawn-colored breeches, white shirt, and dark hair. Like the light that surged on the crest of an incoming wave, he took her breath away.

"Looking for me?" He tossed an orange to her. "I think you will find it the right sweetness."

She inhaled the strong citrus scent. "This is where you learned to identify tropical plants," she accused laughingly. How she missed the island...long sultry nights...what he did to her...felt her muscles tighten as desire warmed her to the core.

He took her hand. "Come."

"Where are we going now?"

"We have unfinished business."

An indulgent smile was his only answer.

She stopped, pulling her hand away. "How can you think of something like that at a time like this?"

"I'm to be a duke soon. My father wants to turn over the responsibility during the next year. I must show you to your chambers." He cuffed her chin with one finger.

"Why, we need to…" She couldn't think of what they needed to do. Those damned eyebrows were tilted her way. Like the faint exquisite music of a dream, he murmured into her ear and her pulse flickered and leapt.

Nicholas dismissed her lady's maid and Alexandra turned to him.

"What will the servants think?"

"Considering that my entire adult life, I've never paid much heed to the way things are "supposed to be," I can't imagine why now I would be doing so. I pay them to be discreet and after two days of celibacy, I want to be alone with you."

He watched her walk around, looking at the pink peacock silk wallpaper, fingering the silver brushes on the vanity and admiring the rose brocade bedcoverings of the mahogany four poster bed. In the glow of the afternoon light, he saw the provocative goddess she had been that first day on the beach. He heard again, the sweet dulcet tones of her voice on the other side of the planks in the hold of the *Santanas*. He saw the woman who dug in the dirt to provide them with sustenance. He saw the woman who mocked him out of his doldrums. His heart hammered in his chest.

He stared at her intently. "If I were a painter, I'd start with making a line of dark sienna against the light behind you."

And still he stared at her. Her hair gleamed like beams of sunlight, cascading down her back and around her shoulders. Something sprang free in his chest. Its newness was at first, painful, but the feeling resolutely exploded forth with a life and vigor of its own. Something marvelous, implausible, and all-consuming.

This woman was to be his wife and carried his child. She was made to be worshipped.

"Ten of my bedrooms in Deconshire could fit in this room. I don't know how I'm going to get accustomed to all of this space..." she turned to him, "...unless I have you to share it with."

He pointed to her dressing room and a long dark corridor. "The connecting door to my chambers."

She licked her lips. "Oh, I suppose that is practical."

He closed the space between them, bent his head, kissing her long and *lingeringly*.

She raised her head and put a finger to her lips and smiled. She undid his cravat, unbuttoned his shirt and eased him out of it. She ran her hands over his chest and his muscles flexed. She pointed to the chair for him to sit, and then pulled off his boots. This new venue where she undressed him left a hard hum of lust flowing through his veins. She ran a finger over him, outlining his rigid manhood.

"Um, I approve," she said and left him there, heat curling inside him.

He leapt up, crossing the distance in two easy strides, spun her around, undid her buttons and untied her corset. Two could play the same game.

Her gown pooled at her feet. He swung her up into his arms and carried her to the big four-poster. He shrugged out of his breeches and lay beside her, her soft breasts teasing his chest.

Alexandra sighed. "The minute I heard your voice on the *Santanas*, I felt safe. You had come like a Guardian angel to protect me."

Nicholas ran a forefinger over her lovely cheek. "You're safe from everything here at Belvoir—except me."

Her soft lips parted with only the slightest urging from his probing tongue. Her arms automatically went around his neck as she drew his tongue into her mouth, then gave him hers. He teased her, tormented her, offered himself to her by thrusting deep with his tongue, then leisurely withdrawing and thrusting again and again, until Alexandra clung to him, her mouth moving back and forth over his in passionate surrender.

He stroked her hair and slid his hand down over her throat to her breasts, circling the dusky crests with his thumb until they stood up proudly. He caressed the line of her back and over her rounded hips. In response, she weaved her soft arms about his neck, splaying her fingers behind his shoulders and back.

He had not imagined that any woman could create such desire in him, could arouse such passions, such a deep tempest. Her scent and heat surrounded him like a sensual miasma. He rolled atop her into the white slant of afternoon sun.

When he entered her, her eyes closed and he saw the soft sweep of her lashes and heard the soft pleading moans as she cried out for him in a sweet pinnacle of release.

How much more entranced could he be? Nicholas exhaled and glanced at the sky framed through the windows. The late afternoon sun prismed through the beveled windows, casting dazzling reds, oranges, yellows, blues and greens.

All her fears should now be eradicated with the imprisonment of Lady Sutherland and Willean. She had told him he was her Guardian angel and embraced him with a delight that filled him with a tenderness so deep he ached inside.

Then why the bothersome doubt that ran frigid along his spine?

He leaned into her, brushing the top of her nose with his lips. "I won't rest until I know you're safe, and you'll never be safe until we figure out who is against the Rutland's."

She tucked her hair behind her ear. "With you, Nicholas, I always feel secure."

He grabbed her hand and placed it on his heart. "I have to return to London for two days on business. If you walk around Belvoir, it will be with guards. And you will not leave the grounds at all.

"Anthony said that Cuthbert Noot, the man who tried to kill him and Rachel, claimed that there was a very wealthy and power-ful man who would stop at nothing. Cuthbert was shot before he could reveal anything."

"Do you think the man Cuthbert talked about was responsible for the carriage trying to run us over at the opera?" asked Rachel.

"Probably because Lady Sutherland denied any arrangement of that event."

Chapter 30

*I*n one of the huge salons in Belvoir, Rachel and Aunt Margaret sat across the table from Alexandra, mired in a myriad of wedding details and mountains of lists. And the number of guests? Dear Lord, it seemed half the country had been invited.

Alexandra marveled at Nicholas's matronly aunt. The elderly woman was a maestro, and in terms of logistics could match wits with the admiralty.

Aunt Margaret looked up from her writing. "The only dark cloud to the wedding is the frightening menace that lurks. From now until the wedding is a perfect venue for *our adversary to attack* while everyone is busy."

Alexandra dipped her quill into ink and scratched across the parchment. "Everyone looks to Lord Drummond—"

Rachel shook her head, leaned over and patted her dog, Casey, an adorable, brown and white, Springer Spaniel. "Not everyone thinks Lord Drummond is responsible. Like you, Alexandra, Duke Cornelius gives me the shivers. He is like holes in Swiss cheese, something is missing."

Alexandra placed the quill down and pushed a finished stack of correspondence toward Aunt Margaret. "Twice he has called me Lucretia."

Aunt Margaret stared at her. "That does not bode well at all. Have you told Nicholas?"

Alexandra sighed. Casey ambled over, rested her dome-shaped head on Alexandra's lap, begging her with those gold-brown eyes. She reached down and massaged the dog behind her ears. "We have been so busy. I mentioned the situation once, but we were interrupted and the circumstance was forgotten."

"To tell you the truth, I don't like him either," said Aunt Margaret. "I never would have absolved him like Richard had after Cornelius abducted Lucretia. Lord Westbrook arrived years later, totally humble, penitent and bearing gifts, enough to charm the devil. Lucretia was long dead and everything was forgiven."

"He told me about the affair on the island, where the Duke put out Cornelius's eye with a sword, defending Lucretia and his banishment by his father."

Alexandra gathered a stack of papers spread like a deck of cards. With a sharp tap, she straightened them in an orderly row. "Don't you see a pattern? Abductions, his *modus operandi*."

"Stay close to Belvoir," Aunt Margaret warned.

"Rachel and I have been invited for tea today at the Duke of Banfield's. Nicholas sent a note saying it was fine to go as long as we have guards," said Alexandra.

"The Duke of Banfield and Humphrey are lovely company and so full of good humor," said Rachel. "I do need to get out a bit."

Aunt Margaret harrumphed. "I don't like it, especially with the Duke and Nicholas called away to London. Not one bit, but if you two are determined and Nicholas said it is fine, then go and enjoy yourselves. That said, enough of the depressing talk. These are to be happy times."

Alexandra picked up her swan's quill and ran the soft feathery end beneath her chin. "It has been my experience that you can always enjoy life if you make up your mind that you will."

"That's what I like about you, Alexandra. You are direct and will make a fine Duchess. We live in a world of circumlocution where one never says what one means let alone performs what they are supposed to do. You are a breath of fresh wind, a remarkably resourceful young lady with wit and ready tongue. Like you, Rachel."

"Why thank you, Aunt Margaret," Rachel and Alexandra chorused, and then laughed at their unison.

A footman arrived with a tray laden with tea, flaky strawberry tarts and currant scones. "I'm to remind Lady Sutherland and Lady Rutland that the coach will await their departure in thirty minutes."

When the servant poured, and then departed, Aunt Margaret eyed them both over her teacup. She took a sip and pursed her lips. "Needs sugar. By the way, how many children do you ladies foresee?"

Alexandra widened her eyes.

Rachel coughed in fits of laughter. "In case you haven't noticed, Alexandra, Aunt Margaret cuts into the matter as with a pen of fire, and pointed in her discussions."

Aunt Margaret precisely dropped two lumps of sugar in her tea. "I'll answer the question. You are both young, healthy, and with many childbearing years ahead of you. Perhaps twelve for each of you."

"Good heavens," said Alexandra, unconsciously placing a hand on her belly, and smiling at the child growing warm and robust inside her.

Aunt Margaret dipped her eyes to where Alexandra caressed her middle. "We have to hurry. I'm guessing the next duke will be born about the same time as Rachel's baby?"

Alexandra's jaw dropped.

Rachel giggled. "Aunt Margaret, does anything get past you?"

Aunt Margaret lifted a brow. "You think they played chess on the island the entire time?"

Chapter 31

Alexandra and Rachel traveled throughout the afternoon, the rain pattering on the roof and continuing to fall as the team of horses pulled the Rutland coach swaying and lurching down the road, becoming bogged down in numerous potholes.

"We are to arrive soon, I trust? I never thought to find myself with morning sickness in the afternoon," Alexandra remarked, her hand splayed over her stomach. She settled into the swabs, perspiring from the stifling heat and humidity. She peeked out the window. Dark low-hanging clouds blanketed the sky, laying the earth in a dismal gloom.

She fretted about going out on a day like today but more than the weather rose a panicking dread in her bones, something didn't seem quite right. Before Nicholas departed for London, he had given her express warning not to leave Belvoir grounds, yet he had sent a missive insisting she go to the Banfield's for tea. "In hindsight, I wish we sent our regrets," she said.

Rachel had been silent, not her normal chatty self, her face taking on a grey hue. She was heavier with child and beginning to show. "This outing, I can assure you will be my last before the wedding. All this bumping and rocking is making me ill. I'd like to curl up in my bed and sip chamomile tea."

The coach began to slow down, and as it came to a complete halt, Rachel leaned forward. "Good, we are here at last."

The words barely out of her mouth, Alexandra heard a loud thump above. Then *bang, bang, bang.* Gunshots! Dear God! Another bang hit and pierced the side of the coach. She yanked Rachel to the floor and covered her with her body. Men screamed. A guard cried out from the top of the carriage, then a thud and thumping sounded and she saw him roll down the back and hit the ground. Another man fell and splashed in a puddle outside the door. Then just as suddenly as it began, the shooting stopped. Then complete silence.

Alexandra frowned and leaned to look out the curtained window. The exit handle rattled. She jerked back and the door flew open and banged violently against the side of the coach. Cool, wet air rushed in.

"Get out!" a low guttural voice commanded from outside and before Alexandra could reach for the pistol strapped to the side of the coach, the other door flew open. A large man holding two pistols, pointed the weapons directly at them, deadly intent in his rheumy eyes.

"Do as they say," Rachel said.

Were these highwaymen to rob them or the machinations of the Rutland enemy? Either way, two pregnant women were vulnerable.

"If ye ladies would remove yerselves from the carriage," said a giant of a man with a gun pointed at her heart. Alexandra stepped into the muddy roadway, keeping to the side of the dead guard face down in a puddle. He had a hole in his back and blood pooled around him.

Nausea rolled in her throat. *Keep your wits about you.*

Her hands shook as she turned to help Rachel down. To the rear of the carriage, three more Rutland guards lay across each other dead. The driver and one remaining guard were standing on the other side bordering a thick forest, their weapons in a pile next to a tree laying over the road, cut to block the coach's progress.

Alexandra counted ten men, a rough-cut mob of filthy beasts, and not highwaymen. Highwaymen worked in smaller numbers. She shuddered. This was a planned event.

The giant beside her plucked at a button-sized wart on the side of his face. *Wart* would be an appropriate name. "His lordship said no witnesses." Wart raised his gun to shoot the driver and guard.

Alexandra shouldered her full weight into Wart. "Run," she screamed.

Caught off guard, Wart tripped over the dead guard, tumbling in the muck. The gun went off, the shot fired into the treetops. Branches and leaves settled over them. The guard and coachman leaped into the forest.

"Get them!" Wart ordered.

Several men rushed into the woods.

Alexandra exhaled. The growing twilight, turned everything indistinct in the fading light and would make it difficult to track the guard and driver through the dense forest. Perhaps they could get back to Belvoir and get help.

Wart slapped the mud off him and pushed her toward the felled tree. "You bitch. Get going before I shoot you. You too." He motioned to Rachel.

Alexandra stumbled, her white slippers slipping in the mud and she shivered as the rain increased.

"Lean on me," Rachel said. "That was foolish but very brave thing to do."

"Keep ye're bloody mouths shut." Wart rasped.

Harnesses jangled, hooves pounded. A coach appeared on the other side of the felled tree. Wart opened the door and his body blocked the seal on the door from her view. He motioned with his gun for them to get in. Alexandra hesitated. Visions of her last abduction swam before her. This time she would not be so lucky.

"I will not leave with you."

Wart shrugged. "Get in or get a bullet through your head."

Alexandra narrowed her eyes. "Why the extra coach? Why not shoot us and be done with it? I believe you are ordered not to hurt us."

Wart swung up his gun in her face. "I get miserable when I'm wet and cold and you never know when this pistol might go off."

Rachel nodded, boarded the coach and held out her hand. Alexandra refused. Wart raised his gun and slammed her on the side of her head.

Alexandra's eyes fluttered open, awareness seeping into her skull. Her body felt leaden, sluggish. Her stomach roiled. She touched her head and groaned. An egg-sized bump grew on the side of her head. The world tilted. Oh, God. Was she going to be ill?

Boosting herself up on one elbow, she realized she was lying in a bed. A beam of light shattered the dark as it pierced through a window, making her eyes hurt. Another wave of nausea rose in her throat. Flopping back down, she draped one arm over her eyes to block out the painful light.

When the nausea calmed, she looked at the unfamiliar silk wall garishly embossed with plumes of ferns and interwoven with long panes of mirror.

Seeing her reflection in the mirror, she gasped. Someone had undressed her. She wore only her chemise. Even her shoes and stockings had been removed.

Wherever she was, it was obvious she was a prisoner. She swung her feet around and to the floor, touching the soft carpet, then tiptoed across the room to the closed door. She turned the doorknob.

Locked.

Her heart sank. She leaned against the door and knocked. "Is anyone there?" Her throat felt scratchy and parched, she coughed. No response. She swung around, scanned for another escape route, right to left...and up above...where she saw her reflection. The ceiling was covered with mirrors.

Seeing a mark on her forehead in the reflection, she reached to touch it. Ouch! It hurt. She withdrew her wet and sticky fingers. *Blood.* She turned and pounded her fist on the door. "I cannot open the door. Does anyone have the key?"

"Alexandra? Is that you? Are you all right?"

A woman's voice. Was that Rachel? Still groggy, Alexandra shook her head, then moved to the other side of the room. What the hell was going on? She had been in the Rutland coach going to the Duke of Banfield's for tea. Shots. They'd heard shots. Men fell dead. A struggle.

She spoke through the wall. "Rachel?"

"I'm here."

"Where are we?"

"The Duke of Westbrook's home."

She shook her head again. Clarity was not her friend. "Why?"

"Think, Alexandra."

A chill clawed up her spine with slow realization...all that had been done to the Rutland family had been the Duke of Westbrook's doing.

"Dear God in heaven. We are his pawns. He will use us to lure Nicholas, Anthony and Duke Richard here."

Alexandra examined the window. No way could she fit through the small aperture. She peered below. Three stories. A wave of vertigo hit her and she waited for it to pass. "Odd, but this room has only one tiny round window, about a seven-inch diameter and too small for me to fit through. There is no escape."

"My window is small and far too risky to climb down in my condition. I've tried picking the lock to no avail.

Alexandra clutched her stomach, her baby growing safe inside. Someone inserted a key into the lock and turned it. She straightened. A quick twist of the doorknob and the door banged opened, revealing the gentleman she had known in her bones was the architect for all the calamities that had befallen the Rutland's.

"Ah, good, you are awake," Lord Westbrook said genially. "Your color has improved. For a few disconcerting hours, I thought you would not wake."

"Why have you brought me here?" She crossed her arms over her breasts. The chemise was too thin to protect her modesty.

"Lucretia, I had to."

Alexandra inhaled. What to do. Play to his delusion.

He scrutinized her. "How do you feel?"

Her hand slid up to her throat. "Better," she lied. "But why did you feel you had to kidnap me, milord?"

"I had to get you away from the Rutland's. They are evil."

Her head snapped up. That voice, so familiar to her now and as frightful as a serpent's hiss. She closed her eyes. Westbrook was the man she had heard behind her that day on the docks, commanding Captain Diogo to take Nicholas aboard the *Santanas* and depart at once.

She opened her eyes, meandered to the far side of the room. Would her shaking legs give out from beneath her? She looked through the thick, wavy pane of glass distorting the world. "Then it is good you saved me."

"I've wanted you in my arms for so long, Lucretia."

"Why bother abducting me?"

The Duke of Westbrook laughed. "You are so beautiful and naïve."

"Why didn't you ask, I would have come."

Alexandra edged away from the window when he stepped toward her. "I do not understand, Lord Westbrook," she said, deliberately pitching her voice so she sounded submissive. "Why have you brought us here?"

Lord Westbrook tilted his head to the side. He carefully deliberated her question. His face changed, embodied a sinister look, as if he was sizing up his quarry.

"I have such wonderful plans for you, Lucretia."

"I do n-not understand." she stammered.

Without warning, he lunged for her and seized her roughly by the upper arms. Surprised by his attack, she screamed, but the muscles in her throat were taut with fear and she barely uttered a sound.

"I'm aware that you are confused by all of this, my dear lady.' His fingers dug into her bare arms and she winced in pain. "I sent the invitations to Belvoir requesting your presence at the Duke of Banfield. I also know Duke Richard and Lord Nicholas are in London for two days. How easy it was to orchestrate their visit to London. No one knows you are here."

Alexandra was repulsed by his touch. She struggled. Her head throbbed from the laudanum and she still felt weak. "What about the driver and the other guard. Surely they will reach Belvoir?"

"What are you talking about?"

"They escaped. The man with the wart on his face did not tell you?" *Divide and conquer.*

"He told me he killed everyone. He will pay for deceiving me."

"Why are you doing this? What did the Rutland's do to you?"

The anger clouding his expression faded as he chuckled. "Lucretia, how could you be so trusting? You must remember the duel between me and Duke Richard...or was it Nicholas? Look at my eye. He thrust a sword into my eye, blinded and disfigured me for life. Don't you remember? Of course not. The Rutland's have convinced you to forget."

Keep him talking. "Why, Rachel?"

"She is breeding another Rutland. She has to die," he said, talking of Rachel's murder as if he were discussing the riddance of a rabbit.

Alexandra shivered. She must save Rachel. "What would Cornelius do to her if he knew she was expecting Nicholas's child? "So how did you arrange the night of Nicholas's and Abigail's kidnapping?"

"The Rutland's are such trusting dolts. Patience was winning the war. Endearing myself to them, gaining their trust as a favorite uncle. Took me years. I paid large bribes to get Percy Devol and Cuthbert Noot out of Newgate as a quid pro quo arrangement. How expedient their grudges equaled mine. Everyone was busy with Abigail's masked ball. My men doused the laboratory with grape-seed oil. Messages were sent out. Richard and Anthony were to die in the explosion."

His plan was what Nicholas and she had discussed for a long time. Now the pieces were starting to fit.

"What happened? Why didn't the Rutland's die?" She already knew the answer. Delay him as much as possible.

The Duke of Westbrook drew back his fist and punched the pillow. Alexandra flinched.

"A delay by that bitch, Abigail. Lord Richard and Anthony grew impatient and departed before I ordered the fire bombs thrown into the laboratory. We were successful in drugging and kidnapping Nicholas and Abigail. Percy and Cuthbert managed their seizures. We took them to the docks and I paid another huge sum to have two ships depart with them...to have them suffer and die."

"Who killed Percy?"

"I had one of my men stationed in Boston to do the trick."

"What about Cuthbert, who killed him?"

As long as she kept up the questioning, she was safe. He liked bragging about his crimes.

"I had Rachel abducted to lure Anthony to an abandon sea captain's house. They were tied up and the house set fire but they made a device to escape. Cuthbert failed, so I shot him. I couldn't have him shooting off his big mouth and directing the authorities to me.

"I did it all for you, Lucretia," he said with adoration. "So, we could be together."

Alexandra licked her lips. Her life depended on her acting ability. "My Lord, I cannot imagine the torment you have been through all this time—"

"But you are not Lucretia. She's dead. Who are you?"

His black eye focused on her as he waved between what was real and what was the past. Would he kill her? *Think.*

"My dear Cornelius, remember that first time we met when you were attending Cambridge? Remember that lovely afternoon we laughed and had tea?"

"To think of all the lonely years without you, my darling, Lucretia."

Alexandra breathed deeply. Her trick worked. "Anthony, Abigail, Nicholas and Duke Richard survived. What is next for them?"

"Don't worry your pretty head. My mind delights with endless possibilities."

Alexandra winced. The man's life was dedicated to destroying the Rutland's. Lady Ursula Sutherland and Willean paled in comparison for their treachery.

His upper lip curled. "I hate all of them. Why are you marrying Nicholas, Lucretia?"

He started to wave into the present again. "I waited for you to rescue me, Cornelius. I was powerless."

"That is why I abducted you. It was for your own good. But you did have devotion to him."

"You know I was powerless."

"Such wisdom you've gained over your years, my lovely. I confess I am pleased with the way it all has turned out. I had a note sent to Belvoir for when Duke Richard and Nicholas return. They will be frantic. They will not have a very nice end, I think."

Outrage strengthened her body and voice. "And your accomplice, Lord Drummond, he helped you in all of this?" She wanted to eliminate all possible enemies.

Lord Westbrook shoved her so she fell on the bed. "Oh dear, your poor head must be muddled if you believe I would have anything to do with Lord Drummond. He is a fool, but so convenient to pin the blame."

He crawled across the mattress until he was on top of her. "How long have I waited to discover what tasty confection is tucked between your thighs."

Alexandra did not bother screaming. Her fingers curved into a tight fist and she struck him. The blow glanced off his cheekbone. Westbrook grabbed her wrist before she could land another blow.

"Nasty bitch!"

She cried out as he squeezed, grinding her delicate bones together.

"Why are you doing this?" she wailed. "Why would you want to hurt Lucretia?" It was like another individual had emerged, a more violent one.

"This is just the beginning of your torments, Lucretia, for your betrayal. For whoring with Richard and bearing his children. How many nights have I lain awake, dreaming of what I'd do to you?

How many whores have I practiced seduction to maim and strangle to death?" he said tightening his hold on her wrist until she feared he'd break it.

"No!" She glanced from the fixed glass eye to the other. The demonic gleam in Westbrook's good eye brought on a wave of panic.

"Your treachery plays in my mind. But this is rich," he said gleefully. "I will destroy the whole Rutland family with one stroke."

"Nicholas will stop you." She ripped off his wig. His bald head possessed the luminescent quality of a cadaver.

He slapped her across the face and her head rang with pain. She opened her mouth to scream. A filthy sheet was thrust in her mouth. Alexandra gagged. She fought and bucked. With her free hand, she swung and hit Westbrook in the eye. He swore and pressed a knife at her throat and she stilled.

"Now, my lovely," he breathed into her ear. "You will do exactly what I tell you." He laughed, his voice filled with malice.

He was truly evil. Void of emotion.

That's better," Westbrook said. "You have been nothing but a bitch who needs to learn obedience. I will take you now." Westbrook ripped at her chemise. A sickening terror crawled up over her belly. His hand clawed up her legs, forcing her thighs to open.

"Where is your Nicholas now? Where is his power to protect you?" His hands were everywhere. He mauled her breasts in a punishing grip, pinching her nipples. She wanted to scratch his disgusting sneer from his face. When she cried out, he laughed, his hot breath on her neck smelled of rotten cheese.

Your Nicholas is seeking the delights of Lady Susannah."

Cornelius lied. Nicholas loved her and he'd come for her. *He promised to protect her.*

Cornelius pressed the knife deeper into her skin, tipping the knife up and licked her blood from the blade. Her stomach lurched. She twisted, inched across the bed toward the oil lamp on the night table. She stretched her hand.

"Did I tell you what I did to my first whore?"

She shook her head. He wanted to brag. Arrogance. Arrogance was good because it diminished perception. "Tell me, my dear Cornelius," she said while fighting him off.

He loosened his breeches. Alexandra turned her head away, bile rising in her throat.

He pulled her face to look at him. "See the row of bottles, placed on the shelf molding bordering the top of the room?"

Her eyes widened in horror. Were those hair pieces? No wonder there was only one small window. The room was a torture chamber.

He laughed, rubbed his ballocks. "Trophies, pickled and preserved. Like dumb neglected lap-dogs, the whores fawned over me never realizing their fate. I scalped them, just like those savages I draw inspiration from in the Colonies. When I'm alone, I come in here and toss myself off by grabbing my cock and pretending I'm slamming it in you, Lucretia."

He had mentioned his fascination with the Indians at the ball. She inched closer to the oil lamp lay on the table. She pressed down into the mattress. She could do this. She survived the *Santanas*, a hurricane, an island. She stretched her hand. Damn. If only she could reach the lamp. "What happened to the second prostitute?" She wiggled provocatively beneath him, felt his arousal.

She strained and stretched her free hand, while he recanted his sick story with zeal. Tears came to her eyes. She condemned self-pity. Surely, her arm would detach. Her fingers seized upon the bottom of the lamp, pulled it closer.

"When I finished with her, I scalped her alive. You should have heard her screams," he panted.

Alexandra knew what he had planned for her. She grabbed the middle of the lamp and smashed it on his head. Glass shards exploded everywhere. He went limp on top of her. She shoved his body off her. Fire spread with oil across the bed and him. Hands shaking, she searched his pockets for the key, the flames whipsawing and burning her hands. The room filled with smoke.

Dear God, she'd be trapped in an inferno. She swallowed the sour taste in her mouth, searched his breast pockets. Nothing. Bending further to explore his inner pockets, she heard him moan. Hurrying, she searched his pants pocket, nearly weeping when she found a set of keys.

Reaching the door, she pushed the key in the lock. *Turn. Please open.* She heard a scream behind her. Saw him get up, a fiery blast, coming to her.

"Lucretia," he screamed just as she flung open the door and ran out. She heard a thump behind her and turning, saw Cornelius writhing on the floor, screaming. He deserved what he got, but she couldn't just let him die like that. She grabbed a rug from the floor and beat on him to stop the fire. But when it was out, he lay there, a charred corpse. Fire licked up the drapes.

She tossed the rug over him, and ran to the next room. Keys jangling, she rammed one by one into the lock. The last one turned and Rachel opened the door. She hugged her. We must go in different directions in case one of us is caught by a guard, the other can still escape. Rachel disappeared toward the left wing and Alexandra pivoted to the right. She passed one hallway after another. The manor was vast. Men's voices snarled below.

She tiptoed down the stairs and peeked around the doorway. Nicholas, Anthony and Duke Richard were held by seven armed men. Alexandra grabbed a candlestick in the hall. Just then, one of the thugs came out of the room. She brought the candlestick up high. When he moved past her, she swung with all her might and hit him over the head. He slumped to the floor.

Smelling smoke, a cold shard of fear jagged up Nicholas's spine. But then he saw her by the doorway. His heart leaped nearly out of his chest. Alive. Thank God, she was alive. A wave of relief washed over him…but her face looked purpled and bruised on one side and she was wearing only her chemise. His blood boiled into a heated rage. He'd kill that bastard Cornelius.

His relief dissolved as quickly, and he warned her away with his eyes to stay hidden. But a guard came out the door next to her. That was when he saw the candlestick in her hand and the deadly look on her face when she swung the candlestick. The guard went down, out cold. Or dead.

Now, the fool woman was trying to take down Westbrook's men. And she was going to get herself killed.

Nicholas turned to the guards holding him. "Just six of you this evening?" *Never a problem.*

One of the thugs smacked his toothless gums together. The edges of his beard and moustache were yellowed with his drool. "What do you mean, just six?"

"Can you do subtraction? Your other companion is obviously rendered useless."

"I don't understand," said the runt of the litter. He was short, narrow shoulders, long arms that dangled and feet that might serve for shovels.

Nicholas growled. "Anthony, do you remember the night in London near Hyde Park and Piccadilly?" *The night we pummeled six hoodlums who attacked us.*

"With pleasure," Anthony said.

"I told you blokes to keep yer mouths shut," the giant said. The wart on his face was spectacular. Could be where his brain was stored. He put his gun down on the desk.

Dimwit. Westbrook didn't hire the brightest. A little more intellect and the giant could be a cabbage.

"Now," shouted Nicholas.

Anthony leaped like a panther, taking care of the two thugs closest to him.

Nicholas zeroed in on the three in front of him. They formed up like an advancing line of slovenly soldiers, hands loose by their sides. In the middle stood the giant with long ape-like arms, feet thick like cotton bales, his neck as wide as a man's hands splayed side by side, and his shoulders, wide enough to hold a double oxen's yoke. His two flanking companions looked like children, folding out in front. They'd receive his first line of attack. Easy enough. The giant would need trimming.

His father grabbed the gun off the desk and swung it on the sixth man.

The thug to the right dropped an iron bar from his sleeve, ready to hit Nicholas. Before he raised his hand, Nicholas hit him with a right hook. The bar clinked on the wood floor and the thug fell face first on the planks. Nicholas kicked the iron behind him for his father to pick up.

The other runt gaped, seeing the fate of the first thug crash to the ground in front of his eyes.

He who hesitates is lost.

Nicholas slammed him with a full-on punch. He crashed over his companion's body.

The surprise was over, and the giant wasn't a total idiot. No, this guy wanted to use his brute strength which meant he believed he was superior. The remedy for hubris was always a humbling defeat and this man's head was held too high, trying to breathe from his own vapors. Like Damiano who was divided in two and met his watery grave. Except there was no ocean nearby for the giant to fall.

Nicholas and the giant stood linked together in a hushed, unchanging rectangle, tense, rocking a little, staying loose, staying limber, eyes locked on each other.

Did the giant wonder why he wasn't retreating? *Come right ahead and find out.*

The giant came, his wart beet-red and with just a trace of uncertainty in his face. His legs braced, his elbow rising, his intention easy to read. He was going to launch himself at Nicholas and bring his fist down on Nicholas's head.

Nicholas charged, a long, fast stride, aiming to finish a helpless opponent, and in less than a second, all the giant's previous certainty disappeared. He collapsed out of a storming move into a defensive panic. His back arched and his elbow raised. With his momentum, Nicholas shoved the giant's arm up, making the big man's punch useless. Nicholas swung high and hard, and with the flat of his knuckles, caught the giant's jaw. He must have smashed into his back molars, assuming he had any, and the hinge of his jaw hung limp. The giant grasped his jaw, unable to speak turned tail and ran.

Alexandra screamed.

Nicholas looked up. *Lord Westbrook?* He looked like a charred piece of meat...and he had Alexandra in his grip and his gun leveled at Nicholas heart. "I've deadly aim, Nicholas."

"Nicholas, Cornelius is the one behind everything." Alexandra fought him. Cornelius gripped her around the neck. Alexandra choked, tore at his arm with her fingers.

"She's right. I bribed the guards at Newgate to get Percy Devol and Cuthbert Noot out. We hated all of you."

"You, sick bastard," said Duke Richard Rutland.

Nicholas took a step closer to Westbrook. He had to get to Alexandra. "All these years, you've harbored a grudge against our family?"

"Stop, right there, Nicholas. I'll shoot her first," Westbrook warned. "Isn't it obvious? You had my Lucretia. I have her now. I will kill all of you."

Nicholas sweated, inched closer. *Lucretia?* Alexandra had told him how Cornelius called her the name of his long dead mother. His obsession with Nicholas's mother never left him after all these years. Alexandra had been uncomfortable about Cornelius from the start. "You have one shot. After that, I'll kill you.

"I trusted you, loved you like a father. Why?" said Nicholas.

"To entice you, to gain your trust I placed a card shark in your path to put you in debt. Your father never knew so heavy in his mourning. I set up the conflicts at Eton so I could bail you out of trouble. The rest was made easy by your propensity for brawling."

Silence combed the air. Her misery choked him as he watched blood drip from her head wound and a bruise swell on the right side of her face. The impulse to murder raged through Nicholas's veins.

Cornelius waved his gun. "I've waited ages for this moment.

"My late father, the imperial Duke of Westbrook," Cornelius said, sneering, "had paternal feelings during his last days. Reversed his banishment of me. He never should have."

"Why shouldn't he have ended your banishment?" said Duke Richard.

A bizarre look gleamed in his one good eye. "Because I killed him."

"You killed your father?" Anthony said, eyes wide with disbelief.

"Why shouldn't I have? Never could please the bastard. I lured him by becoming the penitent son." Cornelius rasped.

Nicholas's father and brother were distracting Cornelius. Good. Smoke curled from the upper floor. Was the house on fire? That would explain Cornelius half-baked appearance. Nicholas crept closer.

"I smothered the bastard with a pillow. Everyone thought he'd died in his sleep."

As Alexandra tried to break away, Cornelius snapped her back, jamming his gun right next to her temple. Alexandra's whimper went straight to Nicholas's heart.

"There is one more," bragged Cornelius.

"One more what?" said Duke Richard. Anthony edged from the other side of the room.

Cornelius rasped out a breath. "Joshua, your son. I have a man in America whom I've paid handsomely to kill him. Joshua will die soon."

"Who did you send to kill Joshua?" said Duke Richard.

Nicholas dove onto Alexandra, shoving her out of the way, and then pitched his body into Cornelius. They grappled on the floor, Cornelius possessing the strength of a madman, Nicholas pummeling him with his fists, months of anger released. The men rolled with Nicholas on the bottom. Cornelius clutched his gun and jammed it on the side of Nicholas's head.

A shot fired off.

Cornelius fell to the right, clutching his heart. Smoke curled from Duke Richard's gun.

Anthony shook Cornelius. "Who did you send to kill Joshua?"

"He's dead, Anthony. I should have killed him years ago," said the Duke of Rutland. "He's wreaked enough evil on this family. I will alert Abigail, your sister and Captain Thorne in Boston to warn your brother, Joshua."

Nicholas stood and pulled Alexandra into his arms.

"Oh, Nicholas, I thought you were in London and I thought I'd never see you again," she said.

"I have an indefinable instinct for danger. The letter I received hailing my father and I to London was suspicious. Partway there, we returned to discover you and Rachel were missing, never dreaming you would go against my wishes and leave Belvoir. The Rutland driver and guard told us of your bravery that helped them escape and returned to Belvoir. They had recognized the Duke of Westbrook's coach and we rode here."

Alexandra turned in his embrace, her hands flat on his chest. "The note I received was from you, wishing for me to visit Lord Banfield and was penned in your perfect scrawl. Cornelius must have had the note forged."

"No doubt." Nicholas wrapped Alexandra in his coat.

"Where's Rachel? said Alexandra glanced around.

"I'm here," said Rachel, rushing into Anthony's arms. "I had made it outside when I heard the shooting. I peeked through the windows and saw everything was under control."

"Are you all right, Rachel?" Anthony scrutinized his wife.

"I'm doing fine. Just get me home."

Nicholas smoothed his hand down Alexandra's back to ease her trembling. How about you? Did Cornelius hurt you?"

"No. I hit him over the head with an oil lamp."

He whispered into her ear, "And the baby?"

"We're both fine," she smiled.

Fire had reached the upper balconies, smoke and flame now charging through the house, crackling and popping.

"Let's get out of here. The whole place will be a tomb of embers," Anthony said.

Duke Richard pushed past them and ordered his men from the outside. "Go in and drag out these thugs. Tie them up. We might be able to get answers out of them about who Cornelius sent to the Colonies to kill Joshua."

Nicholas picked his wife up in his arms and carried her to the Rutland coach. "When you disappeared, when you were snatched in that madman's grip, I thought I had lost the sun, the moon and all the stars. I despaired and feared of losing you, not two emotions I want to repeat."

"In my heart, I knew you'd come. I love you, Nicholas."

Nicholas gazed down at her, nestled up against him, her tousled head resting trustingly against his chest. "How I love you."

Epilogue

Beneath the joyous pealing of church bells, Alexandra clutched Nicholas's arm as they passed through a cheering throng of well-wishers. The new Lord and Lady Rutland made their way to a white and gold open coach, decorated with hundreds of roses, and drawn by four prancing white horses. Alexandra clutched her bouquet of lilies and roses and was handed into the carriage by Duke Richard.

"I am very proud to have you in the family, Alexandra."

Nicholas's father touched her heart. "Thank you," she mouthed. Did the proud duke wipe a tear from his eye?

As the train to her gown of white embroidered satin and lace was tucked in behind her, she turned and waved. Everyone she loved was present except for the King who made his regrets. Aunt Margaret dabbed her eyes. Anthony and Rachel smiled and waved. Samuel, who had given her away, beamed with pride. He had moved from Deconshire to oversee the Sutherland estate with Bainey. The archbishop, Lady Dabney and her son, John were there to cheer them on. Her heart clenched for Nicholas. They had not been able to learn the name of the assassin the Duke of Westbrook had hired and who treacherously sought Joshua in the Colonies.

Vicar Thompson and his children surprised her, traveling all the way from Deconshire. Of course, Nicholas had kept that a secret. Jay, so fine-looking, had been bribed with cake to wear his new suit. Sylvia and Juliana, her flower girls, took to their job with earnest, by throwing rose petals at them.

Nicholas whispered into her ear. "At least it's not apples they are throwing."

Alexandra laughed and gazed at her wedding ring. Nicholas had taken the black pearl he had given her on the island and had it set in a nest of winking diamonds.

She looked at her new husband and her heart burst with pride. Nicholas, handsome in his black velvet frockcoat with gold trim, black breeches and snowy white stockings looked like a prince.

He patted her hand when he caught her admiring him. "Is this the fairytale wedding you dreamed of, Alexandra?"

"Yes, it is my fairytale wedding."

The horses were tapped and the carriage moved forward.

"I have a wedding gift for you. Open it up." He presented her with a rolled parchment.

"You have given me too much." She looked at him quizzically, and then untied a ribbon and unrolled the stiff translucent parchment."

Nicholas cleared his throat. "A special decree through the King. There is an island in the Caribbean named, 'Alexandra Island' and it belongs to you."

She dropped the parchment on her lap and clasped his face with her hands. "Thank you, Nicholas, but what I really want is...you... *Only you.*"

Author's Note

During the eighteenth century, commerce in the Caribbean was plentiful and so were the wicked hurricanes that downed ships and sailors, plummeting them into watery graves. What if you were like Robinson Crusoe and cast ashore a deserted tropical island? Would you know how to survive with nothing else but your strength and knowledge?

In *Only You*, I took artistic license, and blended a mix of Caribbean Islands including, St. Croix, St. Thomas, Dominica, Jamaica, and of course, my beloved Bahamas—the latter of which, I drew most of my inspiration. The Caribbean bursts with adventurous activities, clear waters, and stunning natural sites. The Bahamas is known for its rich history, stunning views, gorgeous turquoise waters, intriguing cays and caves to explore. Of note, are the people, always offering a friendly smile, and warm and welcoming hospitality. So, a delightful story unfolded...

Acknowledgements

Most books wouldn't be written without the help of some special people. I would like to acknowledge Caroline Tolley, my developmental editor and Linda Style, my copy/line editor. Their insight and expertise were indispensable. Hugs also to my spouse, Edward, five children, eight grandchildren, Eugend Dollard, Dr. Marcianna Dollard, Nancy Crawford, Brenda Kosinski, Paula Ursoy, Gabriele and Peter Lorenz, Andrew Albury, and posthumously, Loretta Bysiek—your love and comfort surround me.

Many thanks to the gracious support of Western New York Romance Writers Group.

Finally, a special note of gratitude to my readers. You will never know how much your enthusiasm and support enrich my work and my life. You are the best.

About The Author

Elizabeth St. Michel, the best-selling author of the Duke of Rutland series (of which *Only You* is the third installment), has received multiple awards for her work.

Her first book, *The Winds of Fate*, was a number-one hit on Amazon's list of best sellers and a quarterfinalist for the Amazon Breakthrough Novel Award.

Surrender the Wind, Elizabeth's second novel, received the Holt Medallion and the Reader's Choice Award and was a finalist for the National RONE Award, which honors literary excellence in romance writing.

St. Michel lives in New York and the Bahamas.

Dear Readers,

It has given me pleasure to write, *Only You* for you. There is no greater compliment to me as an author than for my readers to become so involved with the characters that you want me to write more. That said, I will happily write Joshua's story to complete the Rutland Series. Joshua is a spy on the frontier working for the Patriot's in their fight for freedom during the American Revolution.

I'm also happily returning to the Civil War era and the Rourke family. As you know, my first installment, Surrender the Wind detailed the journey of Catherine Fitzgerald, a wealthy New York heiress and legendary Rebel General John Daniel Rourke. My second installment will acquaint us with General Rourke's younger brother, Colonel Lucas Rourke, head of Civilian Spying for the North. Colonel Lucas Rourke is honor bound to uphold the Union and responsible for a vast network of spies. When Confederates abduct him, his only hope is the enigmatic spy who surrenders her heart and soul to save him. Rachel Pierce is the notorious Saint. Witnessing her father's brutal murder by slaveholders, she emerges disciplined in the high art of spying, moving through southern latitudes like a ghost with no trace of her footsteps and defying every one of her enemies without the slightest hint of their knowledge. Caught in a dangerous web of intrigue, they uncover secrets that will prolong the war and cast them both in danger.

Although I can't tell you much more I can promise you this: like my last novels, it is written with one goal in mind—to make you experience the laughter, the love, and all the other myriad emotions of its characters. And when it's over to leave you smiling...

Warmly,
Elizabeth St. Michel

P.S. If you would like to receive an emailed newsletter from me, which will keep you informed about my books-in-progress, please contact me on Facebook or my web-page at elizabethstmichel.com. The greatest gift you can give an author is a review for her work. I would be thrilled to hear from you!